WAKE
UP
CALL

D1710231

VICTORIA ASHLEY

WAKE UP CALL
VICTORIA ASHLEY

ISBN-13: 978-1490906133
ISBN-10: 1490906134

WAKE UP CALL
VICTORIA ASHLEY

For my mom, my family, my boyfriend, my friends and all of the faithful readers that have read this online. Thank you all. In addition, a special thank you to everyone that helped me in getting this book prepared. I couldn't have done it without you.

WAKE UP CALL
VICTORIA ASHLEY

Chapter 1

"No! Get off me."
I woke to the sound of my mother screaming – her shrill
cries ricocheted off the four walls of my dirty bedroom and flew
straight into my heart. It was so loud that it pierced through my
brain and instantly made it begin to throb.
I yanked my favorite fleece blanket over my head as the
tears started to roll down my pink, puffy cheeks.
In the room adjacent to mine, I could hear the racket of my
drunken parents fighting once again; it was always the same.
All that I heard were screams. The sounds blurred until I was
numb.
I knew I couldn't leave my bedroom or else I would end up
experiencing the wrath of their anger so instead I sat with my
head on my knees, helpless. I pulled the blanket around my
shivering frame in the pathetic hope that it would somehow

shield me from this miserable existence, although, I knew that it wouldn't.

"No! Leave her out of this," my mother cried. "It's not her fault!"

I stifled a sob as I clapped my hands against my ears in a desperate attempt to drown out the noise, but I knew that I was being stupid. This agony would never leave me.

The screams were closer now – insistent, outside my bedroom door. My heart pounded against my chest and I felt as if I could vomit at any moment.

I jumped back and hit my head on the filthy cement wall of my private prison as my parents kicked my door open, stumbling inside as I poked my head out from under my blanket.

My unstable father forced my mother onto the wooden floor until she was nearly unconscious, blood seeping from a multitude of open wounds that adorned her frail body.

Then he turned to me and his eyes were so wild, and I screamed and cried, but in the hatred that inhabited his world, my screams were silent. He walked toward me with malice in his step, and I closed my eyes as I anticipated the searing pain that I had grown so accustomed to.

"No, please!"

I woke up dripping with sweat. I threw my hands over my face and exhaled in a pointless attempt to calm my racing mind. It had been over one year since I packed my suitcase, moving to Westville, Florida, and yet the nightmares still haunted me every night.

I stepped into the grubby bathroom of my one bedroom apartment and stared into the smudged up mirror at my mascara-streaked face.

After taking a long, hard look at the lost little girl with the big emerald eyes - lost in a mess of thick, sticky lashes - I pulled my tangled black hair out of my eyes and splashed a handful of icy water over my face. "Good morning to me, I guess," I mumbled to myself before heading back to my single bed.

Running my fingers through my messy hair, I pulled my favorite fleece blanket over my lap. I looked at the small desk and glowered at my bright alarm clock. "Shit!" It was already ten o'clock at night - time to head out to work.

WAKE UP CALL
VICTORIA ASHLEY

I threw the blanket off my bare legs and jumped to my feet, mind racing. Scrambling to the bathroom, I kicked a pair of old jeans out of my way and turned on the steaming hot water. It sputtered out in drips of umber, causing me to squirm.

I stripped out of my favorite black and gray T-shirt and panties and stepped into the stained shower. The steaming water hit my skin and rolled down my body as I tilted my head back and ran my fingers through my hair. I grabbed my old black sponge and scrubbed my sensitive skin roughly in the pathetic hope that it would be able to remove all of the pain that bloomed within me. The pleasure only lasted for a few minutes.

I finished showering in a rush and stepped out before drying my body and wrapping my hair into a tight messy bun in hopes that it would make me look more mature.

It didn't matter anyway - in my sordid line of business, they liked the women to be young, loose and wild. I threw on a black mini skirt, silver tank top and my favorite silver heels and then grabbed my cell phone and called for a taxi.

"1313 Remington Place. Make it quick, please."

When the gaudy, yellow taxi pulled up outside my apartment, I jumped inside.

The driver looked back at me with beady eyes and gripped the steering wheel, his gray hair falling over his aging face. "Ma'am?" he questioned, with a small smile.

"Taste of Poison," I replied hastily. "Fast please. I'm running late."

He swallowed hard and eyed me from the rear-view mirror, his expression uneasy, as I looked at him impatiently and slammed the door shut. "Yes, ma'am." Sadly, I was starting to get use to that reaction.

We pulled up to *Taste of Poison* and I tossed the man a ten-dollar bill through his open window before he drove away in a cloud of swirling exhaust.

The neon sign flashed above me. 'Exotic Dancers' it read in a flamboyant pink text. It made my stomach churn and my eyes water.

I placed my palm over my stomach and started to make my way toward the entrance of the building when suddenly I spotted a drunken man eyeing me – two black pebbles gazing at me with lust. It made me feel so dirty.

WAKE UP CALL
VICTORIA ASHLEY

"Come here," he slurred. "Damn you look so good." His straggly, blond hair fell over his hairy face as he rubbed a hand over his keg of a stomach.

I took off in a sprint, but to my surprise, he was faster than I expected. He grabbed my arm and yanked me to a halt. I took a deep breath and closed my eyes, silently praying that I would be okay.

"Let go, you dick!" I screamed as I slapped his roaming hands away from my body. I turned around in my silver heels and ran to the door as quickly as possible, almost tripping over my own feet.

I turned around. "Go screw yourself!" Then I swung open the door of the hazy bar and stepped inside, my heart pounding with adrenaline.

The music instantly filled my ears as Trinity – a promiscuous stripper – stepped off the stage in her towering heels and gave the audience a tantalizing smile before disappearing behind the red velvet curtain.

I watched as the crowd went wild. Men of all ages filled the crowded joint, making my stomach ache. I held my breath as I walked through them- their faces were so familiar.

I knew that I had no choice though- the strip bar had been my last resort, but it paid the bills so I had to continue or else I knew that I wouldn't survive. Every other job that I had applied to had turned me down, insufficient experience, no transportation, not enough qualification; it was all the same. It had come down to one decision in the end: work at the strip joint or stay out on the streets.

I stopped to glance down at the black marble floor when I felt a heavy, plastic object hit my foot. A grimace ran over my face upon the realization that one of the men had thrown their draft beer at me. He laughed - baldhead shining in the subdued lighting - and reached for another beer from across the table. "Hell yeah! I love this place."

I shook my foot and held my tongue. I couldn't afford to lose this job, and the owner, Mr. Kendal, took the customers very serious. Their satisfaction meant everything, according to him.

I stormed into the dressing room and found an empty table in the corner, away from the other strippers. I didn't like to talk to any of them - they were gaudy, cheap, and loose. I had kept my head down ever since I first started at the club, and that was how I liked it. I had no reason to try to make friends. I never had before and didn't need to start now.

"Hey. Let me borrow some lipstick. I forgot mine."

I looked up to see one of the other strippers leaning above me. Her red hair fell over her overly tanned face as she reached her arm over my shoulder, hovering it above my makeup. I stared at her in silence, my eyebrows raised, as she reached for my pink lipstick. *Okay then.*

I cleared my throat and tilted my head as she opened the lid of the lipstick and rubbed it over her thin lips. Most of the other strippers shared their makeup and clothing with each other, but not me. "You can just keep that."

The young stripper smiled and puckered her lips. "Thanks, gorgeous." Then she kissed the air and ran her hands over her spandex mini skirt, trying to look flirty. "Are you new?"

I blew out an exasperated breath and turned my head away. I didn't have the patience to deal with her questions. "No. I've been working here for about ten months now," I huffed, hoping that she would just go away.

The girl smiled and laughed loudly. "My bad." She held up the tube of lipstick and nodded her head before turning to walk away. "Thanks."

"Yup," I muttered, as I watched her join another stripper, an older woman with short chestnut hair. They both looked back at me and smiled. *I guess you're never too old to get naked for cash.* It was oddly disturbing, making me shiver.

I applied a layer of red lipstick to my full lips and then a thick layer of mascara before I scanned the closet and decided on my uniform for the night – I was going to be a sexy police officer, clad in black leather. I hated all of the costumes, but this was the only one that made me feel in control of what I was doing – a precious feeling, and certainly one that I wasn't prepared to throw away.

I threw the pink, fuzzy cuffs around the belt and looked around the brightly lit room, my stressful eyes scanning over the rows of lit mirrors. It hurt me to know that in just fifteen minutes, I would be out on that stage being eyed by a pack of perverted, sex-deprived animals. I was as low as I could get.

WAKE UP CALL
VICTORIA ASHLEY

~•~

"Avery. It's time," Mr. Kendal stated. "Good luck out there." He flashed his crooked smile as he motioned with his hands toward the exit. "Don't just stand there, go." He eyed me anxiously, while tapping his fingers on the wall behind him.

I nodded my head, took a step toward the door, and waited for the announcement before I stepped out onto the heart-shaped stage. My own heart sank as I took in the sight around me with guarded eyes - it was even more crowded than it had been when I arrived.

The music blared around me as I closed my eyes and swayed to the fast rhythm. I could feel the money flying at me as I reached for my cuffs and clasped them around my wrist, before wrapping my leg around the smooth pole. Every second out here felt like an eternity.

I opened my eyes momentarily and caught the attention of a man standing by the bar, beer bottle in hand. A bolt of electricity surged through my body as he stared at me with curious eyes. He was gorgeous. He lifted his tattooed arm, tilting back his head as he took a long sip of his beer. He had those bad boy good looks with his jet-black hair, leather boots and V-neck t-shirt. It fascinated me and somehow had me curious.

Suddenly the music stopped; however, I remained rooted to the spot, my gaze locked on him, as his calm eyes looked into mine. A collection of rude insults broke my reverie, causing panic to set in. I shook my head, looked out into the crowd, and sighed, remembering where I was. I felt ridiculous. *Great job, Avery.*

I tilted my head to the right once more in an effort to get a proper look at the enigma who had been standing by the bar only seconds before, but he was gone - lost in a sea of faces. My face scrunched up in annoyance, as I headed backstage to change.

Mr. Kendal licked his lips as his greedy eyes wandered over my flesh. "Here's your money - one hundred and twenty three dollars." He arched an eyebrow as he handed me the money. "Not bad for such a short song. We better start seeing more of you soon." The serious look on his face said it all. He wasn't going to give me a choice if I wanted to keep my job. Three nights a week wasn't going to cut it anymore.

I quickly grabbed the money from his outstretched hand and headed for the door as fast as I could on two, silver heels. I was about to leave when suddenly a huge, muscular bouncer grabbed my open hand. My heart pounded as I attempted to pull my arm away.

"Are you going to be okay by yourself?" he questioned gruffly, flexing his huge chest, but not releasing the grip, he had on my hand.

"Yeah, I'm fine," I replied trying to sound calm. "I have a ride coming."

Finally, he released his grip on my arm, pulling a crumpled cigarette out of his shirt pocket. "Okay. Have a great night, ma'am." I nodded my head and turned away.

I cautiously made my way outside in hopes that my friend, Caleb, would already be waiting, but to my surprise, he was nowhere in sight.

I sighed, strolling over to the side of the brick building and pressing my body against it. I wasn't particularly worried about being outside by myself so late at night, but it still would've been nice if Caleb had been here on time. I grabbed my cell phone from out of my clutch bag and was just about to dial his number when I looked up to see his red BMW pulling up next to me. I felt relieved.

He jumped out and walked over to me, brown suede shoes crunching on the soiled ground. "Get in," he said bluntly, before turning on his heel and striding back to the car, eyes glued to his phone.

I rolled my eyes. Caleb had always hated my job at *Taste of Poison* and he certainly wasn't afraid to hide it. He was twenty-five, nice looking, with thick blond hair, amber eyes and full lips. He was definitely attractive, but not for me.

I clutched my bag to my chest and walked over to the passenger door, hopping inside. "Look, I'm fine. I can take care of myself," I said, running a hand through my tousled hair. Caleb continued to glare at me, his eyes narrowed as he continued to text on his phone as usual.

I tried again. "Thanks for the ride," I stammered. "You're really helping me out. I'm barely getting by and I'm behind on all of my bills. All of the money I made tonight is already spent."

He glanced at me and nodded. "No problem," he replied.
"Maybe you can save up enough money to get by and then get a
new job. This is a shitty place for a woman like you." He looked
me in the eye making me uncomfortable.

"Yeah, well maybe I'm not better than this." I turned away
and rested my head against the cool, glass window. I hated these
talks with him. "I'm fine. It's not that bad," I lied.

Caleb turned to look at me but didn't utter a word, although I
knew that he had a lot to say.

The ride passed quickly, I sat in silence and closed my eyes,
fighting the image of the strange man that filled my mind. I had
dealt with others like him before but there was something
different in his eyes. Something that made my stomach ache.

We pulled up to my single apartment and Caleb turned off the
engine. He reached over the seat, placing his hand on my arm. I
jerked away in response.

"What is with you, Avery? Your life isn't half as bad as you
think!"

I turned to him and rolled my eyes. "You don't know anything
about my life," I began. "You've known me for a total of ten
months." I opened the door and jumped out. "Are you coming or
what?"

He looked at me and shook his head, strands of amber hair
falling into his eyes. "Yeah, why not," he mumbled, before getting
out of the car and slamming the door shut behind him.

Caleb knew that the only part of me that I was willing to give
him was my body – I had made that clear to him many times
before, despite the efforts, he had made to get to know me. I
hadn't been able to trust a man ever since my father, and nobody
was going to change that.

We stepped into my single apartment and I instantly gripped
onto his shirt and pulled him to me. The smell of his cologne was
intoxicating. It turned me on. I wrapped my arms around his
neck, draping them around him like a curtain, and pulled his face
to mine. My lips crushed against his as I reached for his tight
pants and worked on the button while pushing him toward the
old, dusty couch that sat in the middle of the floor. We both fell
back onto it and I let the animal within me take control. It was
the only way that I felt safe.

One hour later and we were both tired. I knew that I needed to get rid of him as soon as I could before he started to assume that he would be staying the night. I gathered up his clothes, belt and shoes and tossed them to him roughly.

He sighed in frustration and looked down at his full hands. "So, I take it I'm leaving now."

I averted my gaze from his disappointed expression and bit my lip. I hated myself for being so cruel.

"You know how this works," I reminded him. "I can't give you anything more and I've made that very clear."

He looked at me and chewed his bottom lip. "I was hoping that I could make you change your mind, Avery." He glanced up from his overused phone with a scowl.

I looked him in the eye coldly and shook my head, keeping my distance. "Well you haven't done that yet. So I'll see you later." I knew that he had feelings for me, but I knew that I would never be any good for him.

"Fine," he muttered. "I have places to be anyways."

He gave me one last, fleeting look before throwing his clothes on quickly and walking out my door, slamming it shut behind him. I jumped, closing my eyes, before running my hands through my hair.

I walked into my cluttered bedroom and plopped down on the end of my small bed, fingering my fleece blanket. It was already two o'clock in the morning, but I knew that I wouldn't be able to fall asleep for a long time. I didn't want the nightmares to claim me. I rested my head against the smooth wall and closed my eyes, forcing back the tears.

Chapter 2

The morning arrived and I rolled out of bed, no longer able to force sleep upon myself. The brightness from the sunlight that streamed through my bedroom window hit me so hard that I had to cover my eyes, blindly making my way into the kitchen. I took one look inside my fridge to find it empty.

Sighing, I made the decision to find a local diner instead. I slammed the fridge door shut and made my way back to my room to get dressed. I threw on my lingerie, skinny black jeans and a faded gray sweater without bothering to tame my wild hair.

Once on the street, I noticed so many happy couples - laughing, kissing, and walking. The sight made me sick to the stomach. I set my gaze on the sidewalk in front of me and walked for ten minutes, eyes focusing on each crack in the uneven paving slabs. I was about to turn down another road when suddenly I noticed a small, stark white diner sitting across the street. It was so small that it looked like a two bedroom house; but it was still very picturesque with a stylish black sign hanging outside that read *The Indy Go*. I had never heard of it, but it would have to do. I needed food and fast.

WAKE UP CALL
VICTORIA ASHLEY

I crossed the road and walked over to the entrance. I reached for the silver doorknob and opened the door. *The Indy Go* was – to my surprise - bigger from the inside and a lot cleaner than I had first expected. It had a collection of large booths that sat on a vibrant black and white checked floor. I skirted my eyes over the collection of customers who were currently seated in the various booths before focusing my attention on the counter - complete with a clear glass cooler in the front that displayed all of the desserts: lemon meringue pie, chocolate fudge cake, vanilla ice cream. They looked delicious.

I looked over to the waitress, a cute blond-haired woman, and noticed that she was currently serving another customer, so I found a seat at the closest booth and sat down. A laminated menu sat on the metal table in front of me, and I picked it up and began to leaf through it eagerly, stomach rumbling. Everything managed to sound good at the moment, making it hard to make a decision.

Five minutes later, the cute waitress I had noticed earlier came rushing over and took my order. Her blue eyes seemed distant as she jotted down the corn beef hash, eggs, bacon and a small coffee, that I ordered. She didn't even attempt a smile before taking off in a hurry, her short skirt flapping around her thighs.

I leaned back into the leather booth and pulled out my cell phone to distract me until my food could arrive. I could have called Caleb, but I knew that I had to be more careful with him. Ever since meeting him at the grocery store less than a year ago, he seemed to quickly grow attached to me. It made things hard.

Suddenly, a large plate of eggs, steak and hash browns appeared in front of me, startling me out of my thoughts. I stared at the plate stupidly, before realizing that she'd messed up my order.

"Excuse me," I began. "This isn't what I ordered." The waitress scrunched up her nose, and waved her arm at me, her blond curls flying as she walked away. I sat there in shock, mouth agape, and wondered what had just happened. I knew that she had to of heard me. I said it loud and clear.

A few minutes passed and still she hadn't returned. It was really annoying me and I wasn't in the mood to mess around. "What the hell is this?" I said, before getting up with my plate in hand and walking over to the counter. "Excuse me, is anybody back there?" I yelled.

I set my food on the counter, eyes down, before suddenly a voice broke through the murmur of the diner. "Can I help you with something?"

I looked up to meet two, deep emerald eyes. I felt my pulse accelerate as I realized that I was staring at the handsome guy who I had noticed last night at the bar. He was even more gorgeous close-up – tall, dark and handsome with a strong, muscular frame. The thermo shirt that he wore clung tightly to his chest, making my cheeks turn red.

I promptly turned my head away, embarrassed. I looked back up, black strands of hair cascading around my face, as I forced a smile. "Oh sorry, yeah you can," I said. "I'm having an issue with my food and the service. I would like to speak to the owner please."

He smiled playfully, eyes dancing with amusement, as he leaned across the counter. "My name is Jace and I am the owner. What issue can I assist you with?" he replied, tone professional.

I glowered at him and laughed in his face. *He might be handsome, but he isn't fooling me.*

"Really? Do you want to run and grab the real owner and stop playing these games! I'm not in the mood." I felt bad for acting so rudely, but I was fed up. He probably recognized me from the club, and found it entertaining to mess with me.

His eyes locked onto mine with an intensity that astounded me. "Is there something that I can help you with?" he replied, again. The warmth from his sweet breath covered my face as he spoke, each syllable as smooth as silk. I focused on his full lips in a pointless effort to distract myself from my raging heartbeat. It didn't work.

I backed away, suddenly embarrassed at how close we were. I pressed a hand to my forehead and sighed. "You know what, never mind. I'm not really that hungry anyways." I turned on my heel and hastily made my way out of the door and into the sunlight. *What a waste of time!*

I was about to cross the road when I felt a big, firm hand grip my arm. I pulled away and spun around, confronting the owner of the diner. "Don't touch me..."

Jace stood erect with a serious look on his face. "Let me at least make sure that you eat." He looked down at my arm and noticed my heavy breathing, before releasing his grip. He smiled and pointed toward the door. "Come back inside and I'll cook your food myself, just the way you want it."

I fixed him with a long, hard stare before I let my hunger win. I wasn't sure that I could even manage to make it back home without getting something in my stomach. "Okay, fine. I'll come back in, but only because I need to eat." I brushed past him and made my way back inside and over to the same table that I had been seated at originally.

Jace plopped down in the booth across from me and smirked. He raised an eyebrow, as if waiting for me to speak.

"What?" I questioned, wondering what he wanted.

He let out a cheerful laugh as if it was the stupidest question he had heard all morning. "Well it might be easier for me to cook you something if I knew what you wanted." His muscles flexed through his fitted thermo as he ran his hand through a crop of messy hair.

I felt myself blush. "Oh yeah. Let's make it simple this time. I'll just take corn beef hash and a coffee," I mumbled. "A large coffee.

He nodded in understanding, stood up, and smiled at me. "I think I can manage that." He laughed playfully and walked away while I attempted to keep my cool.

Several minutes later, Jace returned with a plate full of steaming food. He set down the plate in front of me, smiled, and was about to walk away before I waved my hand.

"What's all this?" I questioned. "I told you just corn beef-"

"Just eat it," he said firmly. "I had a talk with the waitress and she explained everything to me. Boyfriend issues. It's no excuse." He leaned against the table and crossed his arms across his chest. "I sent her home; she's usually one of my best waitresses."

I poked my fork into the thick hash and looked up at him. "See, that's why I don't do relationships."

He looked me in the eye before walking away. "Neither do I."

~•~

WAKE UP CALL
VICTORIA ASHLEY

The long walk home from *The Indy Go* was tiring enough, so when I finally arrived at my door to find the newest eviction notice implicitly warning me that I would be 'Kicking dirt on the streets' if I didn't pay my overdue rent pinned up, it rounded off a fantastic day. *Just great. You have got to be kidding me.*

I stared at the pink sheet of paper held up by a rusty, metal pin. I hadn't even realized that it was already the 10th of September and I was still $400 behind from last month's rent. Ryan Smith, the owner of *Hang 'Em Low* apartments, had made it very clear that if I didn't catch up, then I would be kicked out, and – as he had rudely informed me – 'homeless'.

Frustrated, I yanked the freshly printed-paper off of the door, shoved my key into the lock, and turned before running inside and slamming the wooden door shut behind me. I exhaled in defeat, leaning against the door as the thick tears began to stream down my face. I grabbed my head in both hands and allowed myself to fall to the floor – a weeping mess, with no one to turn to except a man who I had sexually exploited. I wiped away a tear and stared down at the paper in my hand with blurred vision before wrinkling it up and tossing it across the room.

I had no idea what I was going to do if I couldn't get the money on time. I knew I needed the money though, and fast – the deadline was tonight.

Sighing, I stood up and pushed myself against the door for support before pushing away and sprinting to the bathroom mirror. Streaks of mascara smoothly ran down my long, wet lashes and covered my red and puffy face. I grabbed a clean towel and started scrubbing it away as roughly as I could in a ridiculous attempt to remove the darkness - inside and out. I scrubbed and scoured my face numb.

I sat on the edge of the sink and stared at myself until my vision blurred. It had to of been for hours. I hated going to the strip club, but I had no choice.

I pushed myself away from the mirror and slowly walked to my bedroom, head low. My alarm clock read 4:38 p.m. - the club wouldn't get busy until the evening, but I would stay all day and night if that were what it took.

I threw every garment I owned out of my creaky, old dresser and onto the wooden floor around me. To fix this disaster, I needed the sexiest outfit I owned. As dirty as it sounded, the men always scoped the strippers out when arriving to see how they looked before the show. It seemed the less you wore, the more they paid. It disgusted me, but I was desperate.

After changing into a slinky red dress complete with golden heels and heavy makeup, I called for a taxi and waited patiently outside my apartment, arms crossed.

The same taxi driver as before showed up. He wore a huge grin on his face and his eyes danced with recognition.

I glanced at him and smiled before jumping into the backseat and digging through my purse for cash. To my embarrassment, all I could find was a creased $5 bill. I suddenly remembered that I had left all of my money in Caleb's car so that he could get me a money order for rent, to try to catch up a bit.

I looked up from my purse to see the old man looking at me through his mirror, eyes suspicious.

"Is there a problem, ma'am?" he questioned. His voice was a bit nervous as he kept looking between the road and me.

I hastily closed my purse and slammed my hand against my forehead. "I only have a five dollar bill," I murmured, knowing that I was screwed.

The taxi driver pressed on the brakes and placed his arm behind him on the black leather seat. "You're going to have to get out then, ma'am," he mumbled. "I'm sorry, but no money, no ride." His eyes were full of regret as he stared back at me, and I knew that he was only doing his job.

"Okay." I closed my eyes and exhaled before tossing him the $5 bill and jumping out of the taxi. If I walked fast enough then I would make it to work in thirty minutes.

The streets were abandoned in the area of town that I was in, and the lack of streetlights made my heartbeat race. *It's not that far. It will be fine.* I reminded myself.

I willed my feet to move as quickly as possible until the back parking lot of the club came into sight, neon lights bathing the collection of cars in a gaudy light.

I slowed down to catch my breath when all of a sudden I heard footsteps behind me. *Is someone following me?* I ran – heels crunching on the ground – as the footsteps sped up behind me. I attempted to turn around to get a glimpse at my pursuer when suddenly my right heel bent to the left and I came crashing down to the ground, knees scraping gravel. I moaned in pain as I looked above me to see an older man – mid-forties - standing above me, piggy eyes boring into mine. It was the same man that grabbed my arm the night before.

He ran his tongue over his cracked bottom lip and smirked as he stumbled to the left. "You're that hot little stripper from last night," he slurred. "Oh yeah. I remember you." He paused to pull his long beard out of his mouth. It got caked with drool as he spit.

I cowered away from him and attempted to crawl backwards on the ground, red dress riding up my legs. "Get away from me," I screamed furiously. "They're expecting me any minute!" I knew that it wouldn't scare him off, but I hoped that it would at least slow him down and make him think.

"Fuck them," he replied, spitting on himself. "I like pretty little girls like you. Let me take you home and you can give me a private show." He reached down, gripping my fragile arm in his strong hands. "I can pay you more than those jerks inside." My body pressed against his as he yanked me to my feet, grabbing a handful of my hair and yanking my head back so that he could force his mouth to my neck.

My body instantly started quaking as the tears escaped from my eyes and ran down my face. I pulled away from him with as much force as I could muster and swung out, fists connecting with the side of his big head. "I don't do private shows. Get your filthy hands off me!" I screamed, my long hair flying, as I struggled to get away. "Let go!" I narrowed my eyes and elbowed him in the stomach, but it had no effect on his sturdy build.

He gripped me tighter and grabbed my face in his big hands. I cried out in pain before he clamped his cruddy hands over my mouth to silence me. I shook uncontrollably.

He put his hairy face inches away from mine and flicked my forehead with his finger. The contact stung, causing me to yelp. "Listen here, you nasty little whore," he screamed, spitting in my face. "If you can get on stage and get naked for a bunch of no good losers then you can come to my home and put on a good show for a single man with a shit load of money." He paused to laugh. "Oh I get it. You like it. You like being a whore and having all of those eyes on you. Don't you?" He pushed his crotch against me and gripped my face tighter in his hands before crushing his oily, chapped lips to mine.

I gasped as he slipped his tongue into my mouth - roaming and rubbing. The familiar taste of alcohol and cigarettes were so strong that it made me gag. I could taste the salty tears as they ran down my face and dripped onto my mouth as he continued to kiss me.

Suddenly, I saw a figure yank the man away from my helpless body and push him down to the ground. My eyes blurred as the creep attempted to stand back up, but the figure pressed his foot onto his chest once more, forcing him back to the ground. The old man cried out, before crawling away on his hands and knees.

I frantically wiped the tears out of my eyes to see if I could catch a look at my rescuer, but it was no good, the tears wouldn't let up.

The tears continued to run down my flushed cheeks. I exhaled in relief – I was safe, finally. I fell back down to my knees and placed my hands over my face. It didn't even matter who I was now left alone with. As long as that creep was long gone, I had a feeling that I would be okay.

I felt a hand rest on my shoulder, fingertips smooth on my exposed flesh. My first instinct was to shake the hand off, but when I heard a familiar voice, I realized it was Jace. Somehow, I could breathe again.

"Let me help you," he whispered. "I won't hurt you." He kneeled down in front of me and gently grabbed my face in his soft, cool hands. I looked up slowly to find myself staring into the same emerald eyes that I had first seen at *The Indy Go*. The softness in them made me weak.

Instead of jerking away, I found myself falling into his firm chest as another round of helpless tears came, hot against my skin. As much as I hated being touched - with Jace, it didn't bother me at the moment. In fact, as I lay in his arms I felt safe for the first time in a long time. I was still alive and it was thanks to him. He didn't have to help. No one did, but he still chose to.

After a few minutes of silence, I collected myself and looked up at him. He was staring down at me with caring eyes. "Thanks," I whispered. "Thank you for helping me. You didn't have to do that." Suddenly, I felt terrible for the way I had treated him earlier. "About this morn-"

He put a finger to my lips to silence me. "I'm not worried about it and you shouldn't be either." His intense eyes lowered to my bruised leg and widened as he noticed the red blood trickling down it. "Shit! Let me clean you up." He grabbed my arm and gently helped me to my feet. "I'll take you to my house and clean you up."

I backed away from his grip and shook my head. As much as I wanted to, I couldn't leave. I had to get that money. "No! I can't. I have to go to work. I need to pay my rent. Its past due and-"

"No," he cut me off. "I'm not letting you work in this condition." His eyes hardened with worry, as he grabbed my purse from out of my tight grip and began to walk away. "Come on."

I stormed up behind him and yanked my purse from out of his hand. He just didn't seem to understand. "No, you don't understand. If I don't get the money by tonight then I'll be out on the streets." I turned on my heels and headed for the door of the club, eyes wild. "I can't live on the streets, again. I won't."

I felt a pair of hands grip my waist as he hoisted me off the ground, face close to mine, as he carried me toward his car like a mischievous child. It both excited and shocked me at the same time. I opened my mouth to scream, but was quickly silenced by his soothing smile and gentle disposition.

He stared into my eyes before opening the door with one hand and setting me down in the passenger seat of the car. He made sure my head was safely inside before shutting the door and getting in himself, muscular arms gripping the steering wheel with force.

"That wasn't so hard. Now was it?" he questioned.

We sat there awkwardly as he pushed his keys into the ignition, started the car, and took off.

I began to play with the strap on my purse nervously before I finally looked up, swiveling my head to the left so that I could focus on his expression. He had such a beautiful profile – full lips, angular jawline, and dark stubble, it made my heart ache, clearly confused by his presence.

I cleared my throat to make sure that I had his full attention. "So, do you come to the club often, because I've never seen you there before last night?" I paused to swallow. "Then you came back today."

He glanced over at me with a smirk on his face. That was when I noticed the lip ring on the left side of his bottom lip. It looked sexy on him. "No actually. Last night was the first time. I saw something that caught my eye so I decided to come back for a few drinks and to clear my head." He mindlessly ran his tongue over his lip ring and bit his lip.

I looked away from him and decided to rub my fingertips on the window next to me. The rest of the journey passed quickly – and I was just about to ask him where the hell we were – before we pulled up next to a big, cream house with a pretty blue door.

He turned off the engine and looked over at me. "Well this is it." He smiled and opened his door before hopping out and stretching. He looked down into the car at me as I sat there, frozen in time. "Well are you coming in or do you want me to bring my bathroom outside and clean you up?" He laughed in amusement and walked to the front door, looking confident and sexy as he let himself inside.

I couldn't help but to notice how good his ass looked in his fitted jeans.

I exhaled, blowing a strand of hair out of my eye, attempting to think clearly. I stepped out of the car and shut the door before standing outside for a moment and trying to decide if it was a good idea to go into Jace's house. I wasn't sure if I wanted to run inside, run home or run back to work.

I stepped through the front door and looked around the living room, dark eyes searching for his figure in the dimness. It looked cozy with black leather furniture, a fireplace, a huge TV, a bookcase and a computer desk that sat in the corner. It was also very tidy and smelled of light, sweet vanilla.

I walked through the hallway slowly and poked my head into the first open door. It was the bathroom – a sterile, blue room - but still, no sign of Jace. I looked down the hallway again and noticed a door that was partially opened, a crack of amber light spilling out and into the hallway.

I slowly walked toward the door, brows arched, and pushed it open. I jumped back in embarrassment as my gaze set firmly on a half-naked Jace. A mess of inky, vibrant tattoos covered his toned back causing me to blush. His muscles flexed with every move that he made, somehow making it hard to breathe.

WAKE UP CALL
VICTORIA ASHLEY

Jace slowly turned around to face me, denim jeans dropping down to his ankles in the process. I stared - eyes wide - like a moron at the defined muscles that led down to his boxer briefs.

He cleared his throat, clearly amused, and gave me a cocky grin. "Do you mind?"

I sucked in a burst of hot, heavy breath and covered my face in humiliation. I was so embarrassed. "I'm sorry; I couldn't find you so I just thought I would check this room. I'm going to take off now. I need-"

"It's fine. Don't act like you haven't seen a guy half naked before." He laughed. "Just think of it this way, I saw you half naked and now you've seen me." He looked me up and down before turning around and reaching for a fresh pair of jeans. "Now we're even." He pulled up his jeans, walked past me, and grabbed my arm for me to follow him. He didn't even bother putting on a fresh shirt and his low hanging briefs were a distraction that I didn't like.

We made our way into the kitchen and he pulled out a chair for me to sit on. "Sit."

His kitchen was a clean gray room with black granite countertops, a glass table with black leather chairs, and a stainless steel fridge.

He placed his hands on my hips and forced me to sit down, gently guiding me to my seat. My heartbeat rattled against my chest as he bent down with a wet, warm cloth. His closeness made my stomach do flips.

"Let me get a good look at it," he said, his rugged voice irresistible. He pulled my dress up slowly so that it was above my thigh, exposing my bruised flesh. Then he took the wet cloth from the table beside him and began to clean off the scrape. His touch was gentle, tender, and careful. It made my cheeks fill with blood as I closed my eyes.

Suddenly, he grabbed my thigh and opened my legs, running his hand along my naked flesh. It gave me goose bumps.

I jerked away and slapped his arm. "What the hell are you doing? I'm not going to have sex with you."

He smiled at me as if it was the silliest question he had ever heard. "Cool down, woman. I am just checking for more cuts. You had blood on your inner thigh." He closed my legs and backed away as if the thought hadn't even occurred to him.

"Besides, if I wanted you naked then your clothes would already be off." He walked over and threw the dirty cloth in the sink before turning on the tap and washing his hands. "Clearly, that's not my intention."

Somehow, his comment bothered me. "So what makes you think that it would be that easy to get me naked?" I questioned with my arms crossed over my chest.

He walked over to me and sat on the table, leaning in so that his lips were almost brushing mine. "I just have my way," he breathed. "That's not the point, but eventually, you'll see. I'm not trying to have sex with you, though. I'm trying to help you. Two different things."

I pulled my face away from his and laughed. "What makes you think that I'll be around long enough to see anything about you?" He clearly knew nothing about me.

He got up and walked away before stopping to look back at me. I just sat there, stiff. "Well, come on."

I stood up and pursed my lips before following him down the cream-colored hallway. He stopped in front of a closed door before opening it to allow me to pass. "You're sleeping in here tonight. Like I said, I want to help you." He stared at me for a sudden, heart-stopping second – his eyes were so brooding. Then he walked away leaving me alone in the room, feeling confused and overwhelmed.

I briefly stared at my new surroundings before rolling my eyes and taking off down the hall behind him. I grabbed his arm and yanked it, forcing him to turn around to meet my fierce gaze. I didn't expect anything from anyone and I never asked for it either. "What's going on? I'm not staying here."

He grabbed my hand and removed it from his arm. "You said that you're having problems at your place. Sleep here tonight and if you like it maybe, we can discuss you being my roommate. I wouldn't want you sleeping on the streets and you don't need to go back to that club. It's too dangerous." He ran his strong hands through his disheveled hair and smirked. "I've been thinking about renting the room out for a while now. The nights can get a little lonely..." His voice trailed off.

I grimaced. 'Mr. Smooth talker' had another thing coming if he so quickly assumed that I was going to just like and trust him "You better not think-"

WAKE UP CALL
VICTORIA ASHLEY

"Don't worry, if I wanted sex from you... you would know. I already told you that," he cut me off, grinning devilishly before trudging into the living room. The defined muscles in his back flexed with each step that he took, causing me to breathe heavily.

He plopped down on the couch and threw his feet up on the glass coffee table. "If you decide that you want to rent the room then I can help you move tomorrow. I am only trying to help you. I owe it to... an old friend." His face softened as he looked up at me.

"Who said that I even want to stay here tonight and what do you mean, you owe it to a friend?" I questioned throwing my arms up in the air. I was confused. He owed a friend. It made no sense.

"Well you might not have much of a choice after tonight, and you wouldn't understand. It's complicated," he said truthfully. "It doesn't have to be permanent. No one deserves to live out on the streets. Save some money and then you can go as you please. I just want to help."

I sighed and turned away from him to walk back down the hallway. He was right about my situation. The thought of spending any more time sleeping on the streets made my insides cringe. It made me feel weak and helpless that I needed help.

"I just... I don't know what to say. This isn't something that I would usually even consider." I pulled my phone out of my pocket as it buzzed. I stared down at the message from my landlord asking me where his money was.

Swallowing, I looked back up to meet Jace's eyes. "I'll stay for tonight, but don't even think about trying anything." I stopped to look back at him, eyes concerned. "I don't have any clothes to sleep in though..."

"I have clothes." He jumped up from the couch and walked past me and over to his bedroom. He came back a few minutes later with a crisp white T-shirt and a pair of black boxer briefs. The thought of them once being on his body, caused me to blush unwantedly.

I reached out and grabbed them from out of his hands. "Thanks. I guess this will have to do." I said, trying to sound as if the thought didn't bother me.

WAKE UP CALL
VICTORIA ASHLEY

"What's your name by the way?" He stood by the door to his bedroom – the sizable bulge in his denim jeans painfully visible to my lustful gaze. *Stop it, Avery!*

"Avery," I whispered. "Avery Hale." The shock of his kindness was so overwhelming that it made me lose my breath, lips trembling as I swallowed a lump in my throat. I genuinely couldn't believe that someone would be willing to help me out so much, it was extraordinary.

I didn't know what it was about Jace – I had only known him for one day, after all – but I felt somewhat comfortable in his home. It was clean and tidy and the smell of fragrant vanilla that drifted through the hallway was certainly appealing. It was my favorite scent and reminded me of home.

I nodded at him before taking off down the cream hallway and shutting myself in the bathroom. I had a mosaic of different emotions running throughout my body, and it made me feel like breaking down. I knew that I had to be strong though.

I straightened up and placed my hands on my hips, exhaling as I stared at the large, exquisite shower that sat in the corner of the room – golden spout gleaming gently in the muted light of the amber bulb that hung above me.

If there was one thing that I wanted, it was a long, hot shower. I needed to scrub away that filthy creep's perverted touch from earlier, before Jace had saved me. I hated being touched. I always had, even as a child it had been difficult for me to allow my parents to hug me - not that they ever had. The thought of that man's greedy hands roaming over my flesh made me nauseous. I didn't even let Caleb hold me when we weren't having sex - no cuddling, holding hands, and sensual massages. I never allowed his embrace.

I turned on the shower and watched as a torrent of steaming hot water spurted out. Then I stripped off my clothes and stepped inside, closing the shower curtain behind me as I allowed the water to wash away my hot tears.

Chapter 3

I slowly opened my eyes to see Jace standing just inches from my face, his minty breath waking me up completely. I jumped back startled, nearly slamming my head into the wall behind me. "What the hell?" I questioned while throwing my hand over my chest.

My heart was beating so hard that I could see my hand moving up and down on my chest.

Silently he reached for my arm and gently pulled it away from my chest, eyes trained on my lips as he pulled me out of bed and over to the pile of clothes that sat on the black trunk at the end of the bed. "You sleep too much." He laughed. "Let's eat some breakfast and run over to your apartment." Without waiting for a response, he walked out of the bedroom, leaving me alone in the confines of my muddled thoughts.

Batting my eyelids lazily, I sauntered down the hallway, stepping into the dim kitchen to see Jace standing in front of the stove with a spatula in his right hand. I knew that Jace cooked, but seeing him in action was quite sexy.

His taut muscles significantly relaxed as he peered over his left shoulder to find me standing in the doorway. I sighed heavily and looked over at the clock. "Why did..." I stopped when I noticed the time. "Oh shit," I squeaked. "It's already eleven o'clock."

He quickly set my cooked breakfast on a plate and turned around, walking over to the kitchen table and setting it down. He looked over at the clock and smirked. "Yeah, that's what it looks like." He pointed at the chair next to the food and then walked over to fix himself his own plate. "Did I wake you up too early? I would've let you sleep longer, but I don't think that your landlord is going to be so patient with you moving your stuff." He paused to grab a fork. "That's of course, if you agree to."

I sat down and forked my eggs while eyeing his back. The gray shirt he wore was snug and revealing. Suddenly, I found my eyes trailing further down his body. It was beginning to be a bad habit of mine.

Finally, I tore my eyes away and shook my head, clasping my clammy palms together. "That's not it," I breathed. "It's just that I went to bed so early last night and I actually slept more than five hours." I looked up to see him striding over to the table and pulling out the chair next to me. "I haven't been able to sleep much for as long as I can remember..."

He looked up warily from his steaming plate of breakfast and leaned back in his chair. He looked cool and collected. "Maybe you just needed to have me close by to sleep." He smirked playfully before shoving his fork in his mouth and chewing slowly. "Seriously though," he whispered. "You're welcome to rent out my extra room. It's already yours if you ask me." His husky voice sent a shiver up my spine.

I nervously ran my hand through my mess of hair and looked down at my plate. I knew that if I looked into the emerald of his eyes again then I would lose control and agree to his crazy offer. "I can't. I don't even know you and I couldn't-"

"It's yours, Avery," he cut me off. "You can't live out on the streets. You saw what happened to you last night. I won't let that happen again." He shoved one last forkful of food into his mouth and walked over to the sink. "I'll go and get dressed and then meet you at the car in fifteen minutes."

I exhaled, tucking a strand of hair behind my ear as his words sank in. Jace was right. It was either stay with him or risk death out on the streets.

WAKE UP CALL
VICTORIA ASHLEY

Fifteen minutes later, we were inside Jace's black Mercedes and heading over to my old apartment. His hands gripped the steering wheel as the car sailed through the empty streets, nearing my old home with each second that passed. The closer that we got, the more nervous that I became.

"I hope that we have enough room in here to grab what you need." He looked over at me as I played with my old ring nervously. "Nice ring."

I quickly slapped his leg and pointed at the road. "Do you mind watching the road?" I snapped, suddenly nervous that Jace would get us in a crash.

He looked down at his leg with narrowed eyes and let out an amused laugh. "What, don't you trust me?"

I hugged my arms to my chest and bit the bottom of my lip. "Please just watch the road," I said firmly. "I hardly even know you. Besides, I learned long ago never to trust anyone. Everyone will hurt you in the end..." My voice trailed off as I leaned further into my seat. The softness of the leather made me comfortable and suddenly tired again, as if I hadn't gotten much sleep.

The smile instantly faded from his face and his gaze set on the road. "That's not the way to live," he breathed. "We'll have to find a way to change that."

I sat in silence as I began to play with my old ring again, gently tugging it on and off as I held back the burst of emotions running through my mind. I felt torn. I knew that staying at my place wasn't an option but yet I didn't even know Jace. How could I be so stupid to agree to his offer?

"Are we close?" Jace questioned, snapping me out of my painful thoughts.

I jerked my head up just in time to see us passing my apartment. The building was old, rotted and covered in moss. I wrinkled my nose. "It's right there. Go back just a little bit and pull over in that parking lot." I pointed over to the tiny parking lot and leaned back into the plush leather of the seat.

Jace pulled into the parking lot and stopped the car as I pursed my lips. "Good luck with that," he murmured, narrowing his eyes as he peered through the windshield and over at the bedraggled man fisting the door.

My heartless landlord stood outside the apartment door, pounding on it as his nostrils flared. "I know you're in there, girl.

Your ass doesn't get naked until at least ten o'clock!" he screamed in rage. "Don't make me open it myself." He was always very persistent. I hated that.

I smiled quickly, appreciative of Jace's help, before opening the car door and running over to the apartment door, ignoring the random faces that watched me. "I'm just here to get my stuff and then I'll be gone," I said, breathless.

He looked over at me with a gleeful smirk creasing his features. A mop of brown curls fell around his greasy, fat face. The scar on his upper lip stretched as he smiled. I always wondered how he got that scar. My guess was by someone kicking the crap out of him. He was a horrid man, and the thought had even occurred to myself on numerous occasions. "I should keep all of your-"

"Be cool," Jace interrupted. "I'm helping her grab the stuff that she wants and then you'll never see her again." I didn't realize he had come to help me and as I stared at his impressive frame towering over the stumpy old man, I felt my heartbeat soar. I'd never had someone stand up for me before. "We'll leave with no trouble. You have my word."

My old landlord crossed his eyes and sighed in frustration as he reached for his set of keys and opened the door. "You have one hour to get your shit out." His voice sneered as he addressed me with a lecherous smile before turning around and hobbling away.

I licked my lips before stepping inside with Jace following closely at my heel. He stood there silently taking in the surroundings of the small apartment. It smelled of sweet vanilla. Just like Jace's place had.

"I think that we can fit most of this stuff in my car." He paced the apartment while muttering under his breath. "You don't need your bed. You can have the one at my house. You don't need that TV, it's small and outdated." He stepped out of the bedroom and into the living room. "I have a dresser, TV and bed that you can have, so I guess all that you really need are just items that you can't live without."

I ran into his back as he stopped and peeked back into my room. "Is the floor your second dresser?" He looked down at the pile of clothes from the night we had first met and grinned. He was teasing me, but I had stuff that was more important on my mind.

I pushed him out of the room and back into the living room. "I can't just let you give me everything." I threw myself onto my worn-out couch and looked up at him as I grunted. The couch was sunken in and hurt my back. "It's too much. Plus I'm not staying long."

He rolled his eyes and walked into the kitchen, grabbing an empty box. "It's easier to do it this way for the both of us." He walked back to my bedroom with me trailing behind him. "It's really not a problem."

He emptied out my dresser clumsily, throwing all of my clothes into the huge box. I looked down next to him to see him surrounded by my panties. A cocky smirk sat on his face. "Nice panties," he winked, cocking an eyebrow as he stared at the assortment of underwear. He looked rather happy.

I ran over and knocked him out of the way. "I think that I should just take care of this." I grabbed for my panties and pushed them under my legs to hide them as I sat on the ground. "You just take that other empty box and pack up all of the bathroom stuff."

He laughed and nodded his head in agreement, turning around and walking out of the door as I tried to calm my racing heartbeat. *This person was making me crazy.*

Thirty minutes later, we were done packing and pulling back into Jace's driveway. I got out of the car and started reaching for the pile of boxes when suddenly I felt Jace's hand on mine.

He looked me in the eye with an intensity that made me shiver. "Do you mind?" he questioned. "I'm the guy so I'll grab all of this stuff. I'll bring it in and let you unpack it."

I backed away from his touch and took a deep breath. He had already touched me more than what I was comfortable with and it was making my insides summersault endlessly. I turned away and smiled as I walked into his house and into the spare bedroom. Jace followed behind, arms piled high with boxes, and set them down on the floor by the dresser. He was more helpful than I expected. It was nice.

He sat on the edge of the bed and watched me as I unpacked. "Can I help you with something?" I questioned. I couldn't understand why he was hanging around so much. I wasn't quite use to the company. I liked being alone.

He stood up lazily and smiled at me. "Take a shower in a bit and get dressed. We're going out tonight." He walked past me and grabbed the strap of the silver dress that was in my hand. Then he looked me in the eye. "I like that dress. I'm sure it looks nice on you." He looked at me briefly before turning away.

I stood up and threw my arms in the air in frustration. Too confused by what he had just said, I didn't even realize that he could be flirting with me. "What do you mean we're going out?" I wasn't in any kind of shape to go out and be social. I had too much on my mind. I stared at him with confusion written all over my face.

He calmly leaned into my door and ran his hands through his hair. He looked as if he hadn't a care in the world. "Some of my friends are picking us up in a few hours and we're going out for a few drinks." He smirked confidently. "It'll be fun. I'm a lot of fun."

I felt my cheeks flush as he ran his tongue over his lip ring. "I don't know about that. I really need to work tonight. I have no money." My voice filled with adrenaline, as I tore my eyes away.

"Who said that you need money?"

I dropped the dress to the floor and pulled a tendril of hair out of my eye. "I don't expect anything from you, Jace."

He grinned and pushed himself away from the door. "Be ready in a few hours, beautiful." Then he was gone, his footsteps echoing down the hallway as I swallowed a lump in my throat.

My mind filled with confusion at the thought of Jace thinking I was beautiful. A cold shiver ran down my spine as I bent over and picked up the dress that Jace said he liked.

An hour passed as I finished unpacking the rest of my baggage in an effort to make my new home feel as personal as possible. Finally, I finished, placing down a bottle of my favorite perfume on the bedside table before turning around and wiping a bead of moisture from my forehead. Unpacking everything had made me surprisingly tired, and I knew that I needed to freshen up especially if I was meeting Jace's friends tonight. As much as I hated the idea, he seemed set on me going and after all of his help, I owed him.

WAKE UP CALL
VICTORIA ASHLEY

Sighing, I walked out of my room and into the bathroom with a towel in my hand. The bathroom was small but very clean with a large shower in the corner.

Brushing a strand of hair out of my eye, I walked toward it and turned the water on before undressing and hanging my towel on a peg. The shower was hot and as I washed myself, I threw my head back and sniffed the air. It smelled of Jace, causing my mind to wander.

I stepped out of the shower and reached for the fuzzy black towel, clutching it between my fingertips as I brought it to my face and exhaled in contentment. I felt so much better after freshening up, however as I opened my eyes the sight that greeted me made me feel like I needed to shower all over again.

Jace stood calmly, toothbrush in hand, by the bathroom mirror, wearing nothing but a pair of tight white boxers. His taut abdominal muscles flexed as he turned around to face me.

Squealing, I grabbed the towel and covered myself up as his gaze set on mine. "Do you mind?"

His eyebrow twitched before he turned around again and tossed his toothbrush to the side before dropping his boxers and stepping into the shower.

I wanted to run and hide.

"We don't have a lot of time to get ready." He poked his head out of the shower and pointed to the shelf. "Can you throw me that towel?"

My insides turned over as I snatched up my clothes, grabbed the extra towel and walked over to stand in front of him. "Haven't you ever heard of knocking?" I threw the towel at him and stormed into my new room.

The image of Jace naked dominated my thoughts, as I got dressed into the little silver dress that Jace had said he liked, did my hair and walked out into the living room.

Jace stood there looking out the window. He wore a white fleece shirt with the top two buttons undone and a pair of fitted jeans. He was cool, calm, and collected. It was as if nothing had happened.

"What the hell Jace? Was it really-"

He walked over cutting me off. "Our rides here come on." He walked to the front door and paused to make sure that I was following. "Come."

~ 34 ~

"I'm coming," I mumbled, while following him outside and pausing at the end of the grass. I wanted to think of a reason not to go, any reason at all, but my mind wouldn't work.

He jumped into the backseat of the little red car and called for me to get in.

I strolled over to the car to see that it was already full. There were two men in the front and two women in the back. They stared at me expectantly, waiting for me to get in.

I backed away and waved my arms in front of me as my heartbeat began to hammer against my chest. "No. There's no room left in there. I'm just staying home."

I turned away to go, however before I had even taken a step forward I felt a large hand enclose itself around my own before I was pulled into the car and onto Jace's lap.

He gripped my waist and then reached over and slammed the door shut. He was dead set on me going. I was stuck. "There's plenty of room for you right here." He snaked his arm around my waist and pulled me closer. It gave me butterflies. "This is my new roommate, Avery," he said to everyone as they sat quietly.

I looked around the car tentatively as everyone introduced themselves. It was as if the car was full of models and as they said hello I couldn't help but feel completely inadequate compared to them all. I was just Avery. I wasn't beautiful, fun or even social.

"Um...hi," I said awkwardly. I found myself leaning into Jace's lap for comfort and it surprised me. I didn't even flinch when his hands rested on my thighs. Truthfully, Jace was the closest I could get to comfort while being trapped with these strangers

The rest of the car ride passed by quickly as Jace's friends chattered amongst each other. I remained silent, eyes trained on the windshield as I tried to calm my racing nerves.

Finally, we pulled up to a large bar called *Legends*. It looked upper class and everyone outside was dressed well. It was very different from what I was used to and as the car pulled to a halt and the door opened, I smoothed down my dress and tried to remain composed.

We made our way inside and past the bouncer. Jace found us a big round table in the back that was spacious enough for the six of us. He pulled out a chair and motioned for me to sit as my eyes wondered around me. All of the workers wore white dressy clothing. I felt out of place. Even Jace wore white.

"What would you like to drink?"

I sat down and fixed my dress so that it wasn't exposing too much skin before I threw my purse on the table and smiled at Jace, trying to look calm. "I would like a Dr. Cherry and Sprite."

He smirked and arched an eyebrow, as if he was a bit confused by my answer. "Oh come on. That's not even going to get you a buzz," he said, nudging my arm playfully as my eyebrow quirked.

I reached out and slugged him on the shoulder. "What makes you think that I want you to get me drunk?" His eyes danced in the disco lights as I stared at him. He looked good tonight, dressed in his snug white shirt and faded jeans, completed with a studded belt that gripped his sleek waist perfectly. No wonder all of the girls kept staring.

He bent down and placed his lips against my ear as a bolt of electricity ran up my spine. "Every girl wants me to," he whispered, before turning around and walking away toward the bar to get our drinks. Goose bumps prickled my arms as I bowed my head and swallowed. I couldn't explain the way he made me feel when he was close to me but I knew that it was dangerous.

A beautiful girl with long blond curls plopped down next to me and popped her gum. She was trying to look sweet, but I could see the mischievous look deep in her eyes. "Hi, I'm Emma." She forced a smile. "Have you known Jace for long? I didn't even know that he had a roommate." Her blue eyes screamed jealousy as she waited for a response.

"No actually," I started. "I just met him a couple of days ago. He's been really great with helping me out." I shifted unfortunately, as she stared at me.

She leaned back in disbelief and blew out her breath. "Yeah I would say so," she said stiffly.

The girl was stunning: a tall, leggy blond bombshell. He had to be sleeping with her.

I played with my hands nervously before finally, Jace returned and set my drink down in front of me. He smiled and nodded his head in Emma's direction. "Emma, Matt is coming with your drink."

She crossed her arms over her ample breast and huffed as her eyes narrowed. She didn't seem too happy about that Matt guy getting her drink instead of Jace. Jace didn't seem to care, though.

Jace sat down across from us and took a gulp of his drink. I watched as Emma slid out of her chair and walked behind him before snaking her arms around his chest. She attempted to kiss his neck, but he pulled away and leaned over the table.

"So, Avery how's your drink?" he asked. "Finish it up and I'll go grab us a couple more. Don't waste them either. I can sit here all night and make sure that you're finishing every last drop." He reached up and pulled Emma's hands away from his chest as if she was nothing more than an irritation. She looked angry.

I turned my head away as Emma turned red and bit her bottom lip. "It's fine. I'll probably just have this one," I responded. "I'm not much of a drinker anymore." I took another sip and played with my straw as I desperately tried to avoid Emma's malicious gaze. It had been five minutes and she hated me already. I hadn't even done anything to her.

Jace smiled and walked over to sit down next to me. "Well tonight you are." He grabbed my drink and held it next to my lips. "I'll make sure that you're safe." His eyes seemed honest. He slammed his drink back quickly and set the empty glass down at the edge of the table. "You deserve to relax a little."

I leaned in and took a big swig of my mixed drink. The cool liquid ran down my throat and awakened every sense. I swallowed it quickly and took one more before setting my glass down on the edge of the table next to Jace's. He was right. I did need to relax.

"That wasn't so bad now was it? I have more drinks coming," Jace announced.
Suddenly a perky waitress appeared with two tall drinks and two shots piled precariously on a small tray. "Here you go, Jace," she said, before placing them down on the table and walking away.

Matt, the dark haired cutie with crystal blue eyes and huge dimples appeared next to Emma and set two glasses down in front of her. She rolled her eyes and grabbed a glass before throwing her head back taking a long sip. Matt watched her with widened eyes and laughed to himself. "How did you end up with a second round of drinks already?" he asked Jace, while eyeing the liquid courage.

Jace nodded his head and grabbed a shot glass handing it to me. His fingers brushed mine and he smiled. "I have my ways."

I looked down into the glass and jumped back when the strong smell hit me. "Really! Jack Daniels," I huffed. Was he seriously trying to get me drunk? I hated Jack Daniels.

Jace grinned and sniffed his shot. "It's not that bad, Avery." He looked happy and as if, he really enjoyed spending time with me.

I couldn't let him think that I wasn't grateful, so before I had a second to change my mind, I squeezed the glass tightly in my hand and slammed the shot down. The liquid burned as it slid through my parted lips and down my throat. The feeling was raw and caused me to cough violently.

Emma sneered as Jace reached over and patted my back.

I pushed Jace's hand away and took a sip of my mixed drink. "I'm fine, seriously," I said, annoyed with Emma's reaction.

Jace downed his shot hungrily and then smiled at me with rich eyes. "You looked pretty hot doing that, just saying." Then he reached over and ran his finger over my lip. I jumped away, and he smiled. "Are you saving some for later because all you have to do is ask for another one and I'll buy it."

I pushed my shot glass away and stifled back a laugh. He was too silly and carefree for me to not to laugh. "I think that I'm good for now," I replied, feeling the drink flooding through my veins. I felt alive and suddenly nothing around me mattered so much.

Emma glared at me dirtily before grabbing Jace by the arm. Her blond hair cascaded around her tanned face as she tugged his arm. "Come on," she breathed seductively. "Let's dance." Her black, low hanging dress did wonders for her perky breast. They were almost on full display as she eyed Jace as if he were her toy.

Jace scratched his forehead as if deep in thought before finally, standing up. His belt glowed in the darkness of the club as he towered over Emma. "I'll be right back," he said to me as a grimace creased his lips. I swallowed, nodding at him before watching as he turned around and followed Emma onto the dance floor. It was obvious that he didn't want to go, but for some reason still did.

WAKE UP CALL
VICTORIA ASHLEY

A group of gyrating bodies surrounded them as they danced together underneath the glare of the disco lights. Emma draped her arms around Jace's neck and began to swing her hips from side to side in a dance of unadulterated lust. My gaze didn't focus on her though – instead, I stared at Jace. His dark hair and imposing frame had me in a daze. He seemed distant as he stared off into nowhere.

Suddenly, a hand tapped me on the shoulder. I looked beside me to be greeted by another member of the group. He was the owner of the vehicle however, we hadn't exchanged words yet. He had short blond hair, golden eyes and a smile that looked as if it could make a girl melt from a thousand feet.

"Hi, I'm Reece," He smiled sweetly. "Come dance with me. I feel a little left out." He lightly grabbed my arm and pulled me to my feet as I brushed a strand of hair out of my eye and smoothed down my dress.

The silver beads shimmered in the disco lights as I followed Reece over to the dance floor. I couldn't believe this was happening to me. Seeing Jace out on the dance floor was somehow enough to convince me to let Reece pull me out there. Either that or I just didn't want to look silly sitting there alone.

I stood by the side of the dance floor frozen for a moment as I tried to decide whether this was a good idea or not. However, after glancing over to see Emma grinding her slutty little body all over Jace and running her hands down his arms, chest and legs I knew I had made my decision. I wasn't going to let her have fun while I sat bored and alone, looking silly, in the big bar.

I let Reece pull me out to the middle of the dance floor as I began to sashay from side to side. It was a new experience for me but it felt good and as I let the music consume me, I felt my body begin to loosen up.

Reece was dancing behind me, smoothly rubbing his body against mine as his hands explored my dress, fast, insistent fingers playing with the silver fabric that clung to my slender frame. However as his hands moved slowly up my dress to my breast I felt a pang of discomfort strike me.

I jumped forward and turned around to face him with narrowed eyes. "What are -?"

WAKE UP CALL
VICTORIA ASHLEY

A thick, husky voice interrupted me. "Let me dance with her." It was Jace. He didn't look pleased as he watched Reece walk away. He smiled at me. "Are you okay?"

I nodded my head.

I swallowed a lump in my throat as Jace grabbed me firmly pulling my body against his. His face was just inches away from mine as he gripped the back of my leg sensually and dipped me backwards until I could smell the Old Spice aftershave that lingered on his neck. It was strong, sweet, and intoxicating.

I felt a blush stain the porcelain of my cheeks as he leaned forward and pressed his face into my neck. Feeling relaxed, I leaned back and extended my neck as I let his body support mine.

The staccato beats of the music surrounded us as we danced together. Jace's body fit mine perfectly. It drove me mad. I should've been mad at him for touching me, yet I was enjoying the moment. Most likely it was due to the liquor.

We continued to dance for what felt like forever and as his body began to get closer to mine, I felt my heartbeat skyrocket.

I tried to calm my racing nerves as I felt the room starting to spin around me. It was all so overwhelming: the music, the drinks, Jace.

Suddenly I felt him grab my hip with hunger written in his eyes. He moaned softly, bowing his head as he exhaled and ran his hands over my silver dress. His breath warmed my full lips, as he looked me straight in the eye.

We were so close and yet so far away. Suddenly, he froze and then frowned before backing away. "I'll be right back." He gently let go of me and walked away leaving me alone on the dance floor.

I stood there breathing heavily, my body wet with sweat. The relentless pounding of my heart was so loud it deafened me. I had no idea what I was feeling but I knew that it was a new experience for me.

Exhaling, I walked off the dance floor, pushing myself past the group of heaving bodies that surrounded me.

Finally, I freed myself, walking over to the table unsteadily as I felt the effects of all of the drinks from earlier. My mind was a whirlwind of emotions: anger, hurt, pain – I was confused.

Suddenly, a husky voice broke my reverie.

"Avery, wait." I heard Jace behind me. He went to reach for my arm, but I shook it off. I couldn't let him get close to me anymore. It was too much.

"Let go, please," My slurred voice shook with emotion.

He ignored my plea, turning me around before placing his hands on my shoulders and looking me in the eye. "What's wrong?"

I exhaled slowly and ran my hand over my face. "I don't know. I just don't feel good. I'm just going to walk home." I grabbed my clutch bag from the table and started for the door, but Jace stopped me in my tracks.

"Are you kidding me? I'm going home too then," he said sternly. "You don't have to leave all by yourself. I made you come so we'll leave when you're ready."

I sighed in defeat before watching as he waved over at his friends, signaling that he was leaving with me.

Emma and a busty red head rolled their eyes and continued dancing while Matt and Reece looked disappointed.

Jace turned to me. "I have a friend leaving right now. He'll give us a ride."

He placed his hand on my lower back and walked me outside and over to his friends car. The cool air flooded my lungs as I stepped over the gravel and into the safety of the car.

It took us about ten minutes to get back to his place and the journey passed by quickly as I listened to Jace converse with his friend.

When we arrived home, I thanked Jace for the drinks and went to my room without another word. I undressed quickly before crawling into my soft bed and enveloping myself in the quilts. It had been a crazy night. A whirlwind of thoughts sped through my mind like a tornado, my parents, my apartment, my past. I just needed to find a level of peace within myself but trying to find it was proving to be just as hard as I had imagined.

I turned off my bedside lamp and let the darkness consume me just as it always had.

Chapter 4

I could smell the booze on his foul breath as he leaned over me and pounded his fist into the wall just inches above my head. "Get your ass out of bed and go to school." He grinded his teeth and his eyes twitched as he stared down at me.

I cringed and gripped the fleece blanket tightly trying to find some comfort. I was confused. It was midnight. Why was he telling me to go to school? If I argued with him then there would be a chance that my world would end tonight. "But-"

He wrapped his burly fingers through my thin hair and yanked my head to the left. "Don't you even think about talking back to me," he spat. "Get your ass up now." He yanked my hair even harder causing me to fall out of bed and land on the cruddy floor. My hand landed in a pile of dirty clothing, soiled with spilt booze. It was most likely, Jack Daniels. It was my father's choice of poison.

"Henry," My mother said, through hiccups. "It's only midnight." She leaned back against the wall and started laughing. Her laugh sounded oddly diabolic and it sent shivers through my body. Why wasn't she trying to help me?

WAKE UP CALL
VICTORIA ASHLEY

I woke up gripping the blanket on my bed so tightly that it almost ripped. The sweat dripped down my face and left a salty taste on my swollen lips, reminding me that it was just a nightmare.

The nightmares had gotten so bad that I sometimes woke up with my whole face puffy and swollen. I couldn't seem to fight the tears. I was too weak. No matter how hard I tried.

I forced my legs to work as I jumped out of bed and quietly ran down the hall and into the bathroom. I tiredly switched on the light and stared into the brightly lit mirror, my clear reflection showing every bit of the lost girl that I'd become. The pain in my eyes, were very distinct as the tears continued to flow down my face and soak my shirt. I hated the way my parents still got to me. It didn't matter how far away I was. It still hurts.

I turned on the cold water, hands shaking, as I splashed a handful of water on my face. The frigidness of the water gave me the chills that ran all the way through my whole body, waking me up completely.

Afterwards, I made my way through the house in search of Jace, not sure, if I really even wanted to find him.

"Hello." I poked my head into the living room, down the hall, and into the kitchen. The house was empty. Where could he have taken off to? I ended up back inside the kitchen, quickly noticing a note firmly stuck to the fridge. I yanked it off, reading it with curious eyes.

I didn't want to wake you. I left ten dollars on the counter for a cab. Meet me at the diner by ten o'clock. I'm sure that you will love your new job.

-Jace

The note fell out of my hand landing like a feather on my bare foot. The words left me speechless. This man didn't owe me anything, yet he was willing to provide me with a place to stay and a job. It was more than anyone else had ever done for me, yet I'd done nothing to earn it.

I plopped down on a kitchen chair and slowly rubbed circles on the side of my head. It helped me to calm down most of the time, although, I wasn't so sure it was going to help me much this time.

My hands shook at just the thought of waiting tables. I had no experience and the feeling left me empty. I didn't want to mess everything up and end up jobless and homeless once again. I couldn't make Jace look bad and at his own diner.

Finally, I looked up from the table to see that I had less than an hour to get ready and to the diner. I panicked.

I jumped up from the chair and ran back to my room, nearly tripping over my own two feet. I flew face first into the dresser as I reached out to catch myself. I quickly opened every single drawer to the dresser, throwing everything that I owned out onto the floor around me. It was really becoming a bad habit.

"Damn. What do I wear?" I held up my favorite T-shirt shortly before throwing it down next to me. Then I yanked out a pair of faded jeans and my only pair of Converse sneakers.

Forty minutes later I was showered, dressed and standing outside waiting for the taxi. The taxi arrived with fifteen minutes left to spare. I sprinted over to the old taxi sticking my head inside to get a peak. To my surprise, it was the same man as the last two times. I had to admit, that I was still kind of embarrassed by our last encounter.

"*The Indy Go*," I said, with a smile, hoping that he wouldn't bring up the money situation.

He looked out the window staring at me as he struggled to roll it down. He tilted his head and took a deep breath. "Do you have cash this time, ma'am?"

I nodded my head

He looked me up and down with a look of surprise on his round face and returned the smile. "Get in," he said. "That place has some good fried chicken. Are you going there for a lunch date?" he questioned.

I shook my head and searched through my purse. "No. I am actually starting work there today." I found the ten-dollar bill, pulling it from out of my purse. "Here you go. Sorry but I'm in a bit of a hurry."

"Sure thing. No problem, ma'am. I'm just your guy," he said proudly.

The rest of the cab ride was silent. I was sure that by me hurrying him had made him feel uneasy about starting up a conversation. It was fine, though. I wasn't much for conversation and never really knew what to say.

We pulled up to the diner with only two minutes to spare. I sat up anxiously and looked out the window. "Thank you." I jumped out the door, taxi nearly still moving, and ran for the door of the diner.

I stopped dead in my tracks and took a long deep breath before reaching out for the door handle. My hands shook as I whispered words of encouragement. "You can do this. Stay calm," I breathed.

I pulled the door open, eyes wide, to see families gathered around the diner, most of them laughing and playing with each other. Little kids playfully chased each other around while their mothers reached out for them laughing and playing back. I swallowed hard as a lump formed in my throat.

"Avery. You made it." Jace suddenly stepped out from behind the counter greeting me with a friendly smile. He looked good, in a plain back tee and dark denim jeans. His smile made it even better. "I'm glad that you woke up in time." He looked excited to see me. It made me strangely happy.

I nodded my head and turned away from the happy families as I fought to catch my breath. "Yes. I did. I got lucky, really." I forced a smile and looked him in the eye. "Thank you."

"Not a problem." Jace ran his hand through his styled hair and waved his arm out in front of him. "Let me show you around."

A short man in about his mid-fifties suddenly stepped out from behind the counter reaching for my open hand. It startled me. His white slicked hair glistened in the lighting as he chuckled and looked me up and down in wonder. Why damn! I'm Winston, the cook. I make all of the great food in this diner." He grinned and looked at Jace, before looking back at me. "You must be, Avery, the pretty new waitress that Jace told me about." He elbowed Jace in the side and raised an eyebrow.

Jace smirked and lightly squeezed Winston's shoulder. "The word I used was beautiful, Winston." He smiled playfully and reached for my hand. He didn't looked embarrassed one bit, having Winston call him out like that. "Come on."

My heart sped up at the sound of the word beautiful. He had said it once and even then, I couldn't believe it. I pulled my hand from out of his tight grip and nervously bit my lip. He touched excessively and it bothered me. "Okay. I'm ready."

Jace looked down at my hand and smiled. "This here is the kitchen." I followed him around the corner and into a tiny kitchen. It was complete with two stoves, a large deep fryer, two freezers and a fridge.

He quickly pointed out the dressings, desserts, salad condiments and breads before guiding me over to the server station. The server station was a tiny area with a computer, napkins, silverware settings and a place to put your belongings.

It was a lot different from the club I had grown used to going to. There were no half-naked girls, fighting for the best outfit or snatching up my makeup, tainting it with their filthy lips.

"Jace," I paused, trying to find a way to thank him. "Thanks again for...this."

Jace smiled, placing his hand on my lower back and giving me a light shove toward the computer. "This is where you will place your orders. The orders will then go back to the kitchen and Winston will prepare your food."

He stepped away from the computer and pointed over to the heated counter right outside the kitchen. That sucker was so hot that I could feel the heat radiating off it. Either that or it was just Jace. Either way, I started to sweat. "That there is where Winston will leave the food when it's ready."

I looked around, confused as to how I was going to manage to pull everything off and make it through the day. I waved my arms in front of me to cool off. It didn't help. "I don't know-"

"Don't worry." Jace cut in. He smiled and looked me in the eye. He always looked me in the eye, making me nervous. In some ways, I believed that he meant to. "I'm sure that it will be a lot to take in, but Stacy will be here to help you."

I glanced up at him feeling a bit overwhelmed. My eye twitched and I secretly tried shaking it off. "I'm going to guess that Stacy was the waitress that messed up my order the other day," I questioned

I felt the presence of someone behind me before a hand gripped my shoulder and squeezed. I swiftly turned around me to see the young girl from the other day. Her blue eyes gleamed with joy as she pushed her blond strands out of her face. "I'm

Stacy," she said. "I'm sorry about the other day. I would like to start fresh." She smiled at me revealing her small set of dimples.

I carefully looked her over taking in her cheerful attitude. She gave off a totally different vibe than the first time I had seen her.

"Yeah sure," I replied, unsure of how to act around her. "Everyone has a bad day once in a while." I smiled small and twisted a finger in my hair. "Thank you."

She gave me a satisfied smile before leaning in and wrapping her arms around me. I instantly stiffened up feeling uncomfortable. "It's okay." She laughed, and something in her laugh told me that she was used to that reaction. "You will get used to me soon enough." She dropped her arms away from my stiff body and walked away with a small smile. "Follow me."

An hour later, I took on my first table, which happened to be an elderly couple that could barely move without my assistance. I was terrified of accidentally hurting them. However, they didn't mind when I made a few mistakes and understood that it was my first day. I had to admit that I got lucky to get them. They helped to ease me in and relax me before taking on the busy day.

Three plates dropped, and six hours later, I somehow managed to make $68.38. It wasn't the hundreds of dollars that I was used to but the business was a lot better than my last job. I had managed to make it through the whole day without some pervert trying to grope me. I could get used to that.

I leaned into the last dirty booth with a smile as I calmly washed off the table. The clock above me read 4:28 p.m. The hours at the diner were Sunday: seven o'clock a.m. to four o'clock p.m. and Monday-Saturday: 8:30 a.m. - 6:30 p.m. It seemed reasonable enough for me. I could actually get back to my old sleeping habits or at least try.

Jace strolled over from out of nowhere, grabbing the towel from out of my hand. I jumped, unaware that he was even close by. He smiled sweetly before bending over and wiping off the table, taking over my job. "How was your first day," he questioned. "Did you do well on tips?"

I clumsily reached into my apron and pulled out my bundle of cash, hoping that he wouldn't laugh. I had no idea what a good waitress made. "I made around $69.00. Is that good?" I questioned.

Jace looked up and over at Stacy as she gathered up her things and headed for the door. "Thanks Stacy," he said smoothly. "We'll see you tomorrow."

Stacy shoved her keys into her mouth while juggling her belongings. She was quite talented. "Sure," She mumbled. "Bye, guys."

Jace stood up, reaching out a hand. "Do you want help?"

Stacy nodded her head and pushed the door open with her foot. "Um...no. I got it." She smiled and headed out the door.

Jace watched as Stacy disappeared before turning back to face me. "Stacy only made $63.00. You must have something special." He grinned and then motioned for me to follow him to the break room. He bent down, picking up a wrinkled up food order, and tossed it into the trash. "You did a wonderful job. I had a lot of regulars tell me how much they liked you," he said, tone professional. "I am very impressed."

I felt my cheeks redden as I turned my head away in embarrassment. I reached out the hand with the money in it. "Here's some money for rent. I know that it's not much, but it's a start."

Jace placed his hands on mine and pushed the money away, his hands lingered for a moment before he pulled them away. "Nope," he said. "I don't want any of that. You don't owe anything until next month. I already paid rent this month." He walked over and turned off the light switches. Then he pointed toward the door and waited for me to follow.

I walked in silence not knowing how to thank him. All that my parents ever did was take from me. I wasn't use to someone giving. The feeling was...different.

He walked in front of me, holding the door open for me as I followed behind him. He locked the door, checking it twice before turning around and smiling. "I am starving." He threw his keys in his pocket and reached for his car keys. "What shall we eat today? It's ladies choice. I would think hard about this because you might not get this opportunity again," he teased.

I laughed softly as I followed him through the gravel and to his car. It was getting dark outside and the cool wind gave me the chills. "Well... let me think here. It sounds like a huge life decision," I teased. "I haven't eaten all day so I guess I should make it count."

WAKE UP CALL
VICTORIA ASHLEY

Jace smiled and stopped in front of the car. "What is your favorite food? What do you like," he questioned. "I know nothing about you yet. All except for the fact that you like to sleep in your underwear," he grinned, obviously teasing me.

I felt my face flush when remembering thinking that I saw him while going to the bathroom in the middle of the night. It was dark and I couldn't quite be sure if it was him or just my eyes playing tricks on me. Clearly, it wasn't just my eyes. I cleared my throat and jumped into the car. I waited for him to get in and shut the door. "Chicken," I mumbled, trying to change the subject. "I love chicken."

He gave me a cocky grin and then shifted the car into drive. "Great choice. We'll stop at the video store, grab a movie and then pick up some fried chicken," he said confidently. "We'll just have a chill night and I can get to know my new roommate."

I smiled at the thought of just having a normal night, with movies and food. Just two people hanging out. I'd never had a night with anyone that didn't involve sex, bars or dancing. I liked that idea.

"Sounds good, but I get to pick the movie," I said playfully.

"Okay, but nothing too girly. I'm a manly man," he said, nudging me in the side as we pulled into the video store.

What he didn't know about me yet was that I didn't have a sensitive side. Girly love movies would do nothing for someone like me.

After spending a good ten minutes searching for a movie, we ended up leaving the video store with an action movie. The man on the cover looked entertaining enough to catch my eye and really, I just wanted to get out of there. There were too many people watching us as if we were some kind of happy couple. It was creepy.

After arriving back to Jace's house we sat down at the kitchen table, dished out the chicken, and mashed potatoes and started eating.

Jace looked over while taking a bite of his chicken and smiled as I played with my food. "So Avery, do you have any family close by?"

My whole body stiffened, hand shaking, as I fought to keep in control. No one had ever asked me about my family and I wasn't prepared to talk about them. "No," I blurted. "I mean...I haven't seen them in over a year." My gaze set down on my plate of food as I spooned my mashed potatoes. Why is he doing this?

The room stayed silent as Jace studied me with a serious face. I was trying hard to keep my eyes away from his, but I found it to be impossible. Finally, he pushed his food away clearing his throat. "How old are you, Avery?" he questioned, in all seriousness.

I looked up, nose flared, as I fought to hold back the tears. I didn't want to talk about my life and it angered me. "I just turned nineteen last month." I shoved a bite of potatoes in my mouth and slowly chewed. "Why? Why do you need to ask me these questions?"

Jace looked surprised as he tilted his head in thought. "I just want to know about you. This is me getting to know you," he paused. "Or at least trying."

I bit my bottom lip and averted my eyes away from his stare. His eyes were making me want to surrender and tell him more than what I wanted to. "Well I just don't like too many questions."

Jace took a few bites of his chicken before leaning in next to me and smiling. "So, you have a fake I.D?" he questioned amused.

I looked up and nodded my head, happy to change the mood. "Yup!" The room went silent again. "What about you, Jace? How old are you? You own a diner and have a great house. You really have yourself together."

"I just turned twenty three a few months ago. The diner was my fathers before he ran off." His smile faded as he looked up at me and leaned back in his seat. "Why haven't you seen your parents in so long? Where are-"

"I don't want to talk about it." I stammered, thinking that I was already in the clear, when clearly I wasn't.

Jace swallowed hard and crossed his arms over his chest. "Well do you have anyone close by? Like maybe a friend or a boyfriend?"

I looked away, eyes watering, as I dropped my fork. "No." I swallowed hard forcing back the lump in my throat. "I've never had a boyfriend and I don't have any friends." I instantly felt stupid for telling him things so personal about myself. I felt weak. "I think that I'm just going to head to bed." I stood up and pushed my chair away. "Thank you for dinner."

A look of hurt crossed Jace's face as he jumped up from his seat and reached for my hand. His grip was firm. He pulled me in for a hug but I backed away from his pull. "Avery," he whispered. "It's okay to talk about things."

I let out a deep breath and relaxed into his strong arms, burying my face into his chest like a child crying to their father. Feeling his moist shirt against my cheek made me feel silly. I felt like a silly child that had lost. It made me angry. I didn't understand why I was allowing myself to let this happen.

He gently rubbed the back of my head and then ran a finger along my cheek. "There, do you feel better?" He pulled away from me looking me in the eye. "It's okay to cry. The strong ones always do." Somehow I doubted that.

I let out a half sob, half laugh when realizing that I did feel a bit better than before. He didn't know much, but he knew more about me than anyone else did. It was a start. "Yes. Thank you," I whispered. "I actually do feel a bit better."

Jace smiled and brushed the hair from out of my face. "Good, now let's go watch this movie." He stared me in the eye for a moment before he walked away and started cleaning up our dinner mess. He wrapped up the chicken box before throwing the plates into the double sink.

I stood there hesitating shortly before reaching for a plate and deciding to help him. "Here, let me help."

Jace grabbed the plate from out of my hand, brushing his thumb over mine. "No. I can take care of this. You can go and set up the movie."

I pulled my hand away and turned away from him, feeling bad for letting him do all the work by himself, but thankful at the same time. "Okay, sure."

I made my way into the living room and over to the coffee table. I stared down at the movie before reaching down and taking it out of the case. If I really thought about it, it would be my first time watching a movie with a man. As cheesy as that sounded, it was true.

My hand slightly shook as I attempted to shove the movie into the player. I kept missing the opening. *Shit. Relax.* I pushed the movie in and smoothed out my shirt before taking a seat on the loveseat.

A few minutes later Jace plopped down next to me scaring me out of my thoughts. He eyed me curiously, as I kept readjusting myself. "Are you okay?" He laughed as I ran my hands over my jeans, wiping the sweat off.

I looked up at the TV, running a hand through my hair. "Sorry," I mumbled. "I'm fine." Really, I wasn't. I couldn't seem to get comfortable being so close to him.

He smiled at me and turned on the TV. "Are you feeling uncomfortable?" He grabbed my shoulder and gently pulled me against his body. It made my stomach flip. "You can lean against me for support. I'm pretty comfortable." He rested his head next to mine and placed his lips next to my ear. "I don't bite," he whispered.

I let out a nervous laugh relaxing my muscles as I fought to stay calm. Just breathe. It's not that bad. "Thanks," I whispered back. "Thanks for everything."

He glanced down at me and brushed the hair out of my face. "Don't worry about it." He smiled comfortably.

He started the movie and we both sat there in a comfortable silence. It felt nice for once just to relax and not have to talk.

The rhythm of Jace's heartbeat against my back helped to make me feel more at ease, although, my body was screaming for me to get up and run. A small part of me just didn't want to. Therefore, I didn't.

Chapter 5

I woke up in the middle of the night uncomfortable and in a daze. That was when I realized that I was still on the couch and wrapped up in Jace's arms.

My heart stopped and suddenly I felt dizzy. I gently wiggled my way out of his grip, attempting to get away without waking him. I was almost in the clear when suddenly; Jace gripped me tighter and bent in pressing his lips against my neck. His lips were soft and gentle causing my breath to catch in my throat.

I quickly caught my breath and stumbled off the couch, landing on the soft carpet. I scrambled to get back to my feet as quickly and quietly as possible. I had never slept next to a man before and I didn't want Jace to know that I had let my guard down with him. I had to learn to be more careful with Jace. I just couldn't seem to think straight around him.

I very carefully made my way down the hallway and to my bedroom, closing myself inside. I stared blankly down at my lonely bed before throwing myself down and pressing my hands to my head.

I quickly pulled the blanket back, crawling under the soft fleece of the blanket. It had always been my safety zone and at the moment I needed safety from myself. I rested my head against the wall behind me, mind spinning, as I twirled my fingers in my messy hair trying to make sense of my own emotions.

A few moments later, I heard footsteps creeping down the hall and then the sound of Jace's door as he softly shut it behind him. How embarrassing, I had probably woken him up by falling out of his arms. I had a feeling that it was going to be tough to face him in the morning. That was if I could even manage to fall back to sleep.

I tossed and turned for what felt like hours before giving up on sleep. I sat up, arms stretched, as I looked around my new room. Everything from the glass table, black trunk, and pictures on the wall were an unfamiliar feeling that made me wish that I had my own home.

Finally, I hopped out of bed and made my way to the bathroom. The door was wide open so without a second thought I stepped inside, flipping on the light behind me.

"Oh shit!" I screamed surprised by the sight in front of me.

Jace stood there in only his underwear while brushing his teeth. He peered over his taut shoulder and grinned with his toothbrush hanging out of his mouth. He looked just as cool and calm as ever. "Good morning."

I felt my eyes wander down to his low hanging boxers that were so low on his waist that even I felt embarrassed. I threw my hands over my eyes and forced myself not to peek. "I'm sorry," I stammered. "I didn't know you were in here." I turned back to the door and started walking away humiliated.

He pulled his toothbrush from out of his mouth and spit in the sink. "It's fine." He walked up next to me, pulling his boxers up. "I'm done now. The bathroom is all yours." He walked out of the bathroom shutting the door behind him.

I stood there shocked and motionless for a moment. I really wished that he would learn to wear clothes more often. I didn't know how much more of his body I could handle. I just needed to erase it from my mind.

I grunted to myself and hopped in the shower.

After taking a quick shower and getting dressed. I stepped into the living room to see Jace throwing on a black leather jacket. He smiled sweetly upon noticing me watching him. "You look nice," he said. "Hey, I'm going to be gone for a few hours. I might bring some company by later so feel free to have anyone over that you please. You're always welcome."

I gave him a long stare before walking over to the loveseat and plopping down roughly. I suddenly flinched when remembering what happened there last night. "Okay. Have fun," I mumbled. I jumped up from the couch and gave Jace a reassuring smile.

Jace gave me a quick look before he headed out the door. I couldn't help but to notice how his eyes lingered down to the loveseat right before he shut the door behind him. I was sure that it was nothing, probably just an eye twitch or something.

I leaned against the leather couch and took a long deep breath. I had a lot of energy and nothing to do for the day. Caleb of course was always an option. He never seemed to be working and in fact I had no idea where or if he even worked. I hadn't spoken to him for almost two days and I was sure that my phone would probably have at least a few missed calls from him by now.

I paced around the living room for a few minutes before heading to my bedroom and pulling my phone from out of my purse. I dialed Caleb's number and surprisingly got an answer on the first ring.

I could hear his light breathing in the phone moments before he even responded. "Look who is still alive," he said playfully. "I've been calling you for two days now." He was trying to play it off, but I knew that he was annoyed. He always was when he didn't hear from me for a few days.

I huffed into the phone and rolled my eyes not really wanting to get into it. "Just come over," I blurted before I could manage to change my mind. "I need to keep busy."

His heavy breathing filled the phone line as I waited for his response. "Fine," he breathed. "I'll be there in ten minutes. I just need to make a quick pit stop first.

"Wait," I shouted before he could hang up. He was eager to get to me and rushing to get off the phone. "I don't live on Remington anymore."

He was silent before he let out a small laugh, clearly confused. "What exactly do you mean? Is everything alright?" he questioned.

"I couldn't afford to pay rent. I had to move," I replied quickly.

WAKE UP CALL
VICTORIA ASHLEY

He grunted into the phone. "I sent out that money order like you asked. They had to of gotten it by now," he said, sounding slightly annoyed.

I let out a deep breath not caring to explain. "I was already behind from last month though. It's a long story. Just never mind." I paused. "I met some guy and he offered to let me rent out his spare room."

I heard him growl into the phone. That wasn't unusual for him. "Tell me where you stay at and you can tell me more when I get there."

"1533 Lighthouse Road. It's a white house with a blue door. It should be easy to find."

I hurriedly hung up the phone before he could say anything else. I was a big girl and I didn't need to explain anything to him. I tossed my phone aside and wandered back to my bedroom in search of my black jacket. It was almost the middle of September and already, I could feel the change in the weather. I didn't mind it though. It was an excuse to keep bundled up and hidden from the outside world. It was what I did best.

I stepped outside taking a seat on the front porch. I leaned my head back, eyes closed, as the light wind blew through my hair and softly kissed my face. It reminded me of older times. Ones that I didn't want to remember. I wanted to be able to feel the cool wind and think of something better. I needed new memories, ones to be proud of.

The sound of screeching tires startled me from my thoughts. I looked up to see Caleb's red car pull into the driveway and jerk to a halt. His face looked stiff through the windshield, and I could tell that he was trying to calm himself down.

He sat behind the wheel for a few seconds before jumping out and walking over to me. He stared down at his feet while chewing on his bottom lip. Then suddenly he looked up with a look of torment in his desperate eyes. "I would've helped you if you asked. You've always known that, Avery." He let out a breath of frustration and tugged on his blond hair. "What are you so afraid of with me?"

I placed my hands in my jacket pockets and looked out into the street. It was quiet and peaceful. How I wished my life could be. "I didn't expect for this to happen. Besides, I could never live with you, Caleb," I replied. "You know this."

WAKE UP CALL
VICTORIA ASHLEY

He looked down into my eyes before taking a seat next to me on the wooden step. "This guy." He paused for a heart beating second. "Are you sleeping with him? I find it a little fucked up that you won't even spend more than a few hours at a time with me, but yet you moved in with a complete stranger," he huffed. "Tell me."

I looked over at him with my nose scrunched in annoyance. He had no right to ask me that question. I didn't belong to him and I didn't have to answer to him. "No, if you must know." I stood up and walked into the house with him following closely at my heels. "That's exactly why I can live here with him," I breathed. "He doesn't want from me what I can't give." I looked behind me, staring him straight in the eye. "You do."

He sat down on the couch and placed his head in his hands. "I care about you, Avery. I understand that you don't want anything more, but I was hoping one day that you would eventually let me in."

If only he could've understood just how impossible that was. I couldn't, even if I wanted to. Truthfully, I didn't want to. He had already been trying for over ten months. I felt nothing.

I decided it was time for a change of subject before I changed my mind about hanging out with Caleb. "Hey lets go get some lunch," I stammered, trying to figure out if it were a good idea to take him to *The Indy Go* or not. "I'm starving."

He looked up a bit surprised with a small smile on his face. We usually never went out in public. It was one of my rules. It was just easier that way but this time things were different. I needed to get things off my mind and keep busy.

"Where do you want to go?" he asked, while standing up and fixing his black flannel shirt. He still didn't look very happy.

I leaned against the wall with my arms crossed over my chest. I forgot to mention the fact that I no longer had to work at the club anymore. That should make him happy. "Oh yeah, I have a new job." I grinned and walked toward the door. "Have you ever heard of *The Indy Go*?"

A small smile crept over his baby face. "The little diner by your old place," he said joyfully. "Yes. I've been there. You went and applied there?"

"My new landlord owns it," I said smoothly, hoping not to upset him more. "Let's grab some food."

The look on his face was not what I expected. He looked almost angry, as if he wanted to choke someone. He shook his head and bit his bottom lip. "The guy that you live with," he questioned. "That's weird. He let you move in and gave you a job. Isn't he some kind of hero," he mumbled.

I silently followed Caleb outside and to his car. He slammed his door behind him and looked down at his phone while shifting the car into drive. "Looks like I have to make another quick pit stop. It will only take a few minutes."

I nodded my head and turned to face the window. It didn't really bother me, but he always seemed to have to make pit stops. A part of me wondered why, but at the same time, I didn't want to know too much about him. It was my way of keeping a distance. "Sure," I mumbled.

He parked his car into the driveway of a small white house with peeling paint and beaten up windows about five minutes away from Jace's house. It looked just about as bad as my place on Remington had. I sat back and played with the seatbelt while Caleb quickly ran inside.

I looked up when Caleb suddenly appeared back in the car. "See, I told you that it would be quick." He strapped on his seatbelt and looked over at me with a smile, looking happier than he had before entering the house. "Now let's go and eat."

I looked at him wide eyed. "Someone is suddenly in a good mood."

He pulled his car into the parking lot of the diner, parking it in the closest parking space. "I'm just happy to be out with you. I was worried for the last two days."

I pursed my lips and reached to take the seatbelt off, before following Caleb out of the car and into the diner. "Okay. Sure," I replied.

We took a seat in the far back of the diner waiting for Stacy to greet us. To my surprise, an older woman that looked to be in her mid-fifties, walked over with a huge grin on her face. "Hi there, folks. My name is Maple and I will be your server." She grinned from ear to ear while eyeing us up and down, brown eyes sparkling with joy. "What can I get you two love birds this morning?"

My stomach twisted at her words. I let out a high-pitched laugh as I waved my arms at her. "Oh no. No, he's not my boyfriend."

Caleb looked up at me with a look to kill as he groaned. "I'm not very hungry. I'll just take some scrambled eggs and some milk." He forcefully pushed his menu across the table with a forced smile. "Thanks."

"I will take-"

"Avery, is that you?" A scratchy voice called from near the kitchen. Winston poked his graying head around the corner and smiled. He looked happy to see me. "Dear, I see that you have met the new waitress."

Maple leaned over into the booth and rubbed the top of my head. It was a soft, motherly touch, that made me feel welcome. "You're such a beautiful young woman." She smiled. "I've heard a lot about you."

I gave her a small smile and nodded my head. It had to of been from Winston and his big mouth. "I'm guessing from, Winston?" I asked.

Her face lit up and she nodded her head. "No. From Jace," she replied. She paused for a moment, looking over at Caleb with curious eyes, before quickly turning her gaze back to me. "What would you like to eat, dear? You always eat free here. That's the boss's orders."

I shifted in my seat feeling a bit uncomfortable. Jace already provided me with everything that I had and now, free food at the diner. It was unnecessary kindness. I stared down at the table and took a deep breath. "I'll just take the breakfast steak and eggs please."

"Coming right up, dear." Her white curls bounced as she wiped her hands over the front of her yellow dress and then clapped them. "You heard that, Winston. Get to work." She smiled so big that I thought her face would rip. "It's so good to finally meet you."

"It's good to meet you too."

Caleb and I watched in awkward silence as Maple walked away and disappeared into the kitchen.

"Great," Caleb mumbled. "Just great."

An hour later, we headed back to Jace's place, Caleb following me inside without a peep. He barely even spoke a word while at the diner and things were starting to get uncomfortable. I just didn't know what to say to him. I never did. It was probably best if he just left. "Maybe you should-"

The swinging of the front door rudely cut me off, before I could manage to send Caleb on his way. Jace strolled in with a very bubbly Emma following at his heels. He looked a little irritated.

Emma puckered her full red lips, while running a hand over her pink shirt that was only a few more breaths away from ripping off. "Hi again," she muttered. Then she tilted her head toward Caleb with a devious smile. "I see that you have company. Nice." She walked over gently placing her hand in Caleb's hand. "He's cute."

Caleb backed away from Emma's unusual greeting, cheeks turning red, as he looked her up and down. "Thanks, I guess." His eyes quickly shot across the room as Jace pulled his jacket off and hung it on the coat hook. "This must be that guy." He raked his eyes over Jace disapprovingly while stepping closer to me.

Jace nodded his head when he acknowledged Caleb being in the room for what seemed to be for the first time. "Yeah, I'm that guy," he said confidently. "Welcome to our home."

Caleb's eyes wandered over Jace's body trying to size him up. Caleb knew that he was good looking but clearly, he had nothing on Jace's bad boy good looks. Caleb had that sweet 'take me home to mommy' look.

We all stood there in awkward silence before Jace turned and headed for the kitchen. "Okay then. Who wants a drink?" The sound of clinking glasses filled the room as we all followed Jace into the kitchen. "Avery, I picked you up some Cherry Mcgillicuddy and Sprite." He set the bottles in front of me and then pulled out a bottle of Jack Daniels, not even bothering to acknowledge anyone else.

Caleb's eyes followed Jace's every move as he leaned against the counter, arms crossed over his chest in anger. "So that is what you drink." Caleb growled in my direction, clearly jealous that Jace knew something about me that he hadn't.

Emma rolled her eyes, clearly not looking too thrilled either. She walked over, snaked her arm around Jace's waist, and reached for his chest. "What about me Jace? Do you have anything for Margaritas?" she questioned, looking me in the eye with a wink. She was trying to get to me, and for unclear reasons, it was working.

Jace laughed while pushing her hand away from his chest. Then he walked over to the fridge and pulled out some Pepsi. "Nope. You'll just have to drink Jack or what Avery's drinking. I was really only thinking about the two of us when I went shopping."

His words somehow caused my heart to speed up. I looked away embarrassed.

Emma peered over at me and rolled her big eyes. "I don't drink that sissy shit," she whined. "Give me some damn Jack." She moved away from Jace, jumping up on the black granite counter as he poured a few mixed drinks for everyone.

Caleb watched my reaction and then smoothly walked over and gripped me by the waist. I instinctively shook him off with a grunt. He knew better than to grab me. He gave me a dirty look, shook his head, and turned to face Jace. "I'll take a couple of shots," he said firmly.

Jace didn't even bother to look over as he grabbed four shot glasses and poured Jack into them. He slid two of the shots across the counter and kept two in front of him. "Enjoy," he said, as they both grabbed their shots and slammed them both back, watching each other with guarded eyes.

After the second shot, Caleb made a sour face and reached up to wipe his mouth off. "That's some good shit."

Jace just gave him a hard look and stepped away pressing his back against the counter. He gave me that calm smile that he usually wore and took a long sip of his drink.

Emma didn't waste any time striding her way over to Jace and planting a kiss on his lips. He stiffened up at first, almost as if to push her away, but didn't.

A pang of unwanted jealousy surged through me, suddenly forcing me to grab my drink and slam it back. I shakily wiped a hand over my mouth and leaned over, grabbing Caleb by the neck. Surprisingly, I found myself pushing him down into a chair and sitting on his lap.

I glanced up shortly to see Jace pulling away from Emma. It was too late by then.

I slammed my lips roughly against Caleb's knocking his breath out. He didn't hesitate before running his hands through my hair and trailing them down my body. I stiffened before pushing his hands behind his back. I still couldn't handle his touch.

"Don't stop," Emma whined.

I glanced up to see Jace looking directly at us with Emma tightly hanging on his neck. A dark look crossed his face as he wiped his mouth off, and clenched his jaw.

Looking at Jace's handsome face made me want to go crazy. I couldn't help myself so I took it out on Caleb. I placed both of my hands on Caleb's face and pulled him closer, nibbling on his bottom lip. It tasted of Jack Daniels. I never cared for it much but was too involved to care.

Jace let out a long deep breath and then grabbed Emma up wrapping her long legs around him. He stood motionless, in a daze at first before walking away. I knew where he was going and I hated it for some reason.

"Ugh!" I grunted. I pushed my way out of Caleb's lap and grabbed him by the shirt. "I want you right now," I blurted, before I could change my mind. "Come on."

Caleb pushed me down the hallway, bouncing off the cream painted walls, before we both fell through my open door. He picked me up with a hunger and threw me on top of my bed, pressing his full lips to mine. "I'm so turned on right now," he moaned. He grabbed for my shirt to take it off but I stopped him. "What?" His eyes jumped around as he stared at me.

I jumped back when hearing a loud bang come from the room next to us. It sounded as if someone had fallen into the wall or rammed it. The thought of Jace slamming Emma into the wall angered me even more.

I roughly kissed Caleb while moaning loudly. I just wanted it to look bad. For some reason I wanted Jace to be bothered like I was. I wanted his heart to sink as mine had.

Suddenly everything went quiet and Jace's room was silent. I pulled away from Caleb waiting for something more to happen, but nothing.

Caleb caught me off guard reaching for my pants and slipping them off. I was too busy listening to Jace's room to care about my pants. "What's wrong," he breathed. "Why are we stopping?"

WAKE UP CALL
VICTORIA ASHLEY

I looked at him speechless, before the guilt finally kicked in and I panicked. I pushed my messy hair from out of my face and fought to catch my breath. "I'll be back. I need to use the bathroom," I breathed.

I pushed myself to my feet and walked down the quiet hall and to the dark bathroom. I didn't even care that I was only in my T-shirt and panties. I just needed an escape.

I ran inside, closing myself in the safety of the bathroom. I took a long look into the mirror and threw my head back in defeat. *I'm acting like an animal.*

I jumped back startled as the bathroom door swung open to Jace standing there in his boxers. A sight I had grown used to.

He looked me up and down, his body covered in sweat, as he fought to catch his breath. I didn't understand what he was doing.

It made my heart race. "Jace, what are you doing in here?" I took a step toward the door to escape but he grabbed a hold of my wrist stopping me in my place. My heart sped up and my breathing became heavy. "Jace."

He looked me dead in the eye and without saying a word; he picked me up and sat me on the edge of the sink. He gripped my face and roughly pressed his lips against mine, causing me to moan. His lips were soft and sweet, just as I had imagined. Although, I wouldn't admit it. Not even to myself.

The taste was too overwhelming; causing my whole body to shake as he gently ran his fingers through my hair and pressed his body in between my legs. I could feel his hands trembling as he placed them on the inside of my bare thighs while sucking my bottom lip.

Suddenly, he pulled away and we both sat there panting and fighting for breath. His eyes were unreadable as he looked me in the eye and shook his head. My body leaned forward involuntarily, and it almost felt as if I were falling off the sink. I braced myself, pulling myself upright again.

"Jace..." I breathed.

He slowly backed away from me and placed his head in his hands. "Shit! I'm sorry, Avery," he said softly. "I don't know what came over me." He turned around and left me sitting on the sink, half-naked and confused.

WAKE UP CALL
VICTORIA ASHLEY

I leaned back against the mirror and fought to catch my breath. I had so many thoughts running through my head, that I felt as if I could faint. He kissed me, and for one quick moment, all of my pain was numbed.

I placed my hand to my lips, softly tracing them, as I squeezed my eyes shut. "Shit."

Chapter 6

I sat against the sink with my legs shaking uncontrollably. I couldn't seem to breathe, no matter how hard I tried.

I gripped the sink tighter, if that was even possible and leaned into the mirror. My skin felt as if it was on fire and I still felt dizzy. I needed a few minutes to catch my breath and wrap my head around what had just happened.

I blew out a deep breath and slowly placed my feet back on the ground being sure not to fall on my face. It took a lot of effort, but I managed to do it. I needed to get rid of Caleb and fast. I needed to be alone, and now.

I crept down the empty hallway, peeking over at Jace's closed door, before stepping back into my room. Caleb sat there pant less and looking eager with his back pressed against the wall. He looked nervous as he watched my every move. It made me nervous. "What's wrong?

I quickly bent over in a panic reaching for my jeans. "I'm sorry Caleb," I breathed. "It's best if you just leave. I'm suddenly not feeling very well."

I struggled with getting my jeans on, falling over like an idiot in the process. I didn't care though. Caleb's eyes were burning into every inch of my body and I couldn't stand to be so naked around him. I wasn't sure why I hadn't noticed until now.

WAKE UP CALL
VICTORIA ASHLEY

Caleb shook his head, slammed his hands down into the bed, and pushed himself to his feet. He silently grabbed for his jeans and let out an exasperated breath. "I really wish that I knew what you wanted." His eyes followed me as I continued to struggle with my jeans. He looked as if he wanted to help but second-guessed himself, stepping away. "I try and try and nothing is ever good enough for you."

I felt horrible for putting him through everything that I had and he was right. He tried so hard and I did nothing in return. I was a horrible person. I couldn't change how I felt.

"I'm sorry Caleb. It's not you," I whispered. I buttoned my jeans and buried my face in my hands full of shame. "I'm sorry."

I could tell by the look in Caleb's eyes that he hated me. I hurt him repeatedly. It was never ending.

He grabbed for his keys and tilted his head back staring at the ceiling. "Let me guess. It's you, right?" He strode toward the door with hate and rested his palm against it. "Don't even answer that." He paused to swallow. "Have a good life."

I stiffly pushed myself to my feet and watched helplessly as he exited the room. He didn't even bother to look back. "I'm sorry," I yelled. "You will never understand. I can't be anything more than this."

I slammed the door shut behind me falling against the door. Tears threatened to form as I rubbed circles on the side of my head in an attempt to calm myself down and gain control.

Instantly following Caleb's exit, I heard footsteps down the hall followed by the vague sounds of Emma and Jace's conversation. I quietly leaned in closer to get a better sound. As stupid as I felt, I still couldn't help myself.

"Jace, I'm sorry that you're sick. Are you sure that I can't do anything...to make you feel better," Emma asked desperately. "I bet I can make you feel-"

"I'm sure Emma," Jace cut in. "It's time for you to leave. You pushed me into bringing you here in the first place." He sounded almost upset as he spoke. "I told you long ago that I was done with this crap. Now please leave."

It was silent for a moment before what I pictured to be the sound of Emma stomping her way out the front door. The door slammed loudly, followed by the faint sound of Jace's fist pounding into a nearby wall. It startled me, causing me to jump away from the door.

My whole body relaxed at the idea of Emma being gone. I wasn't exactly sure why but I hated her at the moment. Just the thought of her alone with Jace made my stomach knot up. The feeling both confused me and greatly frustrated me.

I ran my hands through my hair, lightly tugging it, as I leaned into the door. *Stop thinking about Jace. It means nothing.*

The sound of Jace pacing by my door caused me to look up. I stiffened as his footsteps shortly stopped in front of my door but then quickly continued back to his room. Then they paused again before I heard the slight sound of his bedroom door shutting.

I needed to get out of here and fast.

My hands shook uncontrollably as I called for a taxi. "1533 Lighthouse Road. Fast, please." I hung up and grabbed for my purse to wait outside. I needed something familiar. Something that I was used to.

The taxi arrived shortly after and I jumped in the back without a second thought. It was my escape.

The driver was a younger man, maybe even still a boy. He glanced back at me with big almond eyes and nodded his head. He looked a little on the rough side but surely nothing to worry about. "Where to?" he questioned.

"Umm...*Taste Of Poison*. Step on it," I stammered, as I looked at the boy through the rearview mirror.

His relaxed face suddenly scrunched up with a look of disgust and disbelief, making me feel uncomfortable. "Look." He paused. "A place like that is no good for someone like you," he said stiffly. "It's dangerous."

My heart sped up at the memory of Jace saving my life. If it weren't for him showing up then I could've been hurt badly or possibly even killed.

"Shit!" I blurted. I squeezed the strap of my purse and reached for the handle. "I've changed my mind," I whispered embarrassed. I slowly stepped out of the taxi and softly shut the door behind me.

I watched with my head lowered as the taxi drove away. That should've been my escape. Anywhere more familiar than here would've been fine at the moment.

WAKE UP CALL
VICTORIA ASHLEY

The thought of Jace seeing me vulnerable, sitting on that bathroom sink, made me want to run away and hide. If he felt the way that my heart was racing against his chest, then he had to of thought something was wrong with me. Even I did.

When I looked up, Jace stood leaning against the porch with his arms and legs crossed. My stomach dropped. His melancholic smile made my legs tremble. He nodded his head toward the door and then walked inside leaving the door open for me.

I slapped myself on the forehead and made my way back inside, closing myself in my room. I needed to force myself to sleep. I needed an escape and in any way possible.

~•~

I quickly got ready for work, knowing that Jace liked to arrive early. After what happened last night I didn't want to make him wait on me.

I grabbed for my apron and purse before heading back to Jace's room. I hadn't heard a peep from him the whole morning and it was unusual. He was always running around early in the morning, making some kind of ruckus.

I held my fist above his door, hesitating before I lightly knocked.

When there was no answer, I tried again. "Jace, are you ready to leave for work yet?"

I waited expectantly for the door to open but it didn't. I reached out ready to knock again but paused after hearing a noise from inside his room. It was clear that he was awake. Maybe he just didn't hear me the first time.

"I'm not going to work," he said loudly. "You can just take my car. The keys are in the kitchen."

I opened my mouth hesitating whether or not to question him. It wasn't really my place. I quickly decided against it trying to avoid as much conversation as I could with him. After last night, I wasn't quite sure how to act around him anyhow.

I took off down the hallway and into the kitchen. His keys were setting down on the counter on full display. I quickly swept them up and made my way outside and to his nice little car.

Truthfully, I had only driven once before and that was when Caleb was trying to give me a lesson, which went well. I was a little nervous but pretty positive, that I would be fine going the short distance, as long as I didn't manage to get pulled over.

I jumped behind the steering wheel and adjusted the seat and mirror. Then I nervously shoved the keys into the ignition and started the engine. "It's cool, Avery. You can handle this. It's only like ten blocks."

I took a deep breath and pulled out of the driveway and into the empty street. Everything was going smooth until a car ran a stop sign almost cutting me off.

I slammed on the breaks and caught my breath. "You idiot," I yelled. I slammed my hand into the steering wheel and pressed on the gas as the other car just continued to drive. I was pretty shaken up, but nothing that I couldn't handle.

When finally arriving at the diner, I walked in to find Stacy wiping down a table. She stood there in her short skirt and lacy red top as she hummed to herself.

I stepped up beside her causing her to look up with a genuine smile. "Good morning, sunshine," she gleamed. "You're here pretty early." She glanced at her watch. "8:30 a.m. Sweet! I could really use your help."

I followed Stacy over to the server station and shoved my purse into the cabinet. At least someone seemed happy to see me. Everyone else around me seemed to hate me at the moment. "Thank you, Stacy."

She nodded her head and threw her black apron on. "I hope that you're ready for a busy day," she said excitedly. "Tuesdays are a lot busier than Sundays. Sometimes we even run out of tables, so I will do my best to help you if you need it." She looked eager as she looked around and cracked her knuckles.

I nervously nodded my head in appreciation, as I followed her eyes out into the dining area. There were eight table booths and four round tables that seated four people. I hoped that she didn't mean that all tables would be full all at once. "I'll just do my best," I said nervously.

She nodded her head in satisfaction and threw her blond curls up into a ponytail. "I'm sure that you will do just fine. The customers loved you the other day and you kicked ass." She looked around as if something was missing. Then her gaze set on me. "Where is Jace? Is he sick?" she questioned.

WAKE UP CALL
VICTORIA ASHLEY

I threw my apron on and shrugged my shoulders. "He didn't seem to be sick. He did have his girlfriend over last night," I replied in a cool tone. I didn't want her to see how much it was eating at me, but I couldn't seem to hide it.

She stared at me in silence before bursting out with laughter. "His what?" She threw her towel down on the front counter and rolled her eyes. "Jace doesn't date. I've known him for five years and I have never seen him in a relationship." She paused to look over at Winston as he entered the room. "Oh, hi Winston. Avery's here early today so there will be two of us."

"Hi, ladies. Looking good today," he said with a cheesy grin, and an eyebrow lift. "What is all this gossip about?"

Stacy nodded and patted Winston on the back before she continued. "Like I was saying, of course, Jace has girls because he is gorgeous, but maybe he's too aware of that and that's why he won't commit. I don't know." She shook her head in shame. "He would be quite the catch.".

I looked over at Winston as he nudged me in the side and winked. "Is someone interested in our boss?" He smiled, eyes lighting up. My stomach got butterflies at just the thought, but I quickly shook it off.

"No!" I blurted a little too fast. I hid my face embarrassed as I walked away to get ready to start my shift. "I'm going to freshen up a bit and get started for the day."

Winston and Stacy both laughed as I walked away. I didn't know what they were getting at, but I couldn't worry about them or Jace if I was going to manage to make it through the day.

Fifteen minutes later, I was greeted by my first customer of the day. I walked over and greeted her with the best smile I could manage. "Good morning ma'am. What can I start you out with?" I pulled out my paper and pen leaning into the table to be sure I could hear her.

The woman slowly looked up from her menu and set her hard gaze on me. Her dull brown eyes burned into my green ones as she studied my every facial feature. The woman almost looked sickly, with sunken in eyes and cracked lips.

Letting out a snort, she leaned into the booth and threw her menu down in front of her. She smiled big revealing her blackened and rotted teeth, while looking me up and down. She looked strangely familiar, but I couldn't seem to figure out how.

"Coffee...black," she said firmly. "Make is quick. I have things to take care of."

I nodded my head and hastily walked away to grab the woman's coffee. I wasn't sure what her problem was, but I didn't like it one bit. I wanted to rip her head off and shove it up her ass but I couldn't let my anger get the best of me. This was Jace's diner and he didn't deserve it.

I poured the coffee and walked back over to the woman's booth, placing the coffee on the table.

I got ready to walk away but she quickly reached out and gripped my arm to stop me, her sharp nails digging into my skin causing me to bleed.

I ripped my arm out of her reach and flared my nose in anger. She looked as if she enjoyed it. "Your name?" she questioned deviously.

"It's Avery," I spat. "Don't ever touch me again." I stared down at her as she smirked and played with her coffee.

"Avery. Avery." She said repeatedly. I hated the way my name sounded, rolling off her dirty tongue. "I had a feeling." She waved me off while taking a sip of her coffee and smiling as she watched me walk away.

That was weird.

By the end of my shift, I was exhausted. It felt as if the day was never going to end and I just wanted to get out of there and take a nap.

Stacy had been right; it was a lot busier than Sunday had been. I managed to drop one plate and mess up a few orders but still made it through the day okay. I was still alive anyway.

I gathered up my tip money and purse and walked over to say bye to Stacy.

She glanced up from her table and set her money down. Her pile was thick, probably mostly full of singles. "You did well today. How much did you manage to make?"

I looked down at my bundle of cash and ran my fingers over it, feeling pleased. It was a decent amount and I was excited about being able to save some up. "About $135."

Stacy grinned and reached out for my arm. She squeezed it, but then quickly released it; probably remembering how I had tensed up the last time. That made me happy. "That's really good."

WAKE UP CALL
VICTORIA ASHLEY

I backed away and turned around to leave. The place was very quiet, making me feel somewhat tired. "Thank you for the help. I'll see you tomorrow."

"Yeah, no problem. Tell Jace everything went well today." She paused. "I'm surprised that he didn't even call to check up on us today." She looked bewildered.

I had almost forgotten about Jace. *Thanks Stacy.* My stomach dropped at the thought of facing him. "Okay. I'll be sure to tell him."

I quickly exited the diner before anything more of Jace could be mentioned. I didn't want to get caught up in another conversation like what we had earlier when I had first arrived for work.

~•~

When I arrived back at Jace's house, I walked in to find him sitting at his computer desk with his head in his hands. He glanced up at me when he heard me shut the door. "Hey," he muttered. "How was work?" He questioned before quickly looking away, as if he didn't want to look at me.

I walked over to the couch and slammed myself down on it, feeling confused. I took a deep breath and yawned. "It was really busy. Thanks again-"

"It's fine, Avery," he cut me off. "You can stop thanking me now." He stood up from the computer chair and slowly pushed it under the desk, looking slightly irritated. He leaned over the desk and ran his hands through his tousled hair. "I ordered us some pizza. I've been feeling like crap today so I think I'm going to just eat it in my room."

"Oh..." I muttered, not really knowing what to say.

He looked in my eyes for a split second before he walked toward the hallway. There was a look in his eyes that I couldn't quite figure out. Something I had never seen from him before. "You're welcome to do anything that you would like. Make yourself at home," he whispered.

I sat there on the couch confused as he walked down the hallway and into his bedroom.

A few moments later, the door shut, causing me to jump. It almost seemed as if he were angry with me.

WAKE UP CALL
VICTORIA ASHLEY

I pushed myself into the soft leather couch and closed my eyes. My stomach rumbled but suddenly I didn't feel like eating either. *I can't seem to make anyone happy.*

I sat there for a moment before bursting out the front door and running to the sidewalk. I stopped, running my hands through my hair, before I began walking. Again, I felt as if I needed an escape. I needed to breathe.

The cool wind hit me hard, causing me to pull my jacket tighter around me as I made my way toward the neighborhood playground. I hadn't been able to step foot on a playground in over twelve years. It gave me too many bad memories.

When the worn-out swings came into view I felt a twinge of pain in my chest. It froze me in place for a second, but I forced myself to go on. I stepped up to the swing and leaned in to touch it. I missed that feeling. The one that I should've gotten as a child. The coolness of it gave me chills

My mother gently pushed me on the swing. I leaned my head back in comfort as the cool breeze lightly blew through my hair. It made me smile. Just a little bit at least.

Being at the park was the only time that I felt free. I wasn't allowed to get out of the house often so when I did I always wanted to go to the park. It was like an escape away from the prison that I lived in.

My father usually stayed home drinking his life away in his stupid recliner chair. He gave us one hour of freedom every couple of months. That was all that he would spare.

"Isn't this nice, Avery?" My mother questioned. "It's such a beautiful night."

I leaned my head back far enough to look into my mother's eyes. Sometimes she was there and sometimes I could see she was fading away like my father. Tonight she was there. She was present and beautiful as ever.

I shook my head back and forth and allowed myself to laugh. "Mother can you-"

Suddenly the swing came to a stop and someone jerked on the left chain. I held my breath, knowing deep down inside that it had to of been my father.

"Henry, you should just go back home. Okay, dear." I could tell that my mother was afraid. She always was, but stayed with him because she loved him too much. I didn't understand.

WAKE UP CALL
VICTORIA ASHLEY

"You've been drinking too much," she whined. Her whole body shook in fear as she watched him, her black curls falling down to cover her blue eyes.

My father pushed my mother out of the way. I watched as she crumbled to the ground and her head bounced off the dirt. "Don't you tell me when I've been drinking too much," he slurred. "If I want to push my little girl then I will. You can't stop me. No one ever can."

My mother pushed herself back to her feet and cowered away from him. She watched with wide eyes as my father started pushing the swing.

I could smell the foul stench of the booze that flowed off his breath every time that he breathed. It made my stomach ache.

"Henry, don't push the swing so high. She's only six," she yelled, her voice unsteady "I...I don't want her to fall."

My father let out a wicked laugh. "I'm going too high? I'm going too high? I'll show you high, Joyce," he said, as he pushed the swing higher.

I just sat there and cried. I cried like a little sissy. That's all that I could do. I was helpless. "Daddy, please stop," I cried out. "I can't hold on. Daddy-"

No longer able to hang on, my hand slipped off the rusted chain and I went flying across the park landing on my right arm. A pain shot through my arm as I heard a loud snap.

I grabbed my arm and sobbed as my father stood there and laughed. "Get up girl."

I stopped the swing and wiped away a stray tear. I looked down at my right arm and rubbed it from the memory. It broke in two places that night. I never understood how someone could've been so cruel. I was his daughter he was supposed to love me. Take care of me. He never did and my mother was still with that piece of shit. My life could've been different. I could've been different.

I jumped off the swing and then turned back around giving it one last fleeting look. I would never be able to go to a park and not think about that moment. It was ruined for me. That idiot ruined everything that could've been good.

I glanced up into the night sky, realizing that I should probably get home before it got too dark and cold. I was already shivering and my jacket just didn't seem to help like it should've.

WAKE UP CALL
VICTORIA ASHLEY

The sky was a beautiful sight on the way home as I stared up at the bright stars. It helped to somewhat ease my mind and make me see that some things in the world could be beautiful.

Once arriving back to Jace's house, I decided to sit out on the porch and take it all in. A new job, a new place to stay, and new people in my life. Everything was changing and I didn't know how or what to think. I sat there for a while feeling lost.

I stood up, getting ready to reach for the door, when suddenly Jace stepped out onto the porch. He leaned into the door and smiled at me. "You're back." He looked a bit relieved as his muscles relaxed.

I smiled back and rubbed the back of my head, somehow blushing from his presence. "Yeah I just felt like taking a walk. I was just thinking." I sat back down on the steps not knowing what to say next. Was he still mad? Was he ever mad? I wasn't quite sure.

He looked down, eyeing the steps curiously, before walking over to sit next to me. His bare arm brushed against my jacket, making me shy away, as I remembered our encounter from the other night. I didn't want to get too close and somehow fall into him.

He looked down at our arms, eyes dark, as he shifted. "Did you enjoy your walk?" he questioned. He looked me in the eye for a breath taking moment before quickly looking away.

I let out a deep breath blowing my hair out of my face. "Yeah...I mean." I paused to swallow the lump that was forming in my throat. "My parents... never mind" I shook my head and closed my eyes. I wasn't ready to tell anyone quite yet.

He ran his hands through his hair and let out a deep breath. "Whatever it is, you're here now," he said. "Everyone deserves a chance at happiness."

I looked over at him suddenly getting a strong urge to reach out and touch him. However, I didn't. "Well, are you happy?" I questioned, hoping that he would give me an honest answer.

He gave me a forced smile and turned the other way. I couldn't really read his eyes. "Not as happy as I hoped to be," he whispered.

I reached over and placed my hand on his shoulder. Then I quickly pulled it away. I looked down at my hand and scooted further away from him. "Why haven't you been in a relationship before?" I questioned without thinking.

He smiled and stretched, his arms looking warm and firm as he held them behind his body. He didn't even look bothered by the chill of the night one bit. It almost made me want to curl up in his arms and hide from the cold chill. "I haven't found that special someone yet. I want to know that I really want to wake up to this woman and fall asleep next to her every day of my life. Until I feel that then I'm not willing to give my heart away." He looked down at the porch and played with the rocks by his hand.

"Oh..." His answer made me speechless.

"What about you," he questioned. "Isn't there any guy at all that you've just wanted to spend your time with? Someone to hold you and love you, someone to talk to?" He looked me in the eye waiting for an answer, his green eyes looking soft and genuine.

I looked down at my hands and started picking at my nails. "No, I guess I can't say I've felt that with anyone," I whispered. "I mean, I guess that I just learned long ago that people will always hurt you even when they love you. Therefore, I decided that if I don't let myself love anyone then they can never hurt me. No one has made me change my mind...yet."

He smiled at me before he stood up and walked toward the door. He paused and looked back at me. "Well I hope one day we both find what we're looking for," he yawned. "I'm a little tired. I think I'll go get some sleep." He opened the door and placed his hand on the doorframe. "Goodnight, Avery," he whispered with a smile.

I took a deep breath and watched him as he walked inside. "Goodnight, Jace," I whispered.

Chapter 7

"Avery."

I looked up to see Jace's head poking inside my slightly opened door, his messy hair falling over his eyes as he smiled. He waved his arm and motioned for me to follow him. "Let's go." He grinned.

I shook my head giving Jace a confused look. "Go where," I questioned. "We don't have to work for another hour." My eyes studied his body as he rubbed his chest and then stretched. It made me blush unwantedly. I turned my head away and coughed. "Were we supposed to go in early today?"

Jace bit his lip ring and leaned against the door, shoving it completely open. "We're calling in today," he said playfully. "I'm sure that the boss won't mind." He turned around and waited for me to follow. When I didn't get up, he tilted his head back. "Well..."

I felt a twinge of excitement as I pushed myself to my feet and followed him to the living room. He tossed me my leather jacket and then reached for his own. My mind raced as I watched him slip it on and I really wanted to know what we were doing.

A week had passed since our conversation on the porch and we hadn't spent much time talking since then. It made me nervous.

WAKE UP CALL
VICTORIA ASHLEY

I looked up at Jace as he reached for his keys and opened the front door. The sunlight that leaked through the door was bright, making my eyes sting. I threw my hand over my face. "Where are we going? Shouldn't we be working?" I questioned, again.

"Nah." He nodded his head toward the door and waited for me to walk out first. "Stacy and Maple have it covered. Maple wanted to come in today to keep her eye on Winston. He's been a bad boy lately." He shrugged his shoulders and followed me to the car. "Don't ask."

I went to reach for the door handle but Jace bumped me out of the way. He opened the door and placed his hand on my lower back. "This is going to be much better than working." He gave me a light shove to help me into the car. Then he shut the door and ran over to get in himself.

The car ride was silent as I stared out the window trying to figure out where we were going. I had been living in Westville for over a year and hadn't even taken the time to discover the place. All I ever did was work, eat and go home. I felt lost looking out the window at my unfamiliar surroundings.

We pulled into a parking lot and the brick building read 'Bowling' in green neon lights. I felt panic set in as I watched him stop the car and shift it into park. I had no clue how to bowl. I had never been bowling in my whole life. "Umm...maybe we should just go for a walk. You know-"

"Don't worry. I won't beat you too bad." He smiled and jumped out of the car. He studied me as I got out and closed the door behind me. His eyes set on mine and his smile faded. "Is something wrong, Avery?"

I nervously brushed my hair behind my ear and shook my head. "It's just that..." I paused to take a deep breath. It would be pointless to lie. "I've never been bowling before," I breathed embarrassed.

He stared at me for a second as if he wanted to know more. When I didn't say anything else, he reached over and grabbed my hand, making my skin tingle. "I'm a great bowler. I'm sure that I can teach you some moves."

I pulled my hand away slightly, but he pulled it closer to him so that our hands rested at his side. "I promise not to bite your hand off," he teased.

I felt my whole body get hot as my heart raced. Something inside me screamed to push his hand away, but the bigger part of me, the louder part screamed to never let go. It confused me so I just kept my hand still as it stiffly held his. "You have to promise me something," I said.

He looked over and smiled as he held the door open for us. He stopped and looked me in the eye. "Anything," he whispered.

I averted my eyes away from Jace's distractive lips and walked inside. "Don't laugh at how bad I am." I looked up as he smiled at me.

"I would never laugh at you, Avery," he said firmly. "Then I wouldn't be such a nice guy. My mother raised me in hopes that I would be a better man than my father was. It would be a shame to say that she failed." He pulled me over to the counter and let go of my hand to grab for his wallet. He laid a twenty on the counter and pointed between the two of us. "Two please."

I stared at him in a moment of weakness before looking up at the worker standing behind the desk.

The young woman blushed as she watched Jace chew on his lip ring. *That damn thing.* Her brown curls cascaded around her freckled face as she tilted her head and reached for the money. "That will be $18.50 for two games." She threw the money inside the register and handed him back his change. "What size?" she asked, her eyes never straying from Jace.

Jace looked over at me and crossed his arms across his chest. "Ladies first."

I nervously smiled at the young woman as she stared me down waiting for a response. "A size seven," I replied.

Jace looked pleased as the girl reached for the hideous red and blue shoes and set them on the counter. He pushed them in front of me and leaned in close to the counter. "A size twelve, please," he whispered.

The girl gave him a grin and raised an eyebrow. "Nice," she said with a slightly red face. She grabbed for Jace's shoes and placed them in front of him. Then she looked at me and smiled. "Have fun." She looked back at Jace and winked.

Jace just smiled and reached for his shoes. They were worse than mine were. They were a shitty color brown and green. "What lane?" he questioned, clearly not too amused with her flirting.

WAKE UP CALL
VICTORIA ASHLEY

The girl shook her head embarrassed and pointed directly in front of her. The lane was lit up with a blue and red lighting. "Lane five." She smiled.

Jace raised an eyebrow and looked over at me. "Okay then. Thanks, Helen," he said looking at the girl's nametag with a smile. "Let's go. I'll help you pick out your ball."

I followed behind him as he walked over to lane five and set his shoes on the table. "Thanks. I have no idea how to choose a ball." It was true, as stupid as it sounded. I didn't know anything about bowling. I had only seen it in movies and usually they already had a ball.

He leaned over and picked up a pink ball with the number eight on it. It was scratched up and stained with dirt marks. He held it out and waited for me to grab it. "How does that feel? Too heavy?"

I placed my fingers in the holes and held it out in front of me. "It feels fine...I think," I said unsure. It wasn't too heavy or too light. I guessed that was what I was looking for. *Please don't embarrass yourself.*

"Perfect," he said looking me in the eye. His gaze made my heart feel like it was on fire. His eyes were the most beautiful thing I had seen in my whole life. There was just something in them that gave me a little...hope.

After changing into our bowling shoes, Jace put our names into the computer. I looked up to see that my name was first. Again, I got nervous.

Jace grabbed my ball and motioned for me to follow him to the lane. "Let me show you and then you can do the second throw by yourself. It's pretty easy after that." He waited for me to walk over and then he placed the ball in my hand.

I stuck my fingers into the holes and looked down the lane. How was he going to help me? By telling me how to aim, or how far back to pull my arm before I threw? I was curious. "How are-"

He stepped behind me and placed his arm around me so that it was resting on my hand. *Oh god. This is too close.* He ran his fingers over mine, being sure that my fingers were properly in the holes. "You pull your arm back and then swing it down the middle of the lane," he breathed in my ear giving me chills. "You want to get your arm as straight as you can before you let go." He pulled my arm back and then swung it forward to show me. "Like this."

After a few practice swings it didn't seem as hard as I expected. I gripped the ball tighter in my hand and peered over my shoulder at Jace. He looked relaxed in his white thermo and faded jeans as he looked back at me. I liked him this way. "I think I'm ready."

Jace let go of my arm and stepped away. "Good. Now kick some ass. I need someone that can challenge me," he said playfully. "That person might just be you."

I looked over at him and smiled. "Here goes nothing." I took a deep breath and studied the lane. Then I pulled my arm back and swung it forward, dropping the ball down the lane. Jace and I both watched intently as it swerved toward the middle of the lane and knocked down most of the pins. "Yes!" I screamed.

Jace walked over and wrapped his arm around my waist to pick me up. "Hell Yeah!" He looked down the lane and counted the pins that were still standing. "Only two pins left. You might just kick my ass if I'm not careful." He set me back down and poked my nose. "Don't put me to shame." He grinned. "Not just yet at least."

I reached for the ball as it came back up and held it against my chest. "If I beat you then you owe me lunch." I teased suddenly, feeling confident.

Jace bit his bottom lip and crossed his arms over his chest. His tattoos showed through his thermo, causing me to smile. It was sort of sexy. "Deal," he smirked. "If I win then you have to let me take you to the movies."

I shook my head confused. What would he be getting out of that deal? I smiled and brushed my hair out of my face. "What's in it for you?" I questioned. I tossed the ball down the lane, this time missing completely. *Damn!*

Jace smiled before walking over and reaching for his blue ball. "Getting to spend time with you." He blew on his hand and placed his fingers in the holes before walking over and throwing his ball down the lane. He smiled as his ball knocked down all of the pins. "Nice! I wonder what movies are out right now."

"Oh, shut up." I laughed and stepped up to the lane. I jumped around in place getting out my nerves and then tossed the ball down the lane. It missed completely, landing in the right gutter.

WAKE UP CALL
VICTORIA ASHLEY

"Oh shoot. Gutter ball," Jace said with a slight grin. "Don't let the game wear you out too much. I wouldn't want you falling asleep during the movie," he said joyously. "That would be embarrassing."

I reached over and lightly punched Jace's arm. He jumped back playfully gripping his arm with a pained expression. "Oh stop playing around." I laughed. "That didn't hurt.

He bit his lip and dangled his arm next to him. "I don't think I can move it. It might just be broken."

I lightly shoved him before he dropped his ball and threw his arms around me, his touch causing me to lose my breath. He tightly squeezed me and started tickling my ribs. "Stop!" I screamed through laughs. "I'm going to kick your ass, Jace."

"Umm..."

We both froze and looked up to see a woman in about her early thirties standing above us with her hand on her hip. She was slightly too thin and her dark hair and green eyes resembled Jace's. Her black pants squeezed her hips tightly and her red shirt was too short revealing faded scars that covered her belly. "Aren't you guys a cute couple?"

Jace looked shocked as he helped me to my feet. He stared at the woman in silence before he stepped forward and threw his arms around her. They were both stiff as they hugged each other.

Finally, after a few seconds of awkwardness they both pulled away smiling. Jace leaned in with a look of nervousness as he kissed her on the forehead.

"Jackie, this is my friend, Avery." He reached over and grabbed my arm to pull me closer. "Avery, this is...my sister Jackie." He looked between the both of us before his eyes wandered to behind where Jackie stood.

His sister? I was shocked. I had known Jace for almost two weeks and he had never mentioned a sister before. I just assumed that he was the only child. I knew that his father left his mother when he was sixteen but that was it. Apparently, either one of us talked much about our past or personal lives.

Jackie looked me in the eye and smiled. "Avery. That is such a beautiful name." She grinned revealing her yellowing teeth. She made me nervous. "Such a beautiful girl."

Not knowing what to say, I just smiled and nodded my head.

WAKE UP CALL
VICTORIA ASHLEY

Jace suddenly reached out and grabbed his sister's arm pulling her sleeve up. He turned it around as if he was checking for something. Then he rubbed it and looked behind her again, eyes wild. "Where is he?" he questioned. "I know he's here."

Jackie pulled her bruised arm away and pulled down her sleeve. She gave him a look of disgust and shook her head. "You haven't seen your dear old sister in three years and that's how you greet me," she spat.

Jace pulled his sister's arm and held her close to him. "Stay with me," he demanded. "You don't have to be with Joe. You can stay with us."

Jackie grinned and licked her teeth. "He's my boyfriend and I love him. He's here you know," she said with a wicked grin. "He's waiting for his friend outside." She pulled away from Jace's grip and walked over to me. She placed her hand under my chin and pulled my face up so that I was looking in her eyes. Her eyes were distant, almost empty. "Take care of my little brother. He needs someone in his life. He's never loved anyone but mother and-"

"Jackie," he cut her off. "Don't even think about going there," he said sternly. Then he pulled her hand away from my chin and pointed toward the door as a man walked in. "There's that piece of shit."

Jackie looked behind her and waved her scrawny arm. A thin man with a blond mullet looked over and ran his fingers through his beard. He looked dirty. Like my father when he was hopped-up. It made my stomach churn. I wanted to hide. "Joe, my baby brother is here," she screamed making a scene. "Isn't he so handsome?"

Joe smiled and headed toward us. I watched Jace as his jaw clenched. I was nervous and Joe was getting closer with each passing second. "Baby bro-"

Jace swung out his right fist connecting it to Joe's jaw. Joe took a step back and stumbled into a chair. We all watched in silence as he fell to the floor and pounded his fist on the ground.

Jace leaned over him and grabbed the back of his hair. "If you ever lay your hand on my sister again, I swear I will hunt you down," he said breathless. "I will hunt you down and I will kill you."

WAKE UP CALL
VICTORIA ASHLEY

Jackie ran over and pushed Jace away. Then she slapped him across the face, leaving a mark. His jaw clenched, but other than that, he didn't move a muscle.

"Leave, Jace. You have no right. I'm a grown woman," she said venomously.

Jace grabbed for my hand and pulled me away from the scene. "Yeah, a thirty year old clueless woman." He paused and looked into her eyes. "I wish our love was strong enough. You need help."

"I'm not the only one," she said. Then she helped Joe to his feet and pulled him toward the door. "This is why we don't talk anymore," she yelled back before stepping outside of the bowling alley.

I watched Jace in silence as he watched his sister walk out of the bowling alley and out of his life. The look on his face was so painful that it hurt me. It reminded me of the pain I felt around my parents. I wanted to cry for him.

We both stood there quietly before Jace turned around and shook his head. "I'm so sorry that you had to see that. I ruined the day," he said sourly.

"Jace." I walked over and placed my hand on his arm. "Don't be sorry," I whispered. "Maybe we can continue this another day."

He looked up and smiled. "No." He paused. "You deserve to have a good day. I like seeing you smile." He walked over to his ball and picked it up from the ground, taking one last look at the exit door. "Besides, you still have to kick my ass if you want that lunch." He smirked.

I stifled a grin as I watched him walk over to the lane and toss his ball. He tossed it so hard that it knocked every pin down. I was impressed. "Very nice," I said playfully.

By the end of the game, Jace was the winner. The scores were Jace with a 160 and myself with a 102. I guess it wasn't bad for my first game. *So much for that lunch.*

We left the bowling alley and I was surprised when he pulled up at the diner. I didn't win the game so he didn't owe me lunch. Even though I was starving, I didn't understand. I sat up in my seat and took my seatbelt off. "What are we doing here?" I questioned. "Are we going to work?"

He smiled and turned off the engine. "I don't owe you lunch, but that doesn't mean that we can't go and eat for free." He lifted an eyebrow. "Let's go. I'm starving." He jumped out of the car and waited for me. "Well...come on."

I got out and followed him inside the diner. Maple greeted us with that award winning '*mommy*' grin that she always gave. "It's two of my favorite people. So glad that you guys came in to see me," she said gleefully.

Jace and I followed her to an empty booth, taking a seat across from each other.

Winston stepped out of the kitchen and walked over to the table with a smile. "Do I have company?" he questioned. "Jace, I'll make your favorite." He looked over at me and grinned. "My favorite -"

"Winston," Maple cut him off. "That girl doesn't find you attractive. Get back in that kitchen," she said with a slight grin.

Winston rubbed his round belly and shrugged his shoulders. "Hey, I worked hard to get a body like this," he teased.

Maple pinched his arm and shook her head as he walked away. "I told you he has been being bad," she said to Jace.

Jace leaned back in the booth and laughed. "You always know how to keep him in check. I need a woman like you, Maple," he said squeezing her hand.

Maple blushed and grabbed my shoulder. She looked between the both of us and smiled. Then she fixed her apron. "The usual, sweetness?"

I looked up and smiled. "I have a usual?" I questioned unaware.

She smiled and pinched my cheek. "Of course you do. You always order the breakfast steak and fried potatoes with extra ranch on the side."

I shook my head in disbelief. She was right. I did. I couldn't believe that she had noticed. "Yes, maple. Thank you," I said.

Jace smiled across the table at me as Maple walked away. Then he leaned in, his eyes studying my hands. "I had a lot of fun today." He looked up and licked his lips. "Did you enjoy bowling?"

I looked away from his lips and cleared my throat before my eyes could roam the rest of his gorgeous body. "Yeah. It was nice. I've always wanted to go bowling but just never had the chance."

I swallowed hard and twirled a finger in my hair. "It's not that I couldn't or anything, it's just that...it's-"

"It's okay, Avery," he cut in. "You don't have to explain why you've never bowled before. I'm sure there are others out there." He smiled and slipped his hand across the table, resting it next to mine. "You're so..."

I stared down at his hand before pulling my hand off the table and resting it awkwardly on my lap. *Don't stop there.* "I'm so what?"

Jace smiled as Maple approached the table with our food. "Cute," he said calmly. Then he stood up to help Maple with our plates.

Maple slapped Jace with her towel and laughed. "You sit down. You're not working. I am perfectly capable, young man."

Jace sat back down throwing his hands up. "Yes, ma'am." He grinned. "Thank you."

A smile crossed my face as I watched the two of them. They were so comfortable with each other and I had to admit that it was rather cute.

"You two enjoy each other." Maple paused. "I mean the food." She laughed.

Jace grabbed his fork and looked over at me. "Oh we will."

While eating, I looked across the diner noticing the same strange woman from last week. She sat in the corner of the diner, peeking over her phone in our direction. I could feel her stare burning a hole right through me, making me feel uncomfortable. She kept tilting her phone as if she were taking pictures of us. It was distracting and creepy.

"Jace."

He looked up from his plate of food and set his fork down. "What's up?"

"Do you know that woman that is sitting in the corner behind you?"

He peered over his shoulder and then quickly turned back around. "Nope. I've seen her in her a few times but that's it," he replied. "Why?"

I shook my head, blowing it off. She was probably just hungry. It's a diner after all. "Just curious. She looks familiar. That's all."

Jace looked down at my fork as I played with my steak. "Now eat." He smiled before shoving his food in his mouth. He somehow even managed to make that look sexy.

After eating, Jace tossed a ten-dollar bill on the table for Maple. Then I pulled out a five -dollar bill and threw it down on the table as well. Jace smiled and placed the saltshaker down on top of the money. "That's nice of you," he said.

I just shook my head before following him to the car. Maple was a sweet woman and she deserved money for her hard work. In the whole time that I had known her, I had never seen her without a smile.

After arriving back to the house, we spent the next couple of hours cleaning the house and just hanging out. It was so different from what I was used to and it felt nice. We made some small talk but I still couldn't manage to talk about my past or my family. It was my dark little secret. A monster inside of me that I didn't want to release.

"Thank you for today."

Jace looked up from the loveseat and nodded his head. "Don't thank me. Just promise to do it again someday."

I couldn't help but to look at his arms as he stretched them out behind him. I remembered what it felt like being close to him and my heart flipped in my chest just thinking about being in his arms again. "I'll think about it." I smiled at Jace before heading to my room to be alone. I needed some thinking time. Some time to be alone.

It was my 16th birthday and I was about to go on my first date. I had been crushing on Nate since the fifth grade and I was so excited that he had finally asked me out. I put on my best dress and threw my hair up in a bun. I wanted him to like me as much as I had liked him.

After I was dressed, I looked over at the clock to check the time. "Shoot!" He would be arriving any minute now. I was so nervous. Even more nervous because both of my parents had been drinking.

My heart stopped and I froze when I heard a light knock on the door. I needed to get downstairs so I could answer it before my parents. I couldn't let them ruin my first date. I was half way down the stairs when suddenly I heard a loud bang on the wall and my father mumbling to himself. Shit!

WAKE UP CALL
VICTORIA ASHLEY

My father had the door wide open and my mother was in the background in a T-shirt and underwear. Nate stood there with a worried look on his handsome face. His blue eyes, usually so bright, were now dull and full of regret.

"Kid, do you have any idea what you're getting yourself into," My father questioned. "Look at her." He motioned back to me as I walked up behind him. My whole body shook.

My mother leaned back in her chair and let out a devilish laugh. It sent chills down my arms. My father joined her in laughter and grabbed a hold of my hair. "She's not worth your time. She's not worth anyone's time," he said spitting in Nate's face. "Get out while you can. Run off kid."

I yanked my head away from my father's grip and grabbed the door. "No!" I screamed. "Nate."

Nate took one look into my eyes and I could see the fear in them. He slowly turned away and walked down the sidewalk. My heart broke with every step that he took.

"Come back, please," I cried. He didn't stop or even bother to turn around. He just left. Left me alone and broken.

I felt the anger build up inside of me and I lost it. I wasn't thinking. "Dad!" I screamed. "I hate you both."

My dad looked at me with eyes of fire. He was going to rip my head off. I had never spoken to him like that before. Even my mother froze in her chair. "You, little bitch."

I took off running toward the stairs. My legs gave out and I knew that I was dead.

I sat up in bed screaming. My whole body covered with sweat, as the tears rolled down my face. I grabbed my hair and pulled it out of my face, while glancing up to see Jace standing in my doorway shirtless. The sight startled me.

He didn't hesitate before running inside my room and sitting on the edge of my bed. "Avery, what's wrong?" he questioned while grabbing my face. His hands were soft and warm. "Tell me."

I stared up at him unable to speak. I felt my whole body quake as I started crying even harder. "I...I-"

He wrapped his arms around me and pulled my head against his chest. "Shh! It's okay." He ran his strong hands over my head and face and placed his head on mine. "I'm here. It's okay," he whispered.

I sat there in his arms for what felt like forever. I didn't want to move. It was starting to become a normal routine for us. I leaned closely against his chest as he comforted me with his soft touch.

When I was finally able to collect myself and gain control, I pulled away and looked up at him. "It was just a bad dream."

He looked down into my eyes and grabbed my face. "That was one hell of a dream then. You can tell me about it," he said softly. "Please."

I turned my face away unable to look him in the eye. "It was just a bad memory. One that I would like to forget," I whispered. "My only boyfriend, he..." I stopped.

He pulled my face toward his and rubbed my cheek. "Did he hurt you?" he questioned, his voice shaking.

My legs started shaking as he rubbed my face. "Not him. My parents." I looked down at the ground in shame. "They told him that I wasn't worth his time. He was the only guy that I ever loved," I whispered.

He shook my shoulders and looked me in the eye. He looked angry. "You listen here, don't you ever believe that you're not worth loving. Anyone would have to be crazy to not love you." He turned his head away and clenched his jaw. "I mean...this guy must have just been crazy to not love you back. He was stupid."

He threw his arms around me not even giving me a chance to speak. He leaned back in the bed pulling me down with him. He pulled me into his body and wrapped me in his arms and close to his chest, his bare legs tangled around mine. "I'm going to stay in here with you until you can fall asleep."

I attempted to pull away to look at him. "I'm fine, Jace. Really, you don't have to," I said struggling.

He pulled me tighter and kissed the top of my head. *Damn his lips are soft.* "Your bed is more comfortable than mine and you need to learn to share." He laughed in my ear.

Chills ran down my body as his breath tickled my ear. "Well, I guess if you put it that way," I whispered and then turned around to face him. He had a way of making things not seem so bad. His humor made me smile to myself. "Don't get too comfortable though."

"Thanks," he said in relief. Then he brushed my hair out of my face, wiped my face off, and pressed his lips to my forehead. "Goodnight."

His warm skin brushed against mine and I suddenly felt naked in only my bra and panties. At the moment, I just didn't seem to care. The feel of his skin made me breathless. "Goodnight, Jace," I whispered.

His lips brushed my neck in response and I fell into him even more.

Chapter 8

I rolled over and stretched as my eyes wandered over the empty mattress next to me. The warmth from Jace's body still lingered on the sheets as I reached over, rubbing a hand over the empty spot.

He stayed the whole night! I jumped up in a panic as I attempted to take in the thought of sleeping next to Jace or any man for that matter. Running my hands through my hair, I took a deep breath, and rolled over, burying my face into the pillow.

After climbing out of bed, I calmly gathered my clothing for work, and walked to the bathroom. There was no sign of Jace in sight, so I quickly closed the door behind me and turned the lock, being sure that Jace wouldn't walk in on me, again. The bathroom quickly filled with steam as I stripped off my clothing and jumped into the shower water. The hot water felt nice on my cool skin, helping me to relax, as I fought to calm my racing nerves. I was a nervous wreck and relaxing was one of the many things that I needed to do.

After I showered and got dressed, I walked out into the living room to find Jace sitting in his black leather chair, his hair looking messy and uncombed. His eyes looked tired and strained as if he hadn't slept all night.

"Umm...hi," I stammered. "Get much sleep last night?" I walked over, reached for my jacket, and slipped it on. Then I pulled the ponytail holder from off my wrist and threw my hair up so that it was out of my face.

Jace gave me a surprised look before he pushed himself to his feet and grabbed for his keys. "You can tell," he laughed. "You sure did sleep like a baby though." He grinned and reached for the door to open it. He waited for me to walk out first before he closed the door behind us and locked it. "I hope that you're ready for a busy day. It's the only day of the month that I make my special fried chicken and gravy." He licked his lips and shook his head. "It's delicious."

The awkward look on his face made me laugh. I lightly shoved him toward the car and reached for the handle. "Oh is it? It's so special that you can only make it once a month?" I questioned.

I shut the door in his face before he could manage to answer. He pointed at me through the window and smoothly walked to the other side and jumped in.

He glared over at me and nibbled on his lip ring. It was such a bad habit of his. "The ladies love anything that I put my hands on. I make this chicken from in here," he said pointing to his heart. His smile faded and then he quickly replaced it and started the car. "You'll love...it."

"How do I know that it's really as good as you say?" I teased. "It could taste horrible and we could be really slow today. I don't see you as being a good chicken maker." I grinned and leaned back into my seat while playing with my old ring.

Jace tilted his head and looked over at me, his eyes soft. "You'll just have to trust me," he whispered. "I know how you love chicken. I will make you love mine."

My heart skipped a beat at the word trust. How I wished that I could. "I guess we will just have to see."

The rest of the car ride was silent until we pulled into the diner. I was surprised to see that there were already a handful of customers patiently waiting outside. It made me smile to think that these people were here for Jace. Maybe he was telling the truth after all.

Jace smiled at everyone before unlocking the door and letting Stacy, Winston, and the customers inside. "Good morning, Jan," he said to an older red headed woman, that didn't look very pleasant. "It's good to see you."

Jan smiled evilly and reached out for Jace's arm. "You just better get in there and get me my chicken ready. I'm not getting any younger. Do you see a line full of boys waiting on me? I don't think so."

Jace laughed and helped push Jan through the door. "Yes, ma'am. If there were, I would be the first one in line too." He looked over at me and winked. "I'll have your chicken right up."

Jan grunted and made her way past Jace and over to the first available booth. She stopped shortly after taking notice of Stacy. She eyed her up and down before shaking her head. "Seeing you once a month is getting to be too much for me."

Stacy's baby blues sparkled as she gathered up her things and threw on her apron. She looked amused by the old lady. "Hi, Jan. It's good to see you too." She grinned.

Jan pushed past Stacy and pounded her cane into the ground. "Damn, bubbly girl." Then she scooted into her booth, while shaking her head.

Stacy ignored the old woman's attitude and started humming to herself while smiling from ear to ear. I had to admit she was acting extra bubbly today.

"Spill it," I said.

Stacy glanced over her shoulder and attempted to hide her smile. "I don't know what you're talking about," she said with a giggle. "Can't I just be happy to work? Today Jace is making his-"

"Oh cut the crap." I smiled and leaned against the counter. She wasn't fooling me. "You're smiling so hard that its even hurting me."

She quickly stepped over and placed her hands on my shoulders. Then she started bouncing up and down like a hyped up teenage girl. I could already see where it was going. "I met a guy," she practically sang.

I couldn't help but to laugh. Some girls were just so silly and clueless when it came to men. It never lasted and no one ever truly cared. "That's great...I think," I muttered.

Stacy frowned and took her hands away from my shoulders. "Oh shoot." She slapped her forehead and shooed Winston away as he attempted to join us. "Not now, Winston. Girl talk." He tiptoed backwards and wandered back into the kitchen, trying to be invisible. "That was so careless of me. I forgot that you're single." She paused and pushed her curls from out of her face.

She looked so sweet and innocent. "Tonight, me and you. We're going out." She laughed, eyes wide. "Girl's night."

I threw on my apron and laughed to myself. "I don't know about that. I have something-"

"She's totally free tonight," Jace said from behind us, causing my heart to sink. "You girls should go out and have fun. You both deserve it."

He smiled and patted us both on the shoulder. "Besides, I was planning on walking around naked all night," he said winking at us as he walked away.

We both watched his back as he walked into the diner and shook hands with his waiting customers. He really was something else. I didn't understand how he was so calm and cool about everything.

Stacy's eyes went wide as she threw her hand over her mouth. She looked back over at me and shook her head. "Oh shit! Now that image will be stuck in my head all day," she pouted. "Poor Alex won't like that."

She wasn't the only one. I was already trying to shake the image from out of my head. *Damn him.* I had already gotten a glimpse of him naked and I had to admit that he was damn sexy. *Guess I'm stuck going now.* "What time? Should I take a taxi and meet you somewhere?" I questioned.

She reached over and slapped my arm. "Don't be silly. I'll pick you up," she giggled. "I wouldn't make you take a taxi. That's what friends are for. I'll pick you up at seven."

"Sounds like fun," I huffed. "We better get started."

"Yes we should," she sang. "You can start by helping Jan." She laughed and quickly ran away before I could object.

Oh joy. I looked over toward the grouchy old woman and grunted to myself. I was definitely not a morning person and it was too early to have to deal with a woman like that.

I walked over to Jan's booth and watched as she played with the plastic bag that covered her hair. "Nice hair piece," I muttered.

Jan looked up at me and yanked the bag from off her hair. Then she grunted and shifted in her seat. "These damn booths are so uncomfortable." She puffed up the curls on her head and looked behind me. "Where's that damn bubbly waitress?"

WAKE UP CALL
VICTORIA ASHLEY

I leaned into her table and shrugged my shoulders. "I think you scared her off. Now what would you like to drink?"

Jan smiled and puckered her lips. "Get me a damn coffee with extra creamer," she growled. "And I do mean, extra creamer."

I laughed under my breath and turned my head away. I had no patience to care about my actions at the moment. "One damn coffee coming up. Extra creamer."

I got ready to walk away when suddenly I felt Jan's hand grip my arm. I glanced down, looking her in the eye. "About time they got somebody that's not so damn bubbly around here." She smiled and then released my arm. "I'll take some water too."

"Sure. I'll be right back." I nodded and walked away. The woman wasn't as bad as I expected. I guess old people liked it when people were mean back to them.

We worked through the lunch rush and things didn't seem to calm down until well after two o'clock p.m.

Exhausted, I plopped down into a booth and closed my eyes. I didn't even have energy enough to grab a drink first. I definitely didn't know how I was going to have the energy to keep up with Stacy later tonight.

"You look hungry."

I looked up and tilted my head. Jace stood there looking proud with a plate of food in his hand. "I am. I'm actually starving."

"Good." Jace set the plate down in front of me and smiled. "Don't fall in love too much." Then he walked away and disappeared into the kitchen.

I stifled a laugh as I watched him poke his head through the window of the kitchen and smile. Falling in love has never been a problem of mine. I won't start now.

I took a bite of the fried chicken, covered in white gravy and moaned. It was moist and full of flavor. *Holy shit.* This is delicious. I stuffed a few more bites into my mouth and attempted to hide my pleasure. I didn't want Jace to know how much I enjoyed his chicken. He was too good and he already knew it.

I will never win with him...

~•~

WAKE UP CALL
VICTORIA ASHLEY

Jace sat back on the couch and grinned as I reached for my jacket. Stacy would be arriving any moment and I just wanted to get the night done and over with. "What are you grinning about?" I questioned with my arms crossed.

He threw his head back and laughed. "You will see." He turned on the TV and stretched. "I'm going to have such a relaxing night. I can't wait until you leave so I can start getting rid of these damn clothes," he said tugging on his shirt.

That jerk. He's teasing me. He was enjoying every minute of my suffering. "I still have time. Maybe I will just call and cancel. Then you can keep your clothes on," I smirked. I pointed at my phone and pretended to look for Stacy's number. "Oh there it is."

Jace glared at me and then reached for his jeans. He unbuttoned them and slipped them off before tossing them at my head. "I'm already stripping. You better hurry and leave," he teased.

I threw his jeans down and kicked them. Then I watched in surprise as he stripped his shirt off and tossed it next to his jeans. "Put those back on," I muttered. My eyes set on his firm chest as he threw his hands behind his head and leaned into the soft couch. His body was like a piece of art. It was beautiful. I hated him for that. "Put them on or I'll make you."

Jace raised an eyebrow and kicked his feet up on the table in front of him. "Nah... I'm good. I like it better this way," he breathed. "I feel so... free."

I took a deep breath, walked over, and grabbed his jeans. I attempted to pick them up, but tripped when they caught under my feet. I fell over on my side and landed with my face in his shirt. "Shit!" I screamed. It smelled of fresh body wash.

I heard laughter before Jace walked over and stood above me. "Stop messing around. I think that your rides here. What would she say if she knew that you were on the floor sniffing my worn shirt?"

"What!" I screeched. "I'm not sniffing your..." I jumped to my feet and punched him in the arm. He was having way too much fun teasing me. "Shut up."

He dangled his arm in front of him as if it was broken. "Shit, Avery," he groaned. His face looked pained.

"I'm sorry. I didn't-"

WAKE UP CALL
VICTORIA ASHLEY

He grabbed me up in is arms, tickling my sides, as he laughed. I started squirming around and screaming as I attempted to pull away. "That's so cute," he grinned. "You have such a cute scream. Go ahead. Scream again."

I kicked my foot out and tripped Jace. His leg gave out on him and we both ended up on the floor with Jace on top of me. He smiled down at me and shook his hair from out of his face. "I like this position," he said breathless. Both of his arms were on the ground around my waist. His face was just inches above mine, his breath, warm sweet, as he breathed heavily. "It's my favorite."

I swallowed hard and turned my face away from his. Being that close only reminded me of that kiss. The one that was never meant to happen and that we hadn't talked about since. It made me nervous. I felt as if I could faint.

"Umm..."

We both looked over to see Stacy standing in the doorway. She smiled down at us and shook her head. "Am I interrupting something?" she giggled.

I pushed Jace over and jumped to my feet. Then I lightly kicked Jace in the leg as he laughed, clearly still amused. "Nope, not at all. I was just-"

"Sure," she cut in. "Let's hurry. I made reservations for 'Island Magic'." She grinned from ear to ear. "I haven't been there in ages." She paused and looked at Jace as he stood back up. "Where's your... oh never mind," she said blushing. "We have to hurry."

I gave Jace a dirty look before following Stacy out the door. I shut the door behind us and followed her to her purple jeep. It suited her personality well. "So, what is 'Island Magic'?" I questioned as we both jumped in.

She puckered her pink lips and started the jeep. Her leg was bouncing in excitement as she took off. "It's a fancy restaurant. You will love it," she said with a playful smile.

I looked down at Stacy's little black dress and suddenly felt a little underdressed in my silver sweater, black leggings and black boots. I really wasn't prepared for a night of fancy dining. Actually, I wasn't prepared for the night to happen at all. What I really wanted was to go home and relax in my warm bed. "I'm sure I will." I forced a smile and then looked out the window.

WAKE UP CALL
VICTORIA ASHLEY

Twenty minutes later, we arrived at a glass building. The whole thing was made of glass and as we walked up, I could already see the palm trees, sand, beach chairs and girls walking around in bikinis. It was a crazy sight. I had never even known a place like that existed.

Stacy looked down at my boots as we started toward the door. "I hope those boots are easy to get off. You're going to want to put your toes in the sand. It feels amazing," she breathed. "It's the closest thing to heaven. That and the boys, of course."

I stopped and looked down at my boots. They had a few straps on the side, but were easy to slip off and on. Suddenly, I felt overdressed. Everyone was wearing beach stuff. It was the craziest thing I had ever seen. It wasn't even warm enough to dress that way.

We entered the restaurant and was greeted by the hostess. She wore a lime green bikini with black flip-flops. Her golden hair was pulled back in a braid and she wore a smile that could light up the whole room. "Welcome ladies. You guys look quite lovely tonight." She reached for a couple of menus and winked at me. "Follow me."

Stacy grabbed my arm and pointed at the girls butt as we followed her. "That lucky, bitch," she whispered. The girls butt was flawless. I didn't even know that butts that perfect existed outside of movies. Her skin was perfectly tanned and she had a tattoo of a butterfly on her lower back. She was sweet and beautiful. Picture perfect.

We followed her to a table that was right next to the bar. Four white beach chairs sat around the bamboo table, and a beach ball stuck to the middle. The whole floor was made of glass, but right around every table, it was full of sand.

The hostess placed the menus on the table and smiled at us both. "You ladies have a wonderful date. William will be your waiter." She walked away glancing back at us, with a flirty smile, before she was out of our sight.

I sat down in a chair and pulled my boots and socks off. Stacy did the same. "That was weird," I said.

Stacy grinned and leaned back in her chair. "She's always hitting on the ladies when I come here. I think that she likes us," she said blushing, clearly happy with the attention. "So...?"

I looked at her confused. "So... what?" I questioned while reaching for the menu. *Why is she looking at me like that?*

She didn't take her eyes off me as she opened her menu and grinned. "What's going on with you and Jace? That was a pretty hot scene that I-"

"Oh no," I cut her off. I didn't want her getting the wrong idea. There was nothing between Jace and I. I didn't want anything from anyone. "There is nothing going on. I was just kicking his ass. You know how he can get," I said. I leaned back in my chair and took a deep breath when I noticed that I was gripping onto the table.

Stacy's eyes lingered down to my hand right before I managed to let go. "Seems like a touchy subject to me." She smiled. "So did you eat any of his famous chicken?" she questioned. "It's the best chicken I've ever had. I wonder where he got the recipe."

I did and it was the best thing I had ever tasted. Although, I wasn't willing to admit it. "Yeah. It was fine. Not as good as he said it would be though," I lied. "He probably found it online."

We both looked up when a young man walked up shirtless, wearing only a pair of blue and gray swimming trunks. He had very short blond hair, almost shaved off, hazel eyes, and a masculine jaw line. He smiled revealing a set of perfect teeth as he pointed at our menus. "Hello, ladies. Are you ready to order or can I answer any questions?" I was sure Stacy would have a few questions. He seemed her type. Clean cut and sweet.

Stacy kicked me from under the table and smiled.

"Ouch, Stacy," I whined. "What was that for?" I questioned as I reached for my leg.

She gave me a desperate look and flared her nostrils. "I'm sorry. It was an accident," she breathed. "Hi, William. I have a question." She let out a flirty giggle.

William leaned into the table and smiled at Stacy. "You can ask me anything," he said entertained.

Stacy looked at me and then back up at William. Then she reached over and grabbed my chin. "Do you think that my friend here is pretty?"

I jerked my leg out and kicked Stacy in the knee. I didn't like where she was going with things.

Stacy shifted in her seat and let go of my chin. She cleared her throat and then placed her hand under her chin. "So...?"

William looked over at me and smirked. "Sure. She's beautiful," he answered. He gave me a flirty smile and flexed his muscle as he reached for his pen. "I would take her out."

Not happy with all of the attention set on me, I threw my menu down, and flicked the beach ball. I'm so going to kick Stacy's butt later. "I'll take the cod dinner, please," I said sternly.

William took a step back and shook his head. He looked a little stunned. "Sure, one Cod dinner." He looked over at Stacy and reached for her menu. "How about you?" He asked confused.

Stacy glared at me and shook her head in disappointment. "I'll just take the same. Bring us two Martinis, please," she muttered, holding up two fingers.

William grabbed for our menus and walked away with a forced smile. You could tell that he wasn't used to rejection. "Sure thing."

After William was out of sight, Stacy leaned over and kicked sand at me. "He was gorgeous. What is your problem?"

I rolled my eyes and fixed my ponytail. "I'm not looking for a boyfriend. I'm fine by myself," I muttered. "I don't even know him. You can't just ask a total stranger that." I said, leaning into the table.

She laughed and rubbed her lips together. "Well I just did and he said you were beautiful. Doesn't that count for anything?" she questioned. "If I hadn't already met Alex then I would've gone for him myself. He's hot."

Is this what normal girls do? Find random guys and jump into a relationship. I don't think so. I didn't like that idea and I could never see myself doing that. "Not really. Like I said I'm fine alone."

Several minutes later, William came back with our food. He leaned over my shoulder and placed the plate in front of me. "Enjoy your dinner," he breathed. "Let me know if I can get you anything. Another Martini or my number," he whispered playfully.

His arm brushed against mine as he pulled away and walked over to set Stacy's plate in front of her. "Enjoy ladies." He didn't take his eyes off me as he backed up and walked over to the kitchen. I had to admit, he was cute, but still not enough to make me stupid.

Stacy eyed me as she bit into her Cod. "You could be throwing something good away." She shrugged her shoulders and took a sip of her Martini. "You should just take his damn number. What will it hurt?"

I rolled my eyes and took a bite of my food. What would be the point? I wouldn't be calling him anyways. "I don't think so," I muttered.

William came by a few times to check on us. I could tell that Stacy was still a little disappointed that I wasn't willing to give William a chance, but I tried not to let it bother me too much. Stacy was just trying to do what a real friend would do. This was just another thing that made me believe that maybe I just wasn't capable of a true friendship. Maybe it was best to accept his number, to at least make her night.

I looked up, huffing, as I eyed William. "Hey, William." I stopped him just as he was walking by our table.

He stopped and walked over with a grin. "Can I get you something else?" he asked.

I exhaled while playing with my napkin. I didn't like what I was about to do. It had my stomach in knots. "Yeah, your number," I sighed.

William reached into his pocket and pulled out a piece of paper. He placed it in my open hand and smiled. Then he closed my hand. "I knew you would ask. Call me anytime." He winked at the both of us and walked away.

Stacy clapped her hands and laughed. "You just made my night."

"Great," I muttered.

After Stacy dropped me off, I walked into a dark, quiet house. It was ten o'clock and it was unusual for Jace to be in bed before midnight. He stayed up late and always woke up early.

Without turning on the lights, I blindly made my way over and plopped down on the couch.

"Ouch."

I jumped up startled when I felt Jace underneath of me. I ran over to the light switch and flipped it on. "I'm sorry. I didn't-"

"It's fine, Avery." he cut me off. He blinked a few times trying to adjust to the lighting. "I should probably go sleep in my room anyways. The couch usually hurts my back," he said stretching. "How was your night?"

I reached in my pocket and pulled out William's number. "Well, Stacy talked a lot and the half-naked waiter gave me his number. You tell me," I huffed. I nervously played with the tiny piece of paper.

Jace sat up on the couch and I plopped down next to him. I averted my eyes away from his half- naked body as his silk blanket dropped down to the floor. I guess he was telling the truth about wanting to walk around naked.

It was silent before Jace looked over at me and bit his lip. "Are you going to call him?" he questioned. He looked down at my hand and ran his hand through his hair.

I tossed the number on the table in front of us and laughed. "No need to." We both sat there in silence and stared at the paper on the table. Then suddenly Jace's sister popped into my head and made my stomach ache. I had been curious about what she said the other night. I couldn't seem to get it out of my head. I needed to know. "Tell me about your sister," I whispered.

He closed his eyes and ran his hands through his hair again. He looked nervous. "Not tonight, Avery," he breathed. "I'm too tired." He stood up and rubbed his hand over his stomach. "I'll see you in the morning." He turned around and walked toward the hallway. Then he stopped and smiled. "The chicken was good wasn't it? Just another reason for you to trust me"

I rolled my eyes and leaned back into the couch. I suddenly felt exhausted and couldn't think anymore for the night. "It could've been better," I smirked.

He nodded his head and turned the other way. "A word of advice." He paused. "Don't call that guy." He grinned. "Goodnight, Avery."

I laughed to myself and pulled my jacket off. "Goodnight, Jace." At least I wasn't alone on this one.

Stacy definitely wore me out. Now I knew what he meant...

"Avery, come out, come out, wherever you are."

I cowered back against the wall, hitting my head on the bottom of my bed. I stifled back a cry as the pain shot through my body, causing my head to throb instantly. I wanted so badly to scream, but I knew that it would give away my hiding spot. So, instead I covered my mouth with trembling hands in an attempt to stay quiet.

WAKE UP CALL
VICTORIA ASHLEY

I heard the creaking of the closet door opening, before seeing items of clothing as they fell down around the bed. I knew that my father would check there. He had always found me in the past. "We can do this all night or we can get this over with," my father growled. "You're asking for it you, rotten little brat."

My father's footsteps echoed throughout the little room as he stomped over to the bed and yanked the blankets off. I could hear him breathing heavily as he struggled to free himself from the tangled mess.

"No," I whispered. He was getting closer and my heart was beating faster.

"Henry!" A drunken female shouted. "Where is that little brat of yours? That girl needs to learn discipline," she slurred. "My stash is all gone. That little bitch did something with it."

It was true. I saw the drugs setting down on the toilet and I accidentally knocked the tray over, spilling it into the water. I panicked and cleaned off the filthy toilet the best that I could manage. I knew that my beating would come later. I had been dreading it all day.

The room went silent for a few moments. My eyes widened and I let out a deep breath of relief. I was in the clear. Maybe he had given up.

I was just about to close my eyes and force myself to sleep, when suddenly I felt a firm grip on my ankle, yanking me out from under the bed. My elbow slammed against the leg of the bed and a cry of pain forced its way out through my parted lips.

"I didn't mean to," I cried.

"Avery," Jace whispered. "Are you okay?" His warm breath kissed my cheek as I slowly opened my eyes. I couldn't tell if I was still asleep or if my mind was just playing tricks on me.

I moaned softly as Jace's hand slowly trailed over my shoulder and down my right arm, leaving a trail of goose bumps. His touch was somehow cool and comforting and I didn't want it to stop. *Even if I am just dreaming.*

I blinked a few times, trying to focus, before realizing that it wasn't just a dream. *He really is here.* I groggily turned my head and looked up at Jace as his body hovered above mine. His bare chest moved slowly as he breathed and the look in his eyes was almost painful to look at. It made my heart ache.

"I heard you screaming," he whispered.

WAKE UP CALL
VICTORIA ASHLEY

I turned my eyes away from his gaze and shook my head. The last thing I needed was to keep Jace awake because of my horrible night terrors. "I'm sorry. I didn't mean to wake-"

"Don't be sorry," he cut in. "I don't really like sleep much anyways. All the good stuff happens when I'm awake." He smiled and grabbed my chin. Then a serious look crossed his face. "Tell me what happened, Avery. I want to know."

I took a deep breath and pushed his hand away from my chin. I still didn't know if I was ready for him to know the truth. Maybe he deserved to know something at least. He had helped me more than anyone else ever had.

I swallowed hard and turned away, facing the wall. "I was having a dream about when I was only ten," I paused to swallow again, trying to find courage. "My father, he wasn't a good man. The look in his eyes..." I flinched at the memory. "I still can't get it out of my head." I-"

Jace threw his arms around me and pulled me against his chest. "Stop," he whispered. "Some things are better left unsaid." He slammed his fist into the wall beside him, leaving a small dent. The outburst made me jump.

"I swear that if I ever get the chance to meet that man that he will wish that he never laid..." He stopped and squeezed his eyes shut. His jaw clenched. "It's okay now. I will protect you. No one deserves to be hurt like that."

I quickly turned my face away as tears threatened to form. I didn't want Jace to see me weak. I didn't want anyone to see me that way. "I don't know what to say," I whispered. "I mean, you don't even know me. I don't know you."

Jace jumped up from the bed, walked over to the wall, and leaned his arm against it. He pushed his face into his arm and took a deep breath. "I don't know about that. I think that I know you more than you think."

He walked over to my dresser and picked up my old black and gray shirt. "This is your favorite shirt. You have worn it ten times in just under three weeks." He tossed it back on the dresser, while keeping his eyes on me. It was driving me mad. "And your hair, you always seem to twirl your finger in it when you think no one is looking. Or, the fact that you brush your teeth like five times a day. It doesn't matter, they are already beautiful." He walked toward the door and stopped to peer over his shoulder. "Just like you."

I sat there feeling stupid as I stared up at him speechless. *How does he... why?* My heart sank.

He shook his head, walking out of the room, before I could manage to say anything else. The door shut behind him before he took off down the hall as I listened to his heavy footsteps. Moments later the door to his bedroom shut a little harder than expected, causing me to jump.

Part of me wanted to go and apologize, but the bigger part told me to stay put. I was an idiot and I didn't mean to upset him. Jace didn't deserve that.

I pushed my face into my moist pillow and closed my eyes, defeated and helpless.

What is he doing to me?

Chapter 9

Hours passed before I decided to just get out of bed and face the day. I couldn't stop thinking about Jace and it made it nearly impossible to fall back to sleep.

Groaning, I pushed myself out of bed and sauntered down the hallway in search of Jace. I knocked on Jace's door. "Jace," I questioned. "Are you up?"

There was no response. I waited by the door for a few minutes before I finally gave up and decided to look through the rest of the house. As soon as I walked into the kitchen, my eyes settled on a piece of paper lying on the middle of the dining table.

Be at work by ten o'clock. Don't be late.
-Jace

I crumpled up the paper and tossed it into the trash. I couldn't believe that he had left without waking me up. We always went to work at the same time.

I quickly got ready for work and called for a taxi. The emptiness in my stomach made me feel weak and I really just wanted to get the day over with.

After arriving at the diner, I tossed the driver some cash and jumped out of the taxi. I was getting close to being late and I didn't want to disappoint Jace anymore than I already had.

WAKE UP CALL
VICTORIA ASHLEY

I sprinted over to the diner, gripped my purse under my arm, and opened the heavy door. Without looking, I quickly made my way to the waitress station, bumping into Jace in the process. A bunch of papers scattered across the floor, causing Jace to look down at them while slapping his forehead.

"Get it together, please. Now all of these orders are mixed up and we're already falling behind," he grunted. He bent down and started picking them up, without even bothering to look at me. "Just hurry and go find Stacy."

I got ready to bend down, but Jace grabbed my arm to stop me. He looked into my eyes and then quickly looked away. "Don't worry about it. I can get these," he said firmly.

I turned my head away ashamed. I somehow managed to upset him even more. The one thing that I was trying to avoid. "I'm sorry. I didn't-"

"I said it's fine," he cut in. He looked at me, expressionless and then quickly turned and walked away.

I felt a hand grip my shoulder, causing me to jump away unexpectedly. I turned around to see Stacy, wide eyed, and looking panicked. I'd never seen her that way before.

"Come on, sweetie," Stacy said. "We need to get busy. I'm so behind." She grabbed my arm and started pulling me behind her. "Throw your apron on. I'll let you grab the next table."

Stressed, I grunted to myself and threw on my apron. I couldn't believe that I had managed to mess the day up even more.

Brushing past Stacy, I made my way to the back of the diner, noticing the back of a woman's head as she took a seat in an open booth.

Walking over to the booth, I pulled out my pen and paper and prepared for my first customer. "My name is Avery, what can I-"

"I was hoping I would get you."

I looked down at the woman for the first time since I had walked over to greet her. I had seen the same strange woman a few days before and seeing her again didn't please me one bit.

She grinned revealing her rotted teeth. "Go and fetch me a coffee," she huffed, with a wave of her hand.

I grinded my teeth and shoved my pad of paper in my apron. The last thing that I wanted was to deal with some crazy bitch as soon as I started my day. "Listen here, lady." I leaned into the table and gripped the back of her booth with my right hand. I was tired of taking people's shit. "If you keep talking to me like that then-"

"Feisty. I like that." She laughed. "I guess some things do change." She leaned back in the booth and pushed my hand away, her rough skin scratching against my skin. "Coffee, black."

She ran her hand through her stringy hair and coughed. Her eyes stayed glued on mine, making me sick to my stomach. She sounded as if she were about to cough up a lung. *Who is this nut job?*

I pushed past Stacy in a hurry, and over to the waitress station. I grabbed a coffee mug, slamming it down on the station, as I poured it high with steaming hot coffee, hoping and praying that she would burn the crap out of herself. *Who does this lady think she is messing with?*

I stomped over to the woman's booth and slammed her coffee down in front of her. She looked up stiffly. "Here's your damn coffee," I groaned. The coffee splashed over the sides of the little ceramic mug and spilled on the woman's hand.

She jerked her ashy hand away revealing a piece of paper underneath. She glared up at me and shook the paper off. Then she pushed herself to her feet and smirked, as she slammed the paper back down on the table. "I've changed my mind on the coffee."

She brushed past me, leaving the smell of booze as it lingered off her heavy breath. She almost fell into a young couple's booth, but caught her balance and reached out to open the door. Glancing back in my direction, she nodded her head at the table, and laughed before disappearing. Everyone in the diner stared in disgust.

A wave of relief washed over me as the door to the diner closed behind her.

I reached down to grab the cup of coffee when I noticed that the piece of paper had writing on it. It was written in childish handwriting. Almost even a scribble. It looked like some sort of note.

My heart raced as I reached for the paper and shoved it into my apron. I didn't need anything messing up my work performance at the moment and I knew that if it was meant for me that it would just be something to mess with my head. Maybe even a hate letter or something. I didn't care to find out anytime soon. I already had a lot on my mind and she was the least of my worries.

The rest of the workday surprisingly flew by and Jace somehow managed to avoid me the whole day. It made me angry. I didn't understand why he was so mad. It wasn't even a big deal. I only told him the truth. We barely knew each other.

I stared out the window lost in thought. I watched as the rain splashed against the window and slowly trailed down to the ground. It reminded me of my life. No matter how hard I tried, I couldn't stop falling.

"That was fun," Stacy sang from out of nowhere. I glanced up with a strained smile, as she sat down across from me. Her bright smile faded when she noticed the sour look on my face. The one that I couldn't help but to make. "Is everything okay?" she questioned.

I shifted in my seat uncomfortably. I didn't really care to talk about things. I never did. "I'm fine. Just tired," I breathed. "You know, it was such a busy day."

She smiled and brushed her hair out of her face. "I know how you must feel. I felt the same way when I first started. Don't worry you're doing a great job."

She stood up and reached for her phone. "I have to go. I'll see you tomorrow." She took one step, but then stopped. "Did you call William?" She grinned. I knew she just wanted me to be happy, but something in her eyes told me that she was interested in William. Either way she wanted me to be happy.

I smiled up at her and shook my head. "No. I've been busy." I knew that was a lie, but I didn't want to upset her. She had been trying so hard to make me happy.

Stacy frowned, before looking over at Jace as he rushed by. "We'll talk more about that later." She ran to the door as Jace held it open. "Bye, guys."

Jace waved, but didn't say anything back. That was unusual. Then he turned back and glared at me. "You coming?" he questioned.

I stood up, feeling stupid, and grabbed my things. "Yeah."

The car ride home was silent. I wanted to say something, but didn't know what to say. Everything that I always said was wrong. It had been that way my whole life. No matter what I had said to my father to make him less angry, it always had the opposite effect. Maybe I was just easy to stay mad at.

I looked over at Jace as he parked the car and pulled his keys out of the ignition. "Thanks for the ride."

We both jumped out of the car and headed for the door in an awkward silence. It took him a moment before finally replying.

"You're welcome." he stammered, as he unlocked the door to let us in. He stood there with a hard expression as he waited impatiently for me to enter the house. It seemed as if I were nothing more than an irritation, just as Emma had been.

I need to go. I don't belong here. I brushed past Jace and headed straight to my room, shutting myself inside. I just wanted to be alone. I couldn't stand to even look at Jace and I just wanted to leave: to have my own place again.

I stood against the wall letting the anger slowly build up inside. I could just leave and Jace wouldn't care. No one ever does. After being pushed away for most of my life, it didn't take much for me to get the hint when it was time to move on. I knew my role. The only world I belonged in was my own.

I grabbed for the empty box that I had stashed in my closet and started throwing my clothes inside. My heart raced and my hands shook as I forced myself to move as fast as I could. I could barely even function right. My mind was going wild. I couldn't get out of there fast enough.

I went to throw my hair brush and makeup bag in the box, but missed. I dropped down to my hands and knees and went to reach for the brush, but stopped when my door suddenly swung open.

Jace stood in the doorway with a grim look on his face. He looked down at me on my hands and knees and then over to the box. He shook his head and then walked over to my bed and sat on the edge. "Avery, I've been doing a lot of thinking today and I want to apologize. I just have a lot on my mind." He stood up, reached for my brush, and placed it back on my dresser. "Get dressed. You're coming out with me tonight. I think that we both could use a drink."

At the moment, I couldn't help but to agree to the offer. A drink sounded nice and I desperately needed something to take the edge off. I was in no way like my father when it came to drinking, but a few drinks once in a while to relax seemed to be normal to me. "Sure. I could use a drink...or two."

Jace smiled and walked toward the door. "Be ready in twenty minutes." He stepped out of my room closing the door behind him.

My heart raced at the thought of doing something with Jace. He had a strange way to him that I couldn't seem to figure out.

I waited for his footsteps to stop, before scrambling to my feet and leaning against the dresser.

I reached inside my closet and started throwing my clothes around. I knew exactly what I wanted to wear for the night, exactly what I needed to feel good.

After finding what I was looking for, I threw on my ivory satin corset and my short black skirt. It molded to my curvy bottom perfectly, hanging just below my panty line. I knew that I looked a little trashy, but I felt sexy and that was what I needed at the moment. To feel anything but hurt.

I slipped on my black heels and curled my hair so that it hung loosely around my face and fell down the middle of my back.

After taking a quick look in the mirror, satisfied with my reflection, I walked out into the living room to find Jace standing there with a black button down shirt and a pair of gray dress pants. His sleeves were rolled up to just under his elbows, revealing his tattoos, and his top button was undone, exposing the top of his black undershirt. He looked stunning.

Jace turned around as I reached for my jacket. His mouth dropped open, but he quickly recovered, pretending as if it never happened. "You look..." His eyes trailed down my body and stopped on my nude legs. He coughed and loosened his shirt collar. "Nice." He reached for his jacket and slipped it on. "I don't know if you should wear that though. If you bend over then-"

I laughed, cutting him off. "I think that I'll be fine." I grinned at his reaction and smoothly slipped my jacket on. The look of pleasure on his face, mixed with one of concern, made me smile slightly. "Let's go, Jace. The club is waiting." I walked past him and grabbed for my purse. "You coming?"

He ran his hands through his slick hair and bit his bottom lip, his expression playful. "Oh yeah. I'm coming."

My stomach did flips as we walked outside.

When we arrived at the bar, Jace jumped out and opened the door for me. He grinned as I jumped out and fixed my skirt. "What?" I questioned.

He laughed and nodded his head toward the club. "Nothing. Let's go."

I heard someone whistle as a group of people walked out of the bar and passed us. I just ignored it and kept walking. I wasn't going to let it bother me. *Not tonight.*

Jace clenched his jaw, biting his lip, as one of the men eyed me up.

He placed his hand on the small of my back and leaned over my shoulder as we approached the bouncer. He was a young man with tattoos and a shaved head. "I can take care of this," he assured me.

The bouncer nodded his head and held out his fist. You could tell that they had a good personal relationship. Maybe they had been old friends or maybe Jace was just a regular of the club. "What's up, man?" He pounded his fist against Jace's and motioned for us to enter the bar. "It's crazy in there tonight."

Jace patted the bouncer on the shoulder and thanked him before walking past him and into the bar.

The bar was so crowded that you could barely even walk without bumping into someone. *This is crazy.* I looked around feeling overwhelmed as Jace fought our way through the crowd and over to a little table in the back.

Everyone seemed to be dressed well and the bar was very eye-catching with black marble tables, leather chairs, black and silver tiles, and black lighting that splashed through the dark walls almost like a tie-dye. It made my jaw drop.

Jace leaned in, his lips brushing against my ear. "This will have to do." He grabbed the drink menu and pushed it over to the edge of the table. "I think we both know what we want," he said, looking me in the eye.

A shiver ran up my spine. I wasn't sure why, but it did. "Yeah."

Shortly after taking our seats, we were greeted by a handsome man with chestnut hair and tattoos that covered most of his exposed flesh. His gray eyes sparkled with life as he smiled between Jace and me.

He placed his hand on Jace's shoulder and squeezed it. "Hey, man. It's been forever." He looked over at me and smiled. "What are you guys drinking?" He nodded at me and grinned at Jace. "Is she yours?"

Jace patted the man's back and then shook his hand. "No, man. This is my roommate, Avery." He turned his head the other way and took an exasperated breath. "I'm sticking with Jack and coke and a Cherry Mcgillicuddy's and Sprite for the lady here."

His friend waved over one of the waitresses, a sassy looking blond in a little red dress, and placed the order. Then he took a seat next to me and smiled. "Hi, I'm Max." He leaned in and reached for my hand. His hand felt big and strong holding mine. "Nice to meet you."

Seeing Jace's uneasy expression made me nervous. I pulled my hand out of Max's grip and shifted in my seat. "Nice to meet you too."

Jace glared over at Max and leaned back into his seat. "How's business? He questioned coldly.

Max reached for the drinks as the waitress came back over and tossed her some money. He smiled. "Keep the change." Then he scooted the drinks in front of us. "It's been great. Been keeping really busy." He took a sip of his drink and then licked his lips, cockily. "Yours? Last thing I knew things weren't the greatest."

Jace shrugged his shoulders and glanced over at me. "It's good. We've been busy. Avery here has had her hands full."

I could feel the tension between the two men and I didn't like it one bit. They obviously had some past issues. I nervously grabbed my drink and slammed back the whole thing. I needed a buzz and fast.

Max looked over and grinned. He looked surprised as he watched me set my empty glass back down. "Hard day?" he questioned. "Let me grab you another one."

I looked at both Jace and Max as I ran my hand over my wet lips. They both looked on edge. "Yes and thanks."

Max smiled at Jace and lifted an eyebrow, and then he stood up and walked away.

Jace eagerly reached for his drink and slammed it, as he watched Max walk away. Then he pointed at his empty glass.

"Looks like I need one as well." He pushed his chair away, got up, and walked away leaving me alone.

I sat there anxiously until they both arrived, drinks in hand. They each pushed a glass in front of me and then Jace quickly sat down next to me. He leaned in and stared me in the eye with a forced smile. "Since you're drinking so fast," he muttered.

I looked between the both of them and grabbed my drinks, pulling them right in front of me. Both of the men were expressionless as I watched them. "Thanks, guys." I leaned in and took a sip from one of the glasses. I wasn't for sure, but I was almost positive that it was the one from Jace because Max's lip seemed to twitch as he sipped his own drink. I was too nervous at that point to take notice of which glass I grabbed.

Max looked at me and grinned as a new song started playing over the speaker. He shook his head in approval and reached for my arm. "Come dance with me." He stood up and pulled me with him. I hesitated at first but then let the buzz do the talking. It was only a dance, after all.

"Sure."

Jace eyed us suspiciously, while taking long sips of his mixed drink. His eyes never left us as Max pulled me out onto the crowded dance floor.

Max grabbed my hips, pulling me close to him, but I refused to get too close. I was buzzing, but that didn't mean that I was going let my guard down. He forced out a laugh and looked down at my breast. "How long have you and Jace been messing around?" he questioned.

I glanced over Max's shoulder and caught a glimpse of Jace as he calmly sipped on his drink. "We're not messing around. He's just helping me out." I set my gaze on the ground and cleared my throat. "We're only roommates."

Max dipped me backwards and placed his lips to my ear. "If you're not Jace's then maybe you can be mine," he whispered.

I pushed my way out of Max's grip and pulled my skirt down as I felt it start to ride up my leg. "You don't even know me. Why-?"

Max bit his bottom lip and pulled me closer to him. "You're sexy as hell. Who wouldn't want you?" he questioned, as his eyes roamed my body. "You would have to be crazy-"

"Stop there." I cut in. His words were making me uncomfortable and his firm grip on me wasn't helping. I felt dizzy and suddenly felt sick to my stomach. "The dance is over."

I looked up to see Jace approach us of what seemed to be out of nowhere. He pulled me out of Max's arms and placed his hands on my face, while looking me in the eye. "Are you okay? You don't look so good."

No, not really. The room spun, causing me to hold onto Jace's shirt to keep from falling. I felt the puke slowly rise in my throat so I let go of Jace and ran to the bathroom as fast as I could, almost tripping into an empty chair.

That's not embarrassing...

Once inside the single bathroom, I locked the door behind me and hovered over the shiny white toilet. I grabbed my hair, pulling it out of the way, as the vomit shot out and into the round bowl. There was no stopping it. I placed my hand on the side of the toilet and gripped it as I got down to just a dry heave. The pain shot through my stomach as my body quaked uncontrollably.

After gaining control of my body, I crawled over to the wall and leaned against it, with my hands locked in my hair. There was no way that I would show my face after that.

My head jolted to the right as someone softly knocked on the door, the sound making me want to hide even more. No matter where I went I could never seem to get away from everyone.

"Avery, is everything okay in there?" It was Jace, his muffled voice carried through the door, causing me to feel sick to my stomach again. "Answer me," he demanded.

I pushed myself to my feet and glowered at myself in the mirror. Mascara streaked my face and my lips still had traces of puke on them. I reached out and grabbed for a paper towel. I squirted a little hand soap on it and then soaked it in water. I let out a breath of frustration and then wiped down my hair and face, before rinsing out my mouth.

I froze when I heard another knock. Go away. The knocking stopped, but then just as quickly as it stopped it started again.

Frustrated, I threw the towel into the trash and leaned against the sink. "Jace, please go away," I breathed. "I'm not coming out."

WAKE UP CALL
VICTORIA ASHLEY

I looked over at the door as the handle jiggled. *Nice try, but you're not getting in this time.*

"Avery." Jace slapped the door before finally giving up on the handle. "Just let me in," he complained. "I want to help you."

I bit my bottom lip and crept over to the door. I placed my hand on it and shook my head. "I will stay in here all night until I know that you're gone, so you might as well just go."

I was surprised when a new voice joined in. "Is this girl ever coming out? I really have to pee." A female questioned.

"I'm sorry," Jace responded. "I'm really trying to get her out." He knocked on the door again but, this time with more force. "Avery, please."

I slammed my fist against the door and then pressed my back into it. I don't think so. It's kind of comfy in here. "No."

"Look, my name is Kat." The stranger spoke through the door. "Please let me in. It can't be that bad." She knocked on the door when I didn't respond. "Please! I have to pee."

Deciding that I had to at some point open the door, I slowly cracked the door open to see a gorgeous young woman with red curly hair and a deep set of dimples. She smiled at me and nodded her head.

I noticed Jace out of the corner of my eye looking at us so I grabbed Kat's tiny arm and yanked her into the bathroom, shutting the door behind us.

Kat pulled her arm away and gripped it with her other hand. "Ouch! Take it easy," she whined. She stared at me with her baby blues as if she were trying to figure something out. Then she leaned into the wall and smoothed out her skinny black jeans. "Is everything okay," she questioned. She looked me up and down and smiled. "You look great, so what's the issue?"

I leaned into the sink and wiped an arm over my face. "I'm embarrassed if you must know." My voice shook. I looked into the mirror and wiped more mascara off my face. "It's complicated."

Kat smiled and walked over to the toilet. "I saw you out there. Those men are gorgeous. I can see why things are complicated." She pointed at the toilet and tilted her head. "Do you mind," she questioned. "I really have to pee."

I nodded my head in response and turned my head the other direction. I wasn't use to sharing bathrooms with strangers, but at the moment it didn't matter. I had too much going on to even think.

After Kat finished using the toilet, she walked over and washed her hands. Then she smiled and nodded at the door. "Can we get out of here already?" She grinned and gave me a light shove toward the door. "Come on, gorgeous. The night is still early."

I reached for the door handle and then stopped to pull myself together. I looked over Kat's slim body, curvy hips, and full breast. She was almost perfect. It caused an aching in my chest. "Are you here with anyone?"

She giggled and ran her hands through her red curls, playfully. I could just assume she heard that question often. "I was here with a friend, but he left in a hurry. He can be weird and pushy sometimes." She gave me a confident smile. "Why you ask?"

"No reason," I said, more trying to convince myself than her.

I nodded and opened the bathroom door, letting Kat walk out first. "That feeling sucks."

Jace stood against the wall with Max standing close by. He grinned and pushed himself away from the wall. "I see that you ladies found your way back out," he laughed. "It's a good thing because I was about to send in a search team."

His humor made me loosen up and laugh. He always had a way of making smile, even when I'd rather not. Although, I wouldn't be surprised if he had that effect on everyone. He was handsome, funny and caring. He definitely was something different from what I was used to.

Kat laughed while walking over to stand next to Jace, her body language flirty and sexual, as she stared up at his towering six-foot frame. "Aren't you just cute and funny!" She reached out her hand and grabbed for Jace's. "I'm Kat, and you are?"

Jace smiled, but didn't seem impressed as he shook her hand. "I'm Jace and this is my friend, Max." He pushed Max a little closer to Kat, as Max smirked, and then walked over to stand next to me. "Avery."

I quickly turned the other way in an attempt to get away. "Jace, not now," I demanded. "Leave me alone. I took a step toward the exit.

Jace softly grabbed my arm and pulled me to a stop. Then he turned me around to face him. "Stop running away all of the time. Let someone help you for once." He brushed my hair behind my ear and ran his thumb over my cheek. His touch was gentle and caring. "Please," he breathed.

I felt lost and speechless, just as I always seemed to feel around Jace. Therefore, I said the only thing I could think of. "Okay."

He placed his hand on my cheek and looked me in the eye. His expression was soft. His jaw clenched as he rubbed his thumb under my right eye, causing my heart to sink.

I jerked my face away in response and walked away, taking a seat. I suddenly felt dizzy. "I need to get out of here." I squeezed my eyes shut to stop the room from spinning around me. I didn't want another incident like the one I'd just had moments before.

"No problem." Max walked over and grabbed my hand. He pulled me to my feet and smiled. "I can help you with that," he smiled. "Let's go."

Jace calmly pulled Max's hand away from mine, placing my hand at my side. "No, man. We're all leaving," he said sternly.

Kat reached for Jace's arm and pushed her bottom lip out in a pout. "Wait a minute. I really don't want to be left here alone and I'm not ready to go home." she whined pathetically, while rubbing her finger over his smooth skin. *Who does she think she is touching him like that?*

Jace pulled his arm away and turned to look at Max. Suddenly, I could breathe again. "I don't think-"

"Come on, man." Max walked toward the door and grabbed the handle, holding it open. "You have a big house. Why don't we all just go there for a few drinks?" he suggested. "It can be like old times."

Jace sighed and motioned for me to walk in front of him. "Yeah, I guess." he groaned. "It has been a while since I've seen you, man."

I nervously twirled my finger in my hair and watched Kat and Max step out the door and into the night. I didn't know either one of them and the thought of entertaining them for the night made me feel uneasy.

Once outside, Kat froze and slapped her hand to her forehead. "Oh crap! I forgot that I don't have my car with me," she said, with a slight whine. "Jace, do you mind if I ride with you?" She smiled and picked at her long purple nails while waiting for a response.

Jace rolled his eyes and looked up from opening his car door. "Yeah... sure." He looked unsure and almost a little stressed. He ran his hand through his hair while looking at me. "Come on, Avery."

I felt my stomach knot up as I walked toward Jace's car. "I'll sit in the front." I said, placing my hand in front of Kat to stop her from getting in. Of course, she would automatically think that she would get to sit next to Jace. Not if I had a say in it. "If you don't mind."

Kat looked down at my legs, as I shivered from the cold and rolled her eyes. "Does it really-"

Suddenly, Max reached for my hand and stopped me from getting in the car. "You can give Kat a ride and Avery can ride with me. That way they both can sit in the front." He nodded at Jace and pushed Kat toward Jace's car. "Problem solved. We'll meet you guys there."

I peered over my shoulder as Jace leaned against his car with his arms folded across his chest. His jaw stayed clenched as he watched us walk to the car, his eyes glued to us the whole time. He didn't take his eyes off us until we were inside Max's tiny red Sports Car.

Max watched me as I adjusted my skirt and set my purse on my lap. His eyes were wide as he pulled his seatbelt on. "This way we all win." Max smiled as he leaned over and grabbed for my seatbelt. "Jace and I go way back."

I pushed Max's hand away and pulled my seatbelt over my shoulder. "Thanks, but I can handle it." I smiled weakly at him before looking out the window. There was something about both Max and Kat that made me nervous.

I watched anxiously as Jace jumped into his car and started it, turning on the headlights. He didn't hesitate long before stepping on the gas and pulling out of his tight parking spot.

Max waited a few minutes before pulling out and following behind Jace. He looked over at me and smiled as I played with the buckle of my purse. His smile, even I had to admit was gorgeous. "So, Avery," he started, "how did you meet Jace."

WAKE UP CALL
VICTORIA ASHLEY

I cleared my throat and turned to face him. His dark hair fell around his face as he stared out the windshield with a smirk. "Um... I met him at the diner."

Max peeled his eyes away from the road to look me over. "That lucky, bastard," he muttered.

I looked down toward his muscular arms as he gripped the steering wheel and pulled into Jace's driveway. His arms were significantly bigger than Jace's and you could tell that he dedicated hours of time into working out. I could understand why he was so cocky. "I guess," I whispered.

Just as Max was pulling the keys out of the ignition, Jace jumped out of his car, walked over to my door, and opened it. "Give me your hand." His face was expressionless, once again.

I placed my hand in Jace's as he helped me out of the car without even giving Max a second thought. "Thanks."

Jace glared over at Max as he walked over and unlocked the door. He held the door open and Kat was the first to walk inside.

Kat walked in with wide eyes and started looking around. "Wow! Nice place. I can really see myself spending time here," she said sweetly.

Jace looked at all of us awkwardly before walking away toward the kitchen. "Thanks... I guess."

I followed Jace into the kitchen with Kat and Max following close behind. He didn't look up from the counter as he set out some bottles of booze. "Have fun, guys. I'll be watching TV." He ran his hands through his messy hair and walked away with heavy steps.

"Come on, man." Max called after him. "The night is young. We have catching up to do."

My stomach rumbled at just the thought of booze. I slipped out of the kitchen unnoticed and into the living room, taking a seat on the loveseat.

Jace looked over at me from the couch and then turned away again. He crossed his arms over his chest and then leaned into the couch. "Did you have a nice ride home?" he questioned stiffly.

I shifted in my seat just remembering the awkwardness. "It was okay. He didn't have much to say." I bit my lip and leaned into the arm of the loveseat. "You?" I questioned, eyebrows lifted. I found myself seriously curious.

Jace mindlessly ran his tongue over his lip ring and played with it "She was on my nuts the whole time," he said uncomfortably. "She-"

He stopped as Max and Kat walked in with drinks in hand. Kat smiled playfully and plopped down next to Jace as Max sat next to me on the small loveseat.

Jace sat back and blew out a breath of frustration. "So this is fun."

Kat placed her drink in between her legs and looked over toward Max and I. "You guys look hot together. Are you guys dating?" She winked. "Or maybe just messing around?"

What kind of question is that?

Max grinned and took a long sip of his drink. "I agree. We would be hot together. Right, Jace? I wouldn't mind-"

"No. They're not. They just met tonight." Jace cut in. "Max is an old buddy of mine. We've known each other since we were kids." His lip twitched as he intently watched Max's every move.

Max smirked while taking another sip of his drink, just brushing off the fact that Jace sounded annoyed with him. "Yeah we have, but I haven't seen you in how many years?" he questioned.

Jace looked uncomfortable as he looked Max in the eye. "Let me see...about four years now." He ran his hand through his hair and looked away. "It hasn't been long enough.

Kat leaned closer to Jace so that her arm brushed against his. "That's a shame, boys. We all should get together and hang out. I'm sure the four of us could have a fun time." She crossed her legs in a sexual manner as she looked down at Jace's crotch. "I bet you're a big boy, and great in bed."

"Oh, I am." Jace muttered, looking me in the eye. "To both."

You damn, slut. I cleared my throat being sure to get everyone's attention. "I think that I'm going to bed." I started to get up from the loveseat, but froze as Max gripped my inner thigh.

"Stay, beautiful," he smirked. The party is just beginning."

"Get your hands-"

Suddenly, I was knocked out of the way, as Jace wrapped his hand around Max's throat and slammed him against the back of the loveseat. He leaned in close to Max's ear and jerked him away from me. "Don't you ever put your fucking hands on her again."

I jumped out of the way. Jace might've been smaller than Max, but that obviously didn't seem to matter to him.

Max coughed and pushed Jace's hand away. "Are you serious?" he questioned. He pushed Jace away and stood up from the loveseat. "We've been friends since we were ten and you're going to do me like this? I knew that you were still fucked up. You haven't changed." He flexed his muscles before rubbing his neck. "That's fucked up, bro."

Jace looked shocked by Max's words. He shook his head, brushing off Max's words and then pointed at the door. "I think it's best that you both leave." He walked over to the wall and slammed his fist into it, causing a picture to fall off the wall. It shattered into little pieces as it landed on the corner of entertainment center and then down onto the floor.

Kat jumped up from the couch and grabbed for Max's arm. She looked at Jace and then over to me. "Are you guy's dating or something?"

The room stayed silent.

"If not then you sure do act as if you're in love." She pulled Max to the front door as Max kept his eyes on Jace. "So much for having fun."

With that, they were gone, slamming the door behind them.

My heart pounded violently as Jace stared at me with concerned eyes. He studied me looking confused.

Not knowing what to do, I ran over to the broken picture and attempted to pick up the glass. I jumped back as a piece of glass pierced through my thumb, causing blood to ooze out. "Shit!"

Jace was by my side in an instant. He grabbed my thumb and looked it over. "Shit, Avery," he whispered. "Are you okay?" He pulled my finger to his mouth and lightly kissed it. My whole body shivered at the feel of his soft lips and the warmth of his sweet breath. "I'm sorry you had to see that."

I swallowed hard as Jace pulled me by the arm so that my chest pressed against his. "It's... okay." I managed to get out. "I... um-"

Jace placed his hand on my cheek and gently rubbed his thumb over my lip. My eyes closed involuntarily "You're so fucking beautiful," he breathed. "I don't ever want anyone to hurt you again."

We both sat there in silence, the only sound, being the pounding of my heart. It went wild in my chest making it hard to breathe. A feeling that I only got around Jace. "Jace. Don't say-"

I was cut off as he crushed his lips to mine. His hands shook uncontrollably as he gripped my face, running his fingers over our lips. His lips were soft and sweet, making me want to fall into him and let go of everything. The past. The future. Nothing seemed to matter. Just us.

We stayed like that for a while before we were forced to pull away, us both gasping for air. He gently tugged back on my hair so that I could look him in the eye. *Those eyes.* The prettiest eyes I have ever seen. They were beautiful and caring. So full of everything that I didn't deserve.

Please, stop looking at me that way. I'm no good for you.

I quickly looked down at the ground, pulling my eyes away from Jace's gaze. That was when I noticed the picture. It was of Jace with some woman. They were at some beach running through the water. The girl had short brown hair and big beautiful eyes. She was gorgeous and they looked so happy playing together.

Jace pulled away, nose flared as he noticed me looking at the picture. He turned his head, letting go of my face. "You should go and get a bandage on that cut." He swallowed hard, while gripping the picture frame. "I will clean this up."

I grabbed my cut hand and slowly stood to my feet. "Who is-?"

"Go and clean up, please." he cut in. His body language was tense as he looked away.

I turned my head away in frustration and shook my head. "Yup. I guess I should take care of this." I was somehow mad at him for not opening up to me despite the fact that I refused to do the same for him. It wasn't fair of me to be angry, but I was.

I walked into the bathroom and cleaned my finger off before wrapping it in a bandage. Again, I managed to upset Jace. Not to mention the fact that it was my fault that him and Max were fighting.

Once inside my bedroom, I shut the door behind me and leaned against the wall. My breathing quickened as I ran my fingers over my lips and closed my eyes. Jace's kiss still lingered on my lips, and the sweet taste of him had me on a high. My mind spun as I dropped to my knees and placed my head in my hands. What is wrong with me? Why do I want to scream?

Suddenly, my bedroom door swung open to Jace standing there breathless. His bare chest was hot and wet from the sweat that covered his body and dripped down to the top of his low hanging jeans. I wanted nothing more than to reach out and touch him. To feel the firmness of his bare skin under my fingertips.

"Jace," I breathed.

His eyes pierced through mine as he took a step toward me, causing my back to press up against the wall. He ran his tongue over his bottom lip and grabbed the back of my neck, wrapping his fingers in my hair. A gasp escaped my parted lips as he yanked my neck to the side, running his fingers over my skin, and grabbed my hip. "Do you want me?" he questioned, breathless.

I stared at him in disbelief. I didn't know what to say and I was at a loss for words. "I don't...what?" I questioned, feeling lost.

He stared me in the eye, walked me backwards, and softly pushed me onto the edge of my bed. He slowly laid down on top of me, spreading my legs, as he rubbed his hand up my right arm.

The feel of him sent a shiver up my spine and caused my legs to shake as he placed his body between my open legs. His jaw clenched as he leaned in, placing his lips back to mine.

His body pressed into me even more, causing us both to moan into each other's mouths. Then with shaky hands, he reached under my skirt and gripped my thong in his hand. "I want you so bad," he whispered.

I felt a surge of panic kick in, and without a second thought, I pushed Jace away. *What does he want from me?* The thought of having sex with Jace scared me, as I had never been scared before.

Jace looked down at me breathless and dripping with sweat. "Did I do something? I'm sorry." He instantly removed his hands from my body and gave me a concerned look. "I would never do anything to hurt you or make you feel uncomfortable."

I turned my head away and suddenly my eyes filled with tears. I had been holding so much back and keeping so much from Jace that I could barely even breathe. "I just can't do this," I cried. "I'm sorry, Jace."

He backed away from me and walked over to the wall. He placed his right arm against it and took a deep breath. "Don't be sorry," he whispered into his arm. "You don't have to do anything that you don't want to do."

I slowly sat up and took a deep breath, looking down at my exposed panties. I pulled my skirt back down and then threw my hands over my face. My body jerked violently as the tears spilled out.

Suddenly, I felt Jace's hands around my face as he pulled me into his chest and kissed the top of my head. He had a way with his hands and he always seemed to cup my face in them. It made me feel safe. "Please don't cry," he whispered. "I didn't mean to upset you." He rubbed his thumb over my moist cheek and looked me in the eye. "I don't want you to be scared around me."

I shook his hand away from my face and turned the other way. I hated the thought of Jace seeing me so vulnerable. I had been trying for so long to be strong. "I'm not," I swallowed. "It's not that I'm afraid of you or to be around you. It's that I'm afraid of getting hurt." I instantly blushed at revealing my feelings toward him. Ones that I wasn't even so sure of yet or what they even meant.

Jace grabbed me by the shoulders and looked me in the eye. Then he pursed his lips and gripped a handful of his hair in his hand. "I'm not going to hurt you. I wouldn't," he paused and bit his bottom lip. "I would never hurt you. I promise."

Unable to stay away from Jace any longer, I leaned into him and gripped the back of his neck. I pulled him against me and rested my head on his shoulder. The comfort of his strong arms made me feel safe. "Thank you," I whispered.

Jace smiled and then pulled me down so that we were both lying down on the bed. Then he reached out and pulled the blanket around us. "I'm staying in here with you," he whispered. Then he grabbed my cut hand and held it to his mouth. "Does it hurt?" His warm breath tickled my hand.

My eyes wandered down to my hand and I shook my head. "No," I began. "It doesn't hurt. Not now at least."

Jace smiled sweetly before he pulled my head down to his chest and sighed. "Can I ask you something without you getting upset?" he questioned, hesitantly.

I felt my heart drop to my stomach. I couldn't say no to Jace after all that he had done for me. I owed him some answers. I took a deep breath and pushed my face further into his chest. "Sure," I whispered.

The room was silent for a minute and I could tell that Jace was trying to figure out the best way to ask me. Perhaps he was afraid of me having some kind of meltdown that he wouldn't be able to handle. He shifted a little to the left before he bent down and kissed the top of my head. "Do you ever miss your parents? I mean... have you ever thought about going home?"

My body stiffened in his arms and my heartbeat skyrocketed. "No," I blurted. "I mean no." I paused and gazed up at the ceiling. "My parents hurt me in ways that you will probably never understand."

Jace clenched his jaw and his whole body stiffened. "I understand it more than you think," he said stiffly. "You saw my sister. Her life wasn't always like that." He paused and ran his hands through his messy hair. Then he let out a deep breath and chewed on his lip ring. "The way that my father was..." He swallowed. "That led my sister and me both to make some bad decisions, ones that we can never take back. I can never bring..." He stopped and pressed his hand to his forehead. I could almost see tears glisten in his eyes.

I slowly sat up and looked into his hurt eyes. His eyes were so full of pain and grief that I somehow managed to forget about my own problems for once. I felt so hurt. Not for myself, but for him.

I pulled myself closer to Jace and wrapped my arms around his body. I just wanted to feel him next to me. It gave me a kind of rush that I had never felt before.

Jace pulled me closer to him so that his lips were against my neck, and we both laid there in a comfortable silence.

Chapter 10

I awoke the next morning wrapped tightly in Jace's strong arms. The feel of his skin against mine made me shiver as I rolled over and out of his grip. Again, I somehow managed to sleep through the whole night without a nightmare or even a thought of my parents. It almost seemed as if Jace kept the nightmares away. As crazy as that seemed, I almost believed it to be true.

A small smile crossed my face as I reached over and shook Jace's shoulder. He looked so sexy lying there sleeping and I almost didn't even want to wake him up, but I knew that I didn't have a choice. "Good morning," I whispered.

Jace slowly opened his eyes and stretched, a smile lit up his rugged features. Then he ran his hands over his chest and adjusted his pants. The bulge in his thin pants made me blush unwantedly, as I turned my eyes away. "What time is it?" He yawned.

I glanced over at my phone, which had three missed calls from Caleb. I picked it up and cleared the screen off, not bothering to care what he wanted. It was best for him if I was out of his life anyhow. I did nothing but bring him down. "It's 10:30 a.m."

Jace swiftly jumped up and crawled out of the bed, a worried look on his face. "Oh shit." He ran his hands over his face and yawned again. "We need to get ready for work and fast. The rush starts in thirty minutes." A smile crossed his handsome face before he leaned down and placed a short kiss on my lips, his breathing soft and even as he cupped my face. "I'll skip a shower so that you can take one. Meet me out front in twenty minutes."

I shook my head still in shock from the kiss. I hadn't expected there to be more kissing involved and I had to admit that it shook me up. I bit my lip and scrambled across my room. "I'll be fast. I promise."

Twenty minutes later, we were both ready and out the door. We hopped into his little black car and arrived at the diner with one minute to spare.

The parking lot seemed very empty for the diner to be busy, but Jace still seemed to rush over to the door, holding it open for us to walk in.

We entered the diner to see Winston and Stacy casually leaning against the counter having conversation. Clearly, we'd beat the rush.

Stacy grinned, flashing us her dimples as she ran over and threw her arms around me. She quickly pulled away and fixed her hair. "Guess who's coming to see me today?" She bit her bottom lip and waited for an answer. She looked so sweet and innocent.

Jace and I both looked at each other and then back at Stacy confused. I suppose that it could've been the guy that she was dating, but I forgot his name, so decided to stay quiet.

Stacy laughed and rolled her eyes. "William," she sang, grabbing her apron and tugging on it. "I saw him last night at a party and he said that you hadn't called him so I asked for his number."

Jace rolled his eyes and headed toward the kitchen. "I think that I'll leave you girls alone." He laughed. "Just be ready for the rush." He looked somewhat relieved as he pushed the kitchen door open and disappeared.

I threw my stuff on the waitress station and reached for my apron as it fell on the ground. "What happened to that...?" I froze when I noticed the letter lying on the ground right next to my apron. I had completely forgotten about the letter until then. The sight of it made me slightly uneasy.

Stacy gripped my shoulder and arched a perfectly groomed eyebrow. "Is everything okay?" she questioned. Her eyes anxiously watched mine as I pretended to not be bothered by the letter.

Despite my efforts, my hand slightly shook as I grabbed for the letter and shoved it into the pocket of my apron. Then I quickly struggled with putting my apron on. My nerves were overworking, again. "I'm fine," I stammered. "It's nothing."

Stacy tilted her head and pointed down at the little black apron. "Are you sure? What was on that piece of paper? Was that a letter?" She crossed her skinny arms over her chest and waited for an answer. "So?"

Frustrated, I reached into the apron and gripped the letter in my hand. "It's just something that some crazy lady left for me a few days ago. I'm sure that it's nothing important," I explained.

Stacy looked over as the door opened and a little stubby man walked in. His gray hair was long and messy as it covered his rosy cheeks. The man looked up with warm eyes and waved at Stacy. She waved back and shook her head. "I'll be right back. Don't think that I will forget about the letter," she grunted, and walked away.

I watched Stacy as she greeted the old man and jotted down his order. The letter was now moist as I gripped it with sweaty hands and ran my fingers over the smooth paper. I wasn't sure why, but I had a bad feeling about the letter. There was something so familiar about the woman and the way she'd spoken to me.

I jumped out of thought as Stacy snapped her fingers in front of my face. "Well...?"

I sighed and pulled the letter from out of my apron. I stared down at it, causing my vision to blur. My head spun as I struggled to open the paper. "Fine! I'll read it, but I'm tossing it afterwards. Like I said, I'm sure that it means nothing." I slowly opened the letter and fought for breath as I read the words repeatedly.

"Dammit, Avery," Stacy growled. "What does it say?" She gripped my shoulder and shook me. "You can tell me anything."

I took the letter and crumbled it in my hands. I stared Stacy in the eye before I tossed it into the trash and walked away. I tried to look as calm as possible, but it was the impossible. I wanted to scream. "It's not important," I snapped, as she continued to follow me.

WAKE UP CALL
VICTORIA ASHLEY

Stacy grabbed my arm as I attempted to walk away. "Is that lady harassing you," she questioned. "We can report her."

I shook her arm off and looked up to see Jace staring over at us. He leaned against the doorframe and studied my face, obviously wanting to know what all the commotion was about. "Is everything okay, Avery?" He lifted an eyebrow.

I looked between the both of them before I took off and ran into the bathroom. I felt as if my whole world was crashing down around me and it was hard to breathe.

I fell down to the floor of the bathroom and reached up with shaky hands to lock the door behind me. "Oh shit! Oh shit!" I gripped onto my messy hair and leaned into the door.

"Avery," Jace said into the door. "Please let me help you. You can talk to me."

I tightly closed my eyes and took a deep breath. It was then that I realized that I wanted Jace's help. I needed his comfort. I almost craved it. I reached up and unlocked the door. Then I stood up and walked over to the sink, leaning against it.

A few seconds later, the door opened and Jace walked in with a worried look on his face. He walked over and placed both of his hands on my shoulders. Then he looked me in the eye and sighed. "Tell me what's wrong."

I looked into his green eyes and suddenly felt safe. As if he could make everything go away, but I knew that wasn't possible.

I quickly looked away and prepared to tell him the story. "Remember that creepy lady from a few days ago?

Jace just nodded in understanding.

"She left me a letter the other day," I whispered. "I knew that I knew her from somewhere. I just knew it." I slammed my fist into the sink at the memories.

Jace's arms stiffened as he gripped onto my chin and forced me to look into his eyes. "Tell me," he demanded. "Who is she?"

I closed my eyes and let out a soft cry. "She's my aunt," I cried. "My father's sister."

Jace pulled me against his chest as my body trembled in fear. He ran his hands over the back of my head and pressed his lips against my hair. It made me want to cry even more. "I won't let them hurt you again," Jace said stiffly. "I promise," he whispered, his lips pressed into my hair.

~ 130 ~

I felt my heart stop at his words. I looked up into Jace's eyes as he reached down and wiped the tears off my cheeks. I wanted to believe it. I really did. "I wish I could believe that," I whispered.

Jace just sighed and held me closer.

~•~

"Oh... is that right?" The sloppy woman crushed her face against mine while pressing her sharp fingernail into my forehead. She suddenly pressed with so much force that it caused my neck to bend into my father's shoulder. "You little bitch," she spat. "You owe me some damn money. That shit is not cheap."

I stiffened up and flared my nostrils as my father tightly gripped my hair and yanked me into the side of the bed. I attempted to reach out for the bedpost, but missed and ended up landing on the floor with my face pressed into the frame of the bed. I let out a soft cry as the pain shot through my body and caused my body to quake with fear. "Aunt Pam," I stammered. "I'm sorry."

Aunt Pam gripped a handful of her stringy hair and shook her head back and forth. Then she bent down on one knee and looked me in the eye. Her eyes seemed distant and lifeless. "I don't give a shit." She turned away to face my hopped-up father. "Henry, I told you that you should've aborted that little bitch in the first place."

Then next thing I knew her rough hand connected with the right side of my swollen face. "I will get you back someday. You will pay for this shit one way or another.

"Avery."

I shook my head, in a daze, and looked up to see Stacy standing just inches from my face. She delicately brushed her blond curls from out of her worried eyes and then reached out to grab my arm.

Not wanting to be touched, I shook her arm off and ran my hands over my face. I was too shook up to handle being touched. "I'm sorry," I whispered.

Stacy pursed her pink lips and placed her hands in the front of her apron. She stared at me for a few moments before she pulled her hands out of her apron and held out the crumpled up letter. She looked down at it with a pained look on her face. "I'm sorry, but I needed to know what this letter said. You're my friend and I care about you."

My heart raced and I wanted to vomit.

She smiled weakly and placed the letter into my open palm. "What does that mean," she questioned. "The letter said *'they know where you are and you will always belong to them. Love Aunt Pam.'* please tell me. Are you in some kind of trouble?" she questioned, with frightened eyes. "I'm here for you."

My eyes wandered down to the letter and my heart dropped down to my feet. At least that was what it felt like.

"I can't...," I mumbled. Then I ripped the letter up and shoved it back into the trash. I pushed it down to the bottom of the can and made sure that it was lost in the mess forever. "It's complicated and probably not worth your time. Just forget about it," I demanded.

"But-"

"I mean it." I cut in, looking up to see Winston poking his head out from the kitchen. His white hair covered most of his face as he attempted to hide. He thought he was slick. "I'm fine and we have work to do." I put on a fake smile and nodded my head. "We have a lot to do today. It's almost rush hour and Jace is depending on us."

Stacy gripped my wrist and pulled me over to the corner by the waitress station. Then she grabbed my chin with her other hand and forced me to look her in the eye. "Listen here. You can resist all you want, but I won't give up so easily." She paused and tilted her head to the right. "I care about you. Jace cares about you. You will tell me what is wrong," she demanded.

I forced my gaze away from Stacy's intense stare and looked down at my feet. I had never in my life had someone be so damn persistent and I wasn't sure how to handle it.

Suddenly, my heart started aching. It felt as if it was being crushed. I didn't know what to do, so I freaked out. "You want to know what's wrong?" I shouted. "I'm a worthless piece of crap that came from a worthless family. Don't waste your time on me. You're too good." I paused to choke back the tears. "Jace is too good"

Stacy's eyes went wide as she reached out and attempted to wipe the tears from off my face. It almost looked as if she were about to cry. "Avery-"

"No! Don't," I breathed. "Don't worry about me. I've always known that this is all that I'll ever be. Just a nobody." I slammed my fist onto the counter and then reached over, grabbing my purse off the waitress station, palms sweaty. "I'm out of-"

"Avery."

My heart stopped and suddenly it was hard to breathe. His voice always had that effect on me. It was like poison slowly running through my veins killing me bit by bit. Like a drug that I couldn't get enough of even though I was almost down to my last breath.

Jace took a step forward and grabbed my hand. He slowly trailed his fingers over my face and backed me into the wall. My heart stopped again if that was even possible. "You can't leave," he whispered. "I need you." His warm breath kissed my lips as he bit his bottom lip and placed both of his hands around my face. They were warm and soft to the touch. Too big for my fragile face, although I wanted to bury myself in them. "Breathe. There is no one here but the two of us. Breathe," he whispered.

I slowly took a deep breath and squeezed my eyes shut. I just wanted to disappear. I shook my head back and forth and fought back the tears. I hated looking weak. "I have to go," I said breathless. "I need to get away from here. You have to understand."

Jace pushed me harder into the wall so that I couldn't move at all. He took a deep breath and ran his thumb over my lip. "I can't let you leave," he stammered. "Not now that I have you closer to me than I ever thought to be possible. I want to take care of you." He pulled his hand away from my face and squeezed his hand into a ball. He looked as if he wanted to punch something, but he didn't.

Instead, he released his grip on me and leaned into the counter. He looked up at Winston and Stacy and shook his head. "I'm sorry, guys. This shouldn't be happening here. This is personal stuff. I apologize."

Winston gave Jace a nod and stepped back into the kitchen without a word. He knew better than to get involved. Things were complicated.

Stacy just looked back and forth between the both of us confused. "I don't know what..." She trailed off when the door to the diner opened and William stepped inside with a huge grin on his face. She looked into my eyes and shook her head, in shame. "Oh... Williams here. Great timing," she murmured.

William quickly walked over and reached for Stacy's hand. "Hey, guys," he said, nodding his head at the three of us. "Nice to see you, Avery." He blushed slightly as he looked around the diner, noticing that something was off.

I looked over at Jace to see him turn his head away and run his hands through his hair in frustration. Then I looked over at William and nodded my head. "Hi, William," I said softly, not wanting him to know what was going on.

Stacy looked at William and frowned before she gripped his hand tighter and nudged him in the side. "Let's leave these two alone," she said stiffly.

I waited for them to sit down in an empty booth close to the back of the diner, before I pulled the strap of my purse back up my shoulder, staring at the back of Jace's head. I felt helpless and I had to do the only thing that I knew how to do. "I hope that you understand why I must leave. It has nothing to do with you." My voice shook as I said my last words. "I will be gone by the time you get home."

I saw Jace's shoulder stiffen at my words. He stood there motionless, holding his breath with his hands tightly gripping the counter as I walked away and out of the diner.

Once outside I paused and looked back at the door. Some part of me hoped that Jace would come rushing out asking me to stay. The bigger part of me knew that I had to leave before I could drag Jace down with me. My parents knew where I was and it would only be a matter of time before they came into the diner searching for me. I couldn't be there when that happened. A small part of me was afraid of being sucked back into their lives. Leaving was the only thing that could save me and keep Jace away from their demented ways. I didn't want them to hurt Jace in any way. I wouldn't allow it.

I hesitantly pulled my phone from out of my purse and stared down at the black screen. Then with my hands shaking, I hit the power button and scrolled down to his name. The only one that would be willing to come to my rescue now. Caleb.

WAKE UP CALL
VICTORIA ASHLEY

He answered the phone after two short rings and I could tell by his desperate tone that he would say yes to anything that I asked. "Caleb," I stammered.

The phone was silent for a moment before he answered. "Yes, Avery."

I took a deep breath and glanced back over at the door of the diner. It was clear that no one was coming to stop me. I couldn't wait any longer. My parents could already be on the way for all I knew. "Can I stay with you for a while?" I asked, struggling to keep my voice strong and steady.

I heard Caleb breathe into the phone before answering. "Yes. I'll come get you now." He sounded relieved. "I'm so happy that you called."

I sat down on the curb and nervously tapped my foot on the gravel. "I'm at the diner. I'll be outside waiting." With that, I pulled the phone away, hung up, and shoved it inside of my purse.

Two minutes later, Caleb pulled up and jumped out of the car. He had to of been just a few blocks away when I'd called. *Lucky me.*

His blond hair looked freshly cut and his amber eyes were full of a certain glow that I hadn't seen in him in a while. It was then that I took notice of just how beautiful he really was. I had so much going on before that I didn't even let myself notice. I was determined to block everyone out of my life, making me blind to everything around me. Jace changed that for me. I was blind to that as well. "Are you alright?" he questioned, while reaching for my hand.

I shook my head and let him help me to my feet. I didn't even push his hand away as he held onto my arm for support. He walked me over to his car and I looked up and smiled at him before I got into the car. "I'm fine. Thank you."

Caleb grinned and shut the door before he walked over to his side of the car and jumped in. He looked at me with wonder in his eyes before he smiled and leaned back into his seat. "It's so good to see you. I've missed you." He looked past me and his smile slightly faded as he shifted the car into drive.

"What?" I questioned, as I studied his face. I got ready to look out the window, but Caleb quickly reached out and grabbed my face to stop me.

He looked me in the eye and smiled. "You just look so beautiful. That's all," he whispered. Then he looked past me again and slammed his foot on the gas. "Let's hurry up so that we can grab some of your things."

I felt my heart stop beating at just the thought of going back to Jace's house. I couldn't stand to be around anything that had to do with Jace at the moment. It just hurt too much and I was so close to giving in to my heart and running back inside to be close to him. I couldn't do that. I wouldn't let myself hurt him anymore.

"Not right now." I blurted out. I took a deep breath and leaned into the seat. "We can do that a different day."

Caleb nodded his head in agreement and gripped onto the steering wheel. "Sure. Maybe tomorrow while that guy is still at work. I'm sure he isn't too happy that you're leaving."

"Sure," I whispered. "I'm not so sure if he truly cares." It was the truth. It wasn't as if he attempted to stop me. Maybe Caleb was the only one that would ever care. That still didn't make me want him. Not the way that I wanted Jace.

I'm doing the right thing. Jace will be safe now...

Chapter 11

I took a deep breath and looked out the window as we turned into a driveway surrounded by a forest of trees. The driveway seemed to go on for at least a mile before we pulled up next to a large white house with tremendous glass windows.

The green lawn was perfectly kept with white stones that led right up to a huge square fountain that was lit up with bright blue lights. The sight was actually quite breathtaking and like nothing that I had ever seen before. Caleb must've had a lot of money. Something that I hadn't been aware of. I guess I should've known from his nice BMW.

Caleb peered over his right shoulder and grinned as he pulled up next to a yellow Four Wheeler and placed his car into park. The look on his face was cocky and proud. I didn't like it. It was as if he'd thought he'd won. "What do you think?" he questioned, while pulling the keys out of the ignition, and throwing them down to lay on his lap.

I leaned back into my seat and stiffly pulled my purse closer to my side for comfort. Then I turned my head to look back out the window. "It's... nice," I mumbled, already starting to regret my decision of calling Caleb. It always ended that way. "I didn't realize that you had such a huge house."

Caleb blushed as he ran his fingers through his hair. Then he nodded his head toward the front door which was a beautiful shade of powder blue. "Let's get out of here so that you can make yourself at home," he beamed. "Come on."

Home. My stomach dropped at the thought of Caleb's house being a home to me. I didn't want that and I hated the idea of it.

I carefully stepped out of the car and closed the door behind me. My eyes wandered over to the huge house and my heart started pounding loudly in my chest. The more I looked at the place the more that I realized that I didn't belong there. Truthfully the only place that I ever felt like home was with Jace.

Caleb grabbed my arm snapping me out of my thoughts. "I'm sure that you're going to love it here," he breathed. "There is plenty of-"

"Caleb," I cut him off. "I'm only staying for a few days." I pulled my arm from out of his grip and brushed my arm off. I didn't want him getting any kind of crazy ideas. I was okay with going with him at first, but not now. Not after seeing the victory in his eyes.

Caleb's jaw clenched as he reached for the brass handle of the door and pushed it open. He silently motioned for me to enter the house before he followed me inside and shut the door behind us.

The smell of Jasmine surrounded me as I looked around the spotless house and placed my purse on the red oak table that sat next to the door. I pointed over to the white suede couch and nodded my head as Caleb walked over to the kitchen and opened the fridge. "I'll just sleep here tonight," I said softly, as I made my way over to take a seat on the cozy couch, and possibly my new bed for a while.

Caleb glanced over from the kitchen and shook his head. "Oh no. You are taking my room. I won't have you sleeping on that thing." He shut the fridge and held out a small tray full of fruit and yogurt. "Hungry?" he questioned. He leaned against the counter while waiting for my response.

I silently shook my head and let out a deep breath. I couldn't even think about eating at the moment. I could hardly even find the time to breathe.

"Okay then," he mumbled, his voice laced with aggravation. "Well tell me about this guy that you've been staying with. Did he do something to hurt you? Did he kick you out?" He paused to eat some fruit. "What made you decide to call me?" he questioned desperately.

Just the thought of being around Caleb was making me exhausted. I just didn't have the energy to keep up a conversation with Caleb and the last thing that I wanted to do was tell Caleb about Jace and my personal life. Jace never asked about Caleb so why did Caleb always have so many damn questions?

"I don't want to talk about it," I whispered, trying not to sound rude. "Also, I would rather sleep in a spare room."

Caleb's face hardened as he walked over and took a seat next to me on the spacious couch. He slammed the tray of fruit down on the table in front of us and leaned into the arm of the couch. "That's not surprising. You never talk to me about shit," he snapped. "How do you expect me to help you when you can't even tell me shit about your life?"

I stood up from the couch and stomped over to the door. I didn't have to take crap from Caleb. I just couldn't handle it. I grabbed for my purse and threw it over my right shoulder as I reached for the door handle. "I'm leaving. This was a bad idea."

Caleb jumped up from the couch and threw his arms up in defeat. "Look, I'm sorry. I'm just happy to have you here." He pointed down at the couch and smiled. "Please come back. I won't make you tell me anything that you don't want to." He nervously played with the tray of fruit as he watched me set my purse back down. "I promise."

I stared at the floor as I crossed my arms over my chest. I needed to get out of there as soon as possible. "I will stay here for a few days and then I plan on getting a cheap car and looking for a little apartment," I said, being sure that he understood. "Can we just get through this without any more fighting? I really can't handle this right now. I mean it. I have a lot on my mind."

Caleb quickly took a bite of a strawberry and shook his head. "I already said I would leave you alone," he grunted. "Can I ask you one question though?"

I rolled my eyes in aggravation and nodded my head. All that I wanted to do was run away and go to bed even though it was too early. I just needed to be alone. "I guess."

He ran his hands over his face and studied my every move. "Are you going to keep working at that diner?" he asked, his voice slightly angry.

The thought of leaving the diner killed me. I had no other choice though. My parents would do anything and everything in their power to ruin not only me, but Jace as well. I had to protect him. "No. I will figure something out," I whispered, pain in my voice.

A grin crossed Caleb's once hard face, before he pushed himself to his feet, and strolled across the room and over to a closed door that stood right at the beginning of the long hallway. He slowly trailed his hand over the wooden door before he pushed it open and pointed inside. "This is my room, but I want you to take it while you're here." He smiled as I stepped inside. "The spare bedrooms aren't quite set up for guest. I've been a very busy man."

I nodded my head in understanding and looked around the expensive home. "I've noticed," I mumbled. "I never knew that you had so much...money." I stepped into the master bedroom and took a quick glance around. It was quite spacious and filled with endless expensive crap. It had a king size bed, a large oak dresser with a mirror on top, a hot tub, a gamer area and a very large computer desk. The computer that sat on the desk looked brand new and barely out of the package. A hot tub. Who lives like this? "Wow!"

Caleb leaned against the doorframe and playfully bit his lip as he played with his nails. I could tell he was enjoying every moment and basking in it. "I try not to talk about the money. There are too many people out there that like to take advantage of people." He stopped playing with his nails to look up at me. "You're different. I don't think that I have to worry about that with you." A smile crossed his face as he looked me in the eye. "All of this is yours. Enjoy."

I turned my head away from his gaze. I didn't like the way that it made me feel. He didn't have to worry about anything with me because I wouldn't be around for long. I just needed a few days to get my money and things together and I would be gone. I didn't need anyone to take care of me. I didn't want that. Especially from Caleb.

"You're right," I said stiffly. "You don't have to worry about me. Can I get a little rest before I go looking for work?"

Caleb crossed his arms over his chest and turned his head away from my view. Then he reached for the door and looked up at me. "Whatever you want. That's how it's always worked," he muttered, as he backed out into the hall and shut the door behind him.

The tone of his voice and looking at his face just made me want to scream. He always had a way of making me feel as if I could explode. Maybe that's why I could never stand to be around him for more than a few hours at a time. He would never understand me and I didn't expect him to.

I threw myself down onto the king size bed and squeezed my eyes shut. I hated the feeling of being there with Caleb. I hated hurting Jace, but I only did it because it felt like the right thing to do at the moment. Jace had done nothing but good things for me. This was the only thing good that I could do to repay him. Leaving was the best thing that I could do for anyone. I knew that and had accepted that long ago.

~•~

Despite being exhausted, I couldn't manage to take a nap. My mind spun with unwanted thoughts and all I could manage to do was toss and turn the whole time. The constant sound of Caleb's light footsteps pacing up and down the hallway didn't do much to help that situation either. The more that I tried to sleep the more exhausted that I felt, and the more that I grew annoyed of Caleb. *Go sit down for crying out loud.*

Feeling defeated, I hopped out of bed and ran my hands over my face. I didn't really feel up to doing anything, but I knew that if I wanted to get out of Caleb's place that I would have to start my job hunting right away. I didn't have time to waste just sitting around and moping, although that was what I felt like doing.

After working at Jace's diner for a few weeks I now had enough experience waiting tables that it would probably be easy to just apply at a few local diners. To be honest, I think that I even somewhat enjoyed waiting tables.

I forced my feet to work as I stumbled over to my Converse shoes and threw them on. It had to of been around 5:30 p.m. by now and it would start to get dark at any time. The faster that I moved, the faster that I could escape Caleb.

I swiftly reached out for my purse and threw it over my right shoulder as I yanked the bedroom door open and stepped out into the dim hallway, in hopes that Caleb wouldn't attempt to stop me. Great!

Caleb suddenly stopped pacing and stood frozen in place. He looked as stiff as a statue. He glanced up at me and his eyes went wide. "Hey," he stammered. "Are you going somewhere?" His voice came out shaky, as he looked me up and down.

I took a few steps toward the front door and pushed my purse into my ribs. "Yeah. I'm just going job hunting. I'll be back before you go to bed," I said quickly. "I have to hurry before it gets too late."

Caleb jumped in front of me before I could reach for the door handle. His chest heaved up and down as he blew his breath out. "Let me take you. It will be quicker to just go in my car. I have a stop to make anyhow."

I turned my head away from his creepy gaze and shook my head. He was acting more clingy than usual and I really just wanted to get away. "No," I blurted, not realizing how rude that it sounded. "I mean... I want to walk. I need the fresh air." I rushed over to the door and pulled it open. "Bye, Caleb."

Caleb was silent, obviously at a loss for words, as I shut the door behind me and I took off in a sprint.

The cool breeze playfully brushed against my face, making me feel relieved to get away, as I strolled down the sidewalk in search of my first spot.

Finally, I was alone and could breathe for what seemed to be the first time in forever. My eyes scanned the beautiful night sky, while taking in the sweet smell of freedom.

A few miles down the road, I finally spotted my first diner. It was a small brick building with a sign out front that read 'Blu's Diner.' I took a deep breath suddenly feeling nervous as I stepped up to the door. The glass door had a listing of the hours and it looked as if they were about to close at six o'clock. I only had about ten minutes before closing time and the place looked fairly empty.

WAKE UP CALL
VICTORIA ASHLEY

I reached out for the handle and got ready to pull it open, when suddenly a young man stepped up to the door and flipped over a sign that read 'Closed.' Are you kidding me?

Desperate, I waved my arms at him and attempted to get his attention. "No! I need to apply for a job. I'm not here to eat," I shouted, hoping the young man would understand. I knew how it was when it was closing time and you were just ready to go home, but he had to understand. It was important.

The young man looked to be around my age, with short golden hair and big eyes. His gray eyes looked tired and annoyed as he glared through the window at me, shaking his head in annoyance. He stared at me for what felt like a lifetime before finally, throwing his arms up and reaching for the door handle.

He groaned, looking me in the face as he opened the door and stepped out of the way for me to walk in. "You're lucky I'm feeling nice tonight. He turned away. "I'll go grab my father."

I nodded my head and smiled at him thankful that he was giving me a few minutes of his time. "Thank you. I will be quick."

The kid pointed over at a stool and brushed his golden locks from out of his baby face. His face had almost an innocent look to it, but something told me that he wasn't quite as innocent as he looked. "Take a seat..."

"Avery," I said, as he searched for something to call me. "The name is, Avery."

"Sure, Avery, it is," he mumbled.

I quietly walked over to the red stool and took a seat. The whole diner looked a little worn down, but I guess that meant that it actually got some good use. It would probably be easy to make cash there and I really wanted the chance to find out. It definitely wasn't anything like Jace's diner, which made me sad, but it was hopefully far enough away to not get caught.

A few minutes later a middle-aged man with graying hair walked out and glanced in my direction. The look on his face said that he was just as tired as his son was and just wanted to get out of the diner and to get home.

He came at me with a steady pace and stopped at the stool in front of me. He huffed and looked me over. "I'm sorry, ma'am, but I don't think that I have what you're looking for." He paused to turn away. "Thank you for stopping in."

He got ready to walk away, but I wasn't willing to let him leave just like that and without even giving me a chance to speak. "You don't understand. I need this job and I will do whatever it takes to make sure that you understand that," I said firmly.

The man froze with his hand to his forehead. His face wrinkled up as he frowned and rubbed his eyes. "I wish that I could help you, but I really can't right now. I'm sorry." His voice sounded sincere, which surprised me.

My heart dropped when I realized that I didn't have a shot. He seemed certain that I wasn't needed and I didn't want to waste anymore of his time.

"Fine. I guess I will continue my search then." I jumped up from the stool, disappointed, and walked past him and his son as I reached for the door. "Thanks for your time."

"Wait," The owner called out. "I might have an opening in a week or two. I have a waitress that is planning on moving to Chicago soon. Come back then and we'll talk." He signed as looked over at his son. "We might be able to help you."

My mind spun just thinking about waiting a couple of weeks. I couldn't wait a couple of weeks to get out of Caleb's place. I needed to get out of there now. The wait seemed insane, although I was thankful for their help. I just smiled and pushed the door open. "Thank you. I'll come back in a couple of weeks."

I stepped out into the night and stood motionless on the side of the road. I felt lost and clueless. I really had no idea where I was and I didn't want to spend the whole night searching for the next diner.

At last second I turned back the way I came and decided to head back to Caleb's for the night. I would just have to spend the whole next day searching. I would do it the right way and call for a cab in the morning. Then I would go to Jace's house and grab my things. The sooner I got out of his life the better.

Wanting to check the time, I blindly reached inside my purse to grab my phone. It felt as if I had been gone for hours and it was really starting to get cold out.

When I finally got a grip on my phone, I flipped it open to see one missed call. My heart sped up as I read the name across the screen. The one name that was enough to almost bring me to my knees. Jace Montgomery.

I have to be strong...

WAKE UP CALL
VICTORIA ASHLEY

The walk back to Caleb's house was slightly long and cold, but I didn't mind. I was numb anyways. It was a feeling that I was used to and one that I had almost learned to welcome. The familiarity of it was all that I had known most of my life.

I promptly stepped up to the front of the house and instantly noticed the little purple Sebring that now sat in the driveway. It hadn't been there when I had left and Caleb probably wasn't expecting me to be back so soon.

I stood motionless in the driveway, the cool wind whipping through my tangled hair while trying to figure out if I wanted to go inside or turn back around. Truthfully, the comfort of bed was sounding quite appealing at the moment and my legs were starting to feel a little sore from the walk anyways.

Finally making the decision to stay, I made my way past the Sebring and up to the porch that was slightly lit up by the blue fountain lights that remained on.

I ran my hand over the smooth wood of the porch as I made my way to the door and reached for the handle. The handle was cool to the touch and sent a chill throughout my body. I shivered.

I could slightly make out Caleb's voice as I slowly pushed the door open and stepped into the house.

"Shit. Put that away, Kat," Caleb muttered under his breath, thinking that I he was talking quietly.

I gradually turned my head to my right to see Caleb shoving something in his pocket and waving his arm in front of him as if he was trying to get rid of something.

"Avery. I didn't know that you'd be back so soon." He pointed over to the girl that stayed seated on the couch; her face was looking down toward the black carpet. "This here is my... friend, Kat."

The girl's wave of red curls surrounded her as she briskly whipped her head up to look at me. I knew I recognized the name. Kat's baby blues went wide as she took in the sight of me. "Holy shit." She giggled.

Caleb looked between the both of us with a very confused look on his face. "Is there something that I should know about?" He looked worried.

I shook my head and pulled my hair from out of my face, before rubbing my hands together to get warm. "We've met before. That's all," I mumbled.

WAKE UP CALL
VICTORIA ASHLEY

Kat adjusted her short red dress while laughing under her breath. She looked just as stunning as the last time I'd seen her. It bothered me.

"Yeah. It was quite a night." She paused and looked between the both of us before reaching for her black clutch bag. "Thanks for... you know. I'll contact you soon." She grinned.

Caleb nodded his head and then turned around to face the kitchen. The look on his face was cold and unusual. "Bye, Kat," he said stiffly.

Caleb's eyes seemed to stay glued to Kats every move as she walked through the living room, hips switching back and forth, as she made her way out the door.

We both jumped as the door unexpectedly slammed shut behind her. She was definitely up to something and I didn't even want to begin to think what that something could've been.

The room was silent for a moment as I sought to take things in. I had never seen Caleb act so strange and jumpy before.

The desperate look on his face had my heart racing as he fiddled with his hands. He was definitely hiding something big and I wasn't sure if I wanted to stick around to find out. My first feeling was to grab my things and go, but then again I wasn't quite so innocent myself. "I'll be in bed if you need me," I muttered.

Caleb watched intently as I walked past him and through the hall to the bedroom.

Once inside I shut the door behind me and threw my purse down on the dresser, ready to get some rest.

I slowly spun around in the mirror watching my purple dress as it flowed around me and cuddled my every curve.

I had never owned anything so beautiful in my life and I worked so hard to get enough money to purchase the dress. I worked for three weeks straight in my neighbor's yard helping her pull weeds and plant all of her flower seeds.

I actually felt proud of myself for once and I only hoped that my parents would be proud of me as well.

After one last final spin, I took off down the hall and gripped the railing as I made my way downstairs and to my mother's room.

WAKE UP CALL
VICTORIA ASHLEY

My father would be gone for a few more hours and I really wanted to get the chance to share my happiness with mother. She always seemed less angry when he was around.

There was even a little part of me that believed she would be better if he wasn't around. Maybe even a good mother. The thought of that still gave me some bit of hope. It was all of the hope that I had left.

I just had my fifteenth birthday, and the dress that I bought myself was the only gift that I had gotten. I could tell that my mother felt bad.

As I stepped into my mother's room, my legs gave out on me and I ended up crumpled up on the wooden floor.

The sight in front of me was enough to take my breath away and I felt all of my hope slipping away. My mother lay naked on the ground, her eyes wide open as her body twitched and she struggled to get air. I reached out with shaky hands and grabbed for her arm.

"Mother!" I cried. "Get up. What did you do?"

"You little bitch!"

I looked up to see my father step into the room and reach for my mother's head. "See what you did," he spat. "She can't handle having you around. You made her want to kill herself."

I backed up against the wall and gripped onto the door. My heart stopped and I wanted to die. I struggled to pull myself to my feet as I fought for air through my sobs. "No. I...no."

My father shot to his feet and was standing over me in an instant. He reached out and in one fluid movement, he had me knocked back down to the ground and lying flat on my face.

"Don't just sit there you, little whore. Call 911."

"Avery. Wake up."

I sat up in bed fighting for breath. My whole body was wet and my hands were shaking uncontrollably as I reached for my hair and tugged. I felt as if I was about to hurl or fall over dead. Whichever would happen first. "Jace," I cried.

"I'm not Jace." Caleb's voice soared.

I slowly brought my eyes up to see Caleb standing shirtless in just a pair of blue sweats.

His eyes burned into me as he cracked his knuckles and crawled onto the foot of the bed. "It's me Avery. I won't ever let Jace hurt you again," he spat. "I will keep him away-"

"No," I cut in. "No." I lay back down and pulled the quilt closer to my face. "Jace would never hurt me, Caleb." I shook my head as the tears continued to fall down my cheeks. It made me angry that he would even accuse Jace of hurting me.

Caleb gradually got closer to me until his body was just inches away from mine.

He pursed his lips and then reached out to caress my face. "You can tell me. I have people that can take care of him for you and then we can be together. Just the two of us." His voice came out confident and smooth as if he was sure that's what I wanted.

He was wrong. That wasn't what I wanted and I never would. I backed away from Caleb's touch and turned my head away from his gaze before rolling my eyes.

"No, Caleb," I growled. "You're not listening to me. You have no idea what I want or need so leave Jace out of this."

Caleb's eyes hardened as he reached out and firmly gripped my wrist. He briefly squeezed it before he released his grip and placed his hand next to his side, a look of hate in his eyes.

"I know what you need." He paused. "You don't know what you need." He stood back to his feet and ran his hand over his stomach. "I'll be in the kitchen eating. If I hear you screaming again I won't hesitate to come back in here and crawl in bed with you. I want to make sure that you feel safe." A slight smile crossed his hard face before he turned around and left the room.

A feeling of relief crossed over me as I sank back into the bed and snuggled up in the quilt. Caleb was making me feel really uncomfortable.

As I closed my eyes and tried to force myself back to sleep, I felt an empty feeling in my stomach. Not only had I gone all day without eating, but I was also beginning to remember how safe I always felt when Jace crawled into bed with me. It was a feeling that no one else had ever been able to give me. The thought made me sick to my stomach and a completely new set of tears were threatening to form.

Without thinking, I jumped out of bed and reached in my purse for my phone. I clutched it firmly to my chest and wiped away my tears with my free hand. I wanted nothing more than to talk to Jace, but I couldn't even begin to think about hurting him again. The thought was too unbearable and it left me feeling empty and ill.

WAKE UP CALL
VICTORIA ASHLEY

I carefully crawled back into bed while running my fingers over the smooth phone. I pressed my head into the stiff pillow and then slammed my face into it to try to escape the hurt. I got startled when suddenly the phone vibrated under my touch. My heart did flips in my chest as my stomach dropped to my feet. I knew who it would be and I didn't know what to do. All I knew was that I missed him. I actually missed him.

I guess we'll make that two missed calls...

Chapter 12

Early the next morning, I woke to the sound of Caleb leaving. A wave of relieve washed over me as I realized that was my chance of getting ready and out of here before he could return. After what happened last night, I really didn't want to deal with him again.

I slowly opened the bedroom door, poking my head outside; to be sure, that Caleb had really gone. When there was no sign of him, I sauntered out of the bedroom and down the hall to the bathroom.

I flipped on the light switch, realizing that in the whole eighteen hours that I had been at Caleb's house that I hadn't even bothered to use the bathroom. The sight astounded me.

It was complete with a two-headed shower, a gray granite sink, decorative mirrors that lined three of the four walls, and another Jacuzzi that sat in the back corner. The glass on the shower was crystal clear and looked as if it were brand new. It was incredibly beautiful and over the top. *This is crazy!*

I tiredly stared at my reflection in the mirror and frowned. Pulling my eyes away from the mirror, I slowly let out a deep breath and leaned into the sink for support. I still felt a little weak from my lack of sleep and was finding it hard to function right.

WAKE UP CALL
VICTORIA ASHLEY

Turning on the faucet, I ran my hands through the frigid water and splashed it over my heated face. Even though it was cool in Caleb's house, I still managed to sweat through the whole night. My skin felt hot and my stomach felt ill.

After quickly showering and dressing, I threw on my leather boots and wandered into the living room. I looked around for a few moments before sighing and walking toward the couch.

I got ready to take a seat, when out of the corner of my eye I noticed something sticking out from under the far left corner of the couch. I mindlessly bent down to reach for what appeared to be some kind of tin tray, but quickly realized that I really had no right to go through his things. I didn't want him in my business so I certainly had no right to be in his.

Taking a deep breath, I reached for my phone and called for a taxi. As usual, they had a free driver and said that they would send one right away.

I would have at least ten minutes before the taxi would arrive and my curiosity was starting to get the best of me. As hard as I fought it, a part of me believed that there was more to Caleb than he had led on. The strange way that he acted around Kat made me nervous.

I steadily made my way back over to the couch and bent down to reach for the tray. Once my hand reached the tray, I paused for a moment to look around, even though I knew that Caleb wasn't even home.

I carefully started sliding it toward me when suddenly I was interrupted by the sound of the front door opening. I quickly pushed it back under the couch.

Caleb stared over at me, eyes wide, as he slammed the door behind him. He hastily made his way over to stand in front of me. "Avery," he hissed. "I would appreciate it if you wouldn't go through my personal things when I'm gone."

He leaned above me and pulled my hand away from the tray, his heavy breathing brushing against my ear. "I think I hear your taxi outside. You should hurry," he said stiffly.

I pushed myself back to my feet while looking Caleb in the eye. The look on his face was scared, but vicious. I didn't like it. "Sorry," I mumbled. "I didn't think it was such a big deal. I just thought it was garbage or something."

Caleb nodded his head, reached over to the couch, and grabbed the strap of my purse. His hand shook as he held it out to me with an apologetic smile. "I'll see you when you get back. Good luck on your search."

I grabbed my purse from out of his loose grip and threw it over my right shoulder. Then I turned and faced the door. "Thanks," I said. I gave him one last look before hurrying outside.

The taxi sat outside just as Caleb said. When I approached it, I noticed that it was a different driver. One that I had never seen before.

Sighing, I hopped into the cozy backseat of the taxi and closed the door. I just didn't have the energy to deal with anything and didn't have much hope in finding a job.

A young man, maybe in his mid-twenties, turned around, placing his arm over the leather seat. He had light chocolate skin and big hazel eyes that seemed friendly and outgoing. He flashed me a carefree smile and lifted an eyebrow. "Where to?"

I leaned into the leather seat and threw my purse down next to me. That was when I realized that I had no idea where to even start. "I'm actually not quite sure where I'm headed yet." I frowned and looked out the window.

The driver laughed, causing me to look up at him. He didn't seem annoyed one bit by the situation. In fact, he looked amused. "Maybe I can help." He grinned.

I smiled back feeling a bit relieved. Other drivers had given me hard times in the past, and I didn't expect this one to be so understanding. "I'm looking for a new job." I looked up into his bright eyes and brushed a strand of hair out of my face. "Preferably a diner."

He smiled wider, if that was even possible, and shifted the car into drive. "Cool. Cool. I have a few ideas."

I exhaled and leaned back into the seat. "That's great. Thank you."

After a few minutes of driving, the driver suddenly pressed on the brakes and peered over his shoulder. I sat up, wondering what he was doing.

"Damn! I just remembered that I have a good friend that owns a diner. I could take you there if you'd like. We haven't spoken in a few months, but we're pretty close."

Feeling a bit of hope, I leaned forward in my seat and gripped the back of the driver's seat. If he had a friend with a diner, there would be a good chance that he could talk the person into giving me a job. "That sounds great... um... what's your name?"

"Dexter, but you can call me Dex." He smiled sweetly before pressing on the gas and taking off again.

"Alright, Dex. Tell me about this friend with a diner."

Dex looked at me through the rearview mirror and popped a fry into his mouth. "To be honest I have no idea how the business is going, but he's got a little diner called *The Indy Go*. I promise that it's-"

"No," I blurted and the car went silent. I shifted in my seat a bit embarrassed. "I'm sorry. I appreciate your help, but can we go somewhere else?"

My heart instantly started pounding in my chest and suddenly it was hard to breathe. Out of all of the people in the world, he just had to be friends with Jace.

Dex looked a little perplexed as he scratched the top his head and pulled into a small parking lot outside of a diner called *Jan's Place*. He shifted the car into park and leaned back to look at me. "Don't worry. I won't even ask what that was about..." He trailed off, looking out the window. "What's your name?"

"Avery," I said softly. "And thanks for not asking." I blew out a breath of relief.

"Avery. It's none of my business. I'm just here to help with whatever you may need," he said, matter-of-factly. "Good luck in there. I'll be out here waiting."

I nodded my head in understanding and stepped out of the taxi.

Finally, someone out there didn't ask too many questions. Everyone else in my life seemed to pry into my personal space. Stacy, Winston, Maple and even Jace.

Oh god! The thought of them brought a pain to my chest. My heart sank when I realized that I actually for once in my life had people that cared. I had Jace, Stacy, Winston and Maple. I had them all and I walked out on them.

I stumbled gripping onto the door of the diner for support. My whole body felt weak as my head spun. I hadn't even realized until then that I actually had a decent life for the first time ever and I blew it. Those people were there when I needed them and they never once judged me. People that I had known for just five short weeks cared more about me than my family ever did or could have.

I leaned against the glass door of the diner with my head in my hands, trying to pull myself together. I had too many thoughts running through my head and I had no idea what to do with them all.

I had spent the last fourteen months running from my parents and just when I thought I was in the clear, Aunt Pam showed up to ruin that. *That stupid, vile bitch.*

"Avery."

I snapped out of my thoughts to see Dex standing outside of the taxi with his arms crossed over his chest. He stood six feet tall with a lanky build. The look on his face was friendly, but concerned. "Are you alright?"

I shook my head and steadied myself back to my feet. I didn't want him knowing that I was having a nervous breakdown. I needed to be strong and show the world that I could make it on my own.

"Yes," I said smoothly, trying to sound rational. "I was just trying to figure out what I was going to say to help me get the job. Thank you." I grinned.

Dex nodded his head, looking a bit skeptical. "Good." He smiled. "Just checking."

He gave me a supportive smile as I opened the door to the diner and slipped inside. The poorly lit diner smelled of cheese and garlic, making my stomach growl as I glanced around.

The inside was a lot smaller than the outside and it held six tables that seated four people each. The small tables, which were covered with brown cloths, had one candle burning in the middle of each one, giving off a small lighting.

The whole diner was empty except for one table that had an elderly couple sharing a small pizza. The couple glanced up, smiled and returned to eating.

I jumped back when a hand suddenly gripped my shoulder. "Holy...!"

"Take it easy child."

A small elderly woman that stood about four foot nine, stood behind me with a tired smile on her aged face. Her red hair was tightly pulled back into a bun and she wore a long black dress with a brown apron over it. She looked a little lost as if she had trouble getting by on her own.

"You look familiar." I was a little surprised at first, but finally put it together. "Ah."

Jan's Place. It was the rude old lady from Jace's diner.

My heart sped up and I lost all hope. She was a bitter old lady. I doubted that she wanted help from anyone.

She walked around me before taking a seat on a half broken stool. "What do you want? Some pizza?"

I shook my head, trying to decide whether to even bother. What choice did I really have? "I'm looking for a job."

She gave me a stern look. "You have one."

"Not anymore. I need a new one and fast. Things are complicated and -"

"Have you ever cooked a pizza before?" she cut in, studying my face.

I stopped playing with my purse and a nervous smile crossed my face. "I haven't, but I am willing to learn."

She stared with curious eyes, before speaking. "I suppose I could use a young woman like you a few days a week. My hands are getting a bit fragile and it makes it hard for me to do it all on my own. It really pisses me off."

She nodded and waved for me to follow her to the back of the diner. "Don't just stand there. Come."

I followed close behind, but still kept my distance. She'd probably snap my head off if I were to step on her.

We stepped into a tiny kitchen and Jan pointed over at the oven. It was large and stained with food. Most likely pizza sauce. "There's your new oven. Don't burn yourself. It hurts like a bitch."

My face lit up. Even though she wouldn't be very pleasant to work with, anything would be better than staying with Caleb. "I get the job?"

Jan smiled weakly and waved her arms in front of her. "If you think you can handle it." She coughed and walked back toward the dining area. "You can, right?"

I raised my head and followed behind her, nearly stepping on her heels. I was excited, eager, and almost wanted to hug her. "Of course I can."

WAKE UP CALL
VICTORIA ASHLEY

I stared out into the orange and red dining area, lost in thought, until she gently placed her hand on my shoulder. "I don't have a lot that I can offer you, but I would like you here on Mondays, Tuesdays and Saturdays from ten o'clock a.m. until around six o'clock p.m. Those are the busiest days and hours so you better move that tushy fast."

I nodded my head in agreement and brushed my hair behind my ear. Three days a week wouldn't be much, but it was a start and possibly enough to get me on my feet until I could find more. "That works just fine with me. Thank you." I turned on my heels and headed out the door with a satisfied grin.

Dex sat calmly on the trunk of the taxi, with his phone in his hands. He looked pretty into whatever he was doing and didn't seem to notice me.

I walked up to him and tapped him on the shoulder with a smile. He jumped back, startled, almost dropping his phone out of his hand.

"Shit!" He laughed. "You scared the crap out of me. How did it go?" he asked, jumping off the trunk and sliding to his feet. He somehow managed to make it look smooth.

I laughed at the cheesy look on his face and followed him over to the backseat of the taxi. I smiled up at him as he opened the door for me to get in. "I got the job."

He placed his hand on the small of my back and helped me into the taxi. He looked down at me and smiled his eyes bright with joy. "Hell yeah! That's great. When do you start?"

I waited as he hurried to get back into the taxi before replying.

"Monday," I replied. "She said that she really only needs me on Mondays, Tuesdays and Saturdays. It's not exactly what I was looking for, but it works for now. I really need to find an apartment now and I'll be set."

Dex looked back at me and gave me a cocky smile. He had a nice smile and his face was pretty easy on the eyes.

"What?" I questioned, as he kept looking at me.

"I think that I can be of some help there was well," he said with confidence. "

Taking a deep breath, I leaned into the seat and closed my eyes. "Take me anywhere you have in mind. It would be nice if it is closer to Jan's though."

"Sure thing."

Dex took me around to a few places, but they were either too expensive or already taken. After about two hours of searching, we stopped by a little duplex about five minutes away from Jace's house. Being so close to Jace had me feeling nervous and sick to my stomach.

The nice man who owned the place showed me around the cute little one bedroom place, but then informed me that the place wouldn't be ready for another week. He said that he would give me two days to think about it and then he was going to give it to the next person that showed interest. I really had a lot to think about.

After getting back into the taxi, I asked Dex to take me to one last place. It was the middle of the day and I was pretty positive that Jace would be at the diner, still.

"I need you to take me by Jace's house. I need to grab a few things."

Dex gave me a surprised look, but took off toward Jace's house anyways. "Did you live with Jace?" he questioned.

Biting my lip, I nervously twirled my hair around my finger. "Yeah. I'm moving out though. I will only be a few minutes. I just need to grab a few things."

My heart sank to my stomach as we pulled into Jace's driveway. His car was gone as I expected. "Thanks, Dex. I'll be right back."

Dex gave me a worried look as he watched me get out of the taxi and walk into the house.

The smell of Jace's body Old Spice body wash hit me as soon as I stepped into the door. The smell was so sweet and familiar that it made me want to crawl into my old bed and fall asleep. I closed my eyes and sniffed the air, before running to my old room to pack.

After grabbing a bag full of my things, I walked into the living room and stared down at the leather couch. That was the first place that I fell asleep in Jace's arms and slept the whole way through. That was a very important moment for me, and one that I would never be able to forget. It was one of my first happy memories.

WAKE UP CALL
VICTORIA ASHLEY

Just as I was walking back out the door, I noticed a new picture hanging on the wall. It was small and hard to see so I walked over to the wall to look.

A wave of sadness washed over me as I took in the sight of Jace and me in his car. It was taken the night that he took me bowling. We were both laughing as Jace pretended to lick my face.

He had snapped the picture of us in the car on the way home. It came out a bit blurry, but looked rather nice. *Dammit, Jace. What are you thinking?*

A flood of tears ran down my cheeks as I stepped outside into the cool air and slammed the door behind me. My first thought was to fall to the ground and curl up, but instead I reached up with my free hand to wipe the tears away.

I couldn't let Dex see me crying after just leaving Jace's house. I wouldn't want him to get the wrong idea.

As I opened the door to the taxi Dex quickly fumbled with his phone until he finally dropped it down in his lap. He looked up with a guilty look, but quickly covered it with a smile. "Ready to go?"

I hesitated whether or not to ask him what he was doing, but decided against it, jumping back into the safety of the taxi. "Yeah. I just need to get out of here."

I can't let Jace find me looking so weak....

Chapter 13

He stared me in the eye, walked me backwards, and softly pushed me onto the edge of my bed. He slowly laid down on top of me, spreading my legs, as he rubbed his hand up my right arm.

The feel of him sent a shiver up my spine and caused my legs to shake as he placed his body between my open legs. His jaw clenched as he leaned in, placing his lips back to mine.

His body pressed into me even more, causing us both to moan into each other's mouths. Then with shaky hands, he reached under my skirt and gripped my thong in his hand. "I want you so bad," he whispered.

"Shit!"

I sat up in Caleb's bed and threw my hands over my sweaty face. It was then that I realized just how rapidly my heart was beating. It always managed to beat that way whenever I thought about Jace and only then.

Slowly placing my feet on the floor, I pushed myself out of the bed and reached over to the table in search of my ponytail holder. I threw my hair up so that it was out of my sticky face and quietly crept over to the door. I was surprised when I heard not only Caleb's voice, but also the voice of another man. It had to of been at least four o'clock a.m.

WAKE UP CALL
VICTORIA ASHLEY

I carefully pressed my face against the door, being sure to be as quiet as possible and took a deep breath. The other voice sounded angry, almost enough to scare me.

"I told you that you had one week. One fucking week." The other man growled.

"And I will have it in two days." Caleb paused for a moment and I leaned further into the door. "I ran into a little difficultly, but it will be taken care of soon. Trust me."

It was silent for a moment before the other voice spoke. When he did, it sent chills down my spine.

"It better be. I'll be back in two days. Two days," he hissed. "If your little problem isn't taken care of, then I will take care of it myself."

I pressed my body against the door and waited for what sounded like the front door opening and then closing. Then I shook off the chill of the conversation and pulled open the door to let myself out. As much as I didn't want to see Caleb, I really had to use the bathroom and knew that I couldn't wait much longer.

Caleb was pacing the kitchen as I stepped out and carefully shut the door behind me. I tried my best to creep down the hall unnoticed, but was unsuccessful. Caleb's voice stopped me dead in my tracks.

"Avery."

I turned on my heels, but kept my head down toward the hardwood flooring. I couldn't bear to look Caleb in the eye at the moment.

Truthfully, I almost felt scared. Scared of what Caleb would do if he knew that I overheard his conversation. "I'm just using the bathroom, Caleb."

The room was silent as I waited for Caleb to respond.

"Look. Whatever it is that you heard-"

"I didn't hear anything. I don't know what you're talking about." I ran my hand through my hair and yawned. "I just woke up because I had to use the bathroom."

Without another word, I took off down the hall and closed myself inside the bathroom. My head was still spinning from the conversation and I had no idea what the two of them were even talking about. *Could it of been possible that he meant me*? "No," I mumbled to myself, not wanting to believe it.

WAKE UP CALL
VICTORIA ASHLEY

I leaned into the sink and took a few deep breaths. Finally, I understood why I always said no to Caleb when he wanted me to stay at his house. I always knew there was something a little off about him. He always took it so well that I wanted nothing more than a sexual relationship from him, but there was always that look in his eyes that said he wanted to do something about it.

I waited for a few minutes before I left the bathroom in hopes that Caleb would go to bed so that I wouldn't have to see him again for the night. I had nothing to say to him. All that I wanted was to make it through the night so that I could wake up early and go looking for an apartment.

To my luck, the kitchen was empty, meaning that Caleb must've decided to go to bed.

I walked quietly into the bedroom and shut the door behind me. I got ready to walk over to the bed when I noticed a shadow in the corner of the dim room. I jumped.

"Caleb," I muttered, scared half to death.

I blindly reached over and flipped on the switch to see Caleb leaning against the wall with his arms crossed over his bare chest. He gave me a friendly smile and walked over to stand at the foot of the bed.

"I just thought maybe you could use some company." He pointed down at the bed and grinned. "Come here. I'm not really tired and the couch is a little stiff." He rolled his shoulder as if it hurt.

The thought of Caleb in bed with me angered me. I didn't want to be anywhere near him.

"No," I said firmly. "If you want to take your bed back then you can. I don't think I can sleep anymore tonight anyways." I reached for my leather jacket and slipped it on.

Caleb hurried over and reached for my purse at the same time as I did. "Where are you going?" He kept his eyes on mine, not loosening his grip on my purse.

I snatched my purse from out of his hand and threw it over my shoulder. I didn't have to explain myself to him and I wouldn't. "I'll just be back," I muttered.

His eyes studied my every movement, sending chills up my spine as I opened the door and dashed through the house to get outside and into the early morning air.

WAKE UP CALL
VICTORIA ASHLEY

It was still dark outside, but somehow I managed to feel safer outside than I did inside the house with Caleb. I had to get out of there and fast.

I heard the door open behind me, but I ignored it and kept walking.

First thing in the morning, I was going to grab my things and call Dex. He gave me his personal number in case I ever needed a ride again. He said that he stayed on call most of the time because he really needed the cash to save up for college. I would be more than happy to give him a call.

The more that I walked, the colder that it got, but I didn't care. I actually welcomed the feeling. It reminded me that I was alive.

It was quite strange. The things that I had been feeling for the last few weeks were so intense and unlike anything else, I had ever experienced in my life. No matter how hard I tried to deny it, I had Jace to thank for that. I think.

After about an hour of walking, I noticed that I had been circling the same block repeatedly. Looking up to see where I was at, I noticed that I was just down the street from Jace's house.

I took a deep breath and threw my hands in my hair as I stood staring over at Jace's house. The place that I once called a home. Every part of me wanted to go there, just open the door, and crawl in bed. Maybe even with Jace. Just being in his arms was a feeling that I missed. To be honest there was no better feeling in the world.

I gradually found myself getting closer and closer to his house until finally I was standing at the bottom of his steps, the cool wind whipping through my hair and smacking me in the face, as I stood there frozen in place.

The house was dark and I got a feeling of peace knowing that Jace was inside sleeping.

I willed my legs to work until I found a spot on the stairs and took a seat. The cement felt cool through my clothing and made me shiver up in a ball with my arms wrapped tightly around my body.

I leaned my head back into the wooden railing and closed my eyes to rest. Just for a minute. The longer that I sat, the heavier that my eyes got. I tried repeatedly to open my eyes until finally I gave up.

WAKE UP CALL
VICTORIA ASHLEY

~•~

The porch light flickered on, waking me from my short sleep. My heart dropped to my stomach as I scrambled to get back to my feet. I couldn't let Jace find me sitting outside his house like some kind of idiot.

I ran off his porch and somehow managed to trip over my own feet, sending me landing on my face. I quickly pushed my arms out in front of me and pushed myself back to my feet. Without looking back at the house, I took off in a sprint and made my way down and across the street.

The walk back to Caleb's house seemed to go by quickly as I found myself standing at the end of his horribly long driveway. I could tell by the brightness of the sun that it had to be at least seven o'clock a.m. by now.

I couldn't believe that I had let myself fall asleep on Jace's porch and not to mention that I almost got caught.

Once I got closer to Caleb's house, I noticed a brown Station Wagon sitting toward the side of the garage.

It seemed as if Caleb always had some kind of company. It was annoying and strange.

Shaking my head, I reached for the door and let myself inside. The house was surprisingly quiet as I walked inside and set my purse on the table.

"There you are," Caleb squeaked. "I was worried about you. You've been gone for hours." He stepped out from behind the curtain and threw his phone down on the couch. "I've been calling you all morning."

I shrugged my shoulders, not caring what he thought. It wasn't his job to worry about me.

"I was fine. My phone was in my purse. You know that I never pay attention to it." I reached into my purse and grabbed my phone out. "No one ever calls me..." My voice trailed off when I noticed six missed calls. Five from Caleb and one from Jace that was sent at 6:15 a.m. I swallowed hard. "I'm fine."

I shoved my phone in my coat pocket and turned toward the hallway.

"Wait," Caleb shouted.

I slowly turned around and shook my head. "Caleb. I have places to go. I'm leaving after I-"

"There's someone here to see you." He grinned, pleased with himself. "I wanted it to be a surprise for a later time, but I was worried about you so I gave him-"

"There's my little girl."

The room went silent, as my father stepped into the kitchen, with his arms out in front of him.

My heart stopped at just the sight of him. He stood there with his old flannel jacket and graying hair, looking at me as if I was truly his little girl.

His face and hands were bruised and bloody and he looked as if he was on a mission.

Fighting to catch my breath, I dropped to my knees and tightly gripped the carpet for support. I placed a shaky hand over my chest and gripped my hair with the other. My body started quivering as the bile rose in my throat and threatened to spew out.

"No," I spat. "No! No! No!" I said while furiously shaking my head. I wanted it to all be a dream. For the man standing before me to just disappear.

Caleb looked between my father and me before he leaned down and gripped my shoulder. "What's wrong?" he questioned. "Your dad is so happy to see you. Are you in shock? I know that it's been a while." He smiled and ran his hand over my arm.

I shook Caleb's hand off my arm and crawled over to the corner. My heart was racing so hard that it became hard to think straight. *Why? How?*

"Avery, honey," my father said sweetly, his malodorous breath reeking of booze. "Your mother and I have missed you very much. I think that it's time you come visit your mother," he slurred, stumbling to the left.

I refused to look up even though I knew that my father was getting closer with each passing second. I was so confused that I just wanted to scream. Why was he acting as if he cared? It was all an act and I wouldn't be stupid enough to fall for his game.

"Go away," I stammered. "You can't control me anymore. I won't let you," I screamed. Inside I was terrified, but I wasn't going to let him take me away.

WAKE UP CALL
VICTORIA ASHLEY

My father bent down and placed his hands on his knees for support. The look on his face was just as distant as I had always remembered.

He inched forward in an attempt to touch my face, but I pulled away. "I don't know what you're so upset about." He snickered. "Your mother and I have faith that you have changed your life around. You don't have to worry."

The words that he spoke left me in a daze and a bit confused. He was trying to turn things around and make me the bad guy. "But-"

"Avery, you're a good person," Caleb cut in. "Don't be ashamed. Your father told me everything. You're not that same person."

I slowly tilted my head up to look both Caleb and the scum in the eye. "Caleb, shut the hell up."

I pushed myself to my feet and waved my arms out in front of me in order to give myself more space. I felt as if I was suffocating. "And you..."I said looking at the man that was supposed to be my father." Get the hell out of my life. I hate you," I spat while shoving him out of my way.

My father reached out and gripped my arm. "You listen here. You are coming with me and I don't give a shit about what you say." His grip tightened as he pulled me toward him and slammed me into the wall, his nails digging deep into my flesh. "Your mother is dying."

My heart dropped. Tears started pouring down my face and my palms started to sweat. The look in his blue eyes softened at the mention of my mother and I knew right away that he was telling the truth.

I stood there frozen against the door as Caleb watched with shocked eyes from beside us. "Dying?" I managed to choke out.

My father loosened his grip on me and leaned against the wall next to me. He threw his hands to his bloodied face and then up to tug on his messy hair. "She doesn't have long to live. You have to come see her," he muttered. "She misses you." He stumbled over, but smoothly caught himself before he could fall.

My mind spun as I slowly slid down the wall and placed my hands on my knees so that I wouldn't fall on my face. I felt as if I could vomit or pass out.

WAKE UP CALL
VICTORIA ASHLEY

Deep down inside my mother wanted to be good. I could always see it in her eyes. The way they always softened when he wasn't around to hurt her. *Shit! Hurt her. That bastard!*

My eyes trailed over to my father's bruised and bloodied knuckles. "You piece of shit," I growled. "You did it to her." I placed my hands on the wall behind me and pushed myself to my feet.

Caleb's eyes went wide as he reached out and touched my arm. "Your mother is dying. How can you accuse-"

Without thinking, I swung my right arm out connecting it to Caleb's stomach. The impact hurt my hand, but it didn't stop me. Then I reached out, connecting my fist to my father's left cheek, as he grabbed my arm again. It felt good to hit the man that had hurt me my whole life. "I hate you both," I screamed.

My father gave me that look. The one I had grown to remember. The one that has frightened me my whole life.

I took off running through the hall with my father following behind me. My heart raced as his footsteps got closer. I could hear Caleb not too far behind my father and I panicked.

I reached for the bathroom door and flung myself inside, slamming the door behind me. I quickly fumbled with the lock and then fell into the sink in relief.

My body jumped involuntarily as the pounding on the door began.

"Get out here you, little bitch," my father spat through the door. His voice was venomous and hateful. He pounded again, making my heartbeat skyrocket. "I will break this door down. Do you hear me?"

I backed away from the sink and crawled into the bathtub for safety. It was something that I did numerous times as a child while trying to escape my father's wrath. I knew that it wouldn't save me, but it never stopped me from still doing it.

"Go away," I screamed, while throwing my hands over my ears and pressing firmly against my head to drown out the noise.

"Maybe you should give her some damn space," Caleb said firmly. "Pam never told me that she hated you so much. This was not what I expected."

I shook uncontrollably as I listened to them argue outside the bathroom door. Their voices began to blend and suddenly I was lost.

WAKE UP CALL
VICTORIA ASHLEY

I squeezed my eyes shut and frantically started searching for my phone. If it were in my purse then I'm screwed. "Where is it? Shit!" I mumbled.

Finally, I felt the bulge of my phone through my leather jacket. I stared down at my phone, trying to see my contact list, but my vision blurry from the unwanted tears that wouldn't seem to stop.

"I'll give you some time to cool off. I'll be out here waiting for you." My father's voice taunted me from through the door. "Told you I'd find you."

I let out a deep breath and relaxed against the cool tub as I reached up to wipe away the tears. The mascara streaked my hand as I pulled it away and continued my search.

Dex told me that he would always be available if I needed a ride. I really didn't have many other choices unless I wanted to wait for taxi service.

It took me a few minutes, but I finally found his name. My whole hand shook as I firmly pressed the call button.

The phone rang three times before he answered. His voice sounded half asleep.

"Hello. It's pretty early. How-"

"Dex," I cut him off. "I need you to get me. I need to leave right now. Please hurry," I cried into the phone. As hard as I tried to hold back the tears, I couldn't. "It's me... Avery."

"Shit, Avery." he said in a panic. "Are you okay?"

I reached up to wipe my face off as I continued to cry into the phone. "No. I need to get out of here. Just hurry."

"You're at the same place as before?" he questioned with worry.

"Yes. Call me right when you pull up and I'll come out," I whispered, trying to think of a plan. "Come now." My voice shook as I struggled to get the last words out.

"I'll be there." He hung up.

I hung up the phone and clutched it to my chest. I couldn't believe that he found me. I thought that I was free of him for good.

A few minutes later, there was a light knock at the door.

I sat on the edge of the tub and kicked it with my boot. "Go away," I screamed. "I'm not going anywhere with you."

"Avery," Caleb said softly. "It's me. Can we talk?"

WAKE UP CALL
VICTORIA ASHLEY

There was no reason for me to talk to him. After seeing my dad and hearing that he knew Aunt Pam, it became very clear to me that he was dealing drugs. That would be the only thing connecting them.

"There is nothing to talk about. You don't know shit about me and I want to keep it that way. Go away," I growled.

It was silent for a few minutes before I heard noise outside the door again. It sounded as if someone had fallen against the door.

"You listen here you, selfish little girl," my father hissed. "Your mother is going to die and you won't even go and see her. What kind of a person does that make you? You're no better than me." He laughed. "That's why no one will ever love you and you will never know what love is," he sang his voice teasing and hateful.

The tear stopped and suddenly I felt like exploding. How did he know what I was capable of when I didn't even know myself?

"Go to hell!" I screamed at the top of my lungs. I screamed so loud that it hurt. It took everything in me not to cover my ears from myself. "You are wrong."

I heard laughter on the other side of the door that made my blood boil. "You are still that stupid little girl. I thought that you grew out of that stage." He slammed his fist into the door and then fiercely turned at the knob. "Stupid little-"

I lost it. Something inside of me took over and I ran over to the door and yanked it open, body shaking and heart pounding in my chest.

My father stood there unsteady on his feet as he glared up at me with shock in his beady eyes. "I'm not that same girl," I said bravely. "I'm all grown now and I'm not going to take your crap anymore."

He stumbled into the wall while reaching out for my coat. His hand missed and he nearly fell to the ground. His eyes burned into me as he pursed his thin lips, the graying hair covering most of his mouth. "You get back here. I drove a long way to get your ass," he hissed.

"Go to hell," I shouted, as I brushed past his drunken body. I was getting out of there. I had to.

I ran past Caleb as he attempted to grab my hand. "No Caleb."

Caleb shook his head and wiped something off his nose. I could tell by the look in his eyes that he was drugged up. "I'm sorry," he muttered. "I didn't know."

I threw my arms up in the air and then reached for my purse. I hated Caleb for this. I hated him for bringing hell back into my life. "I'm out-"

"Stop!" My father cut me off as he reached for my purse. "You're not going anywhere." He yanked me by my purse so that I was in his reach, then he reached for my hair and yanked me down to the ground.

A screech escaped my parted lips as my head bounced off the table leg, sending a wave of pain throughout my head.

I could see Caleb behind my dad as he attempted to reach for his arm to pull him away, but my dad shook him off and came at me anyways.

Before I knew it, his hand was around my throat and squeezing. "Let go," I whined, fighting for breath. "Stop-"

We all froze as the door to the house swung open to Jace standing there. The look on his face was fierce as he looked down at me on the ground and then to my dad that still had his hand on my throat. His strong jaw clenched as he stepped into the house.

My heart pounded at the sight of him.

"Let go," Jace demanded. "I won't hesitate to fucking kill you, you piece of shit."

My dad looked up at him as if was just his imagination. Then a smirk crossed his twisted face. "Screw off. It's none of your business." He pushed me further into the floor as he began to dig his nails into my neck.

I desperately grabbed at his hands attempting to pry them from my neck.

"You piece of..." Jace's words trailed off as he gripped my father's neck, placing him in a headlock. "Let go or I will snap your fucking neck."

My dad's grip on my neck loosened, but then suddenly his fist connected with my right eye as a smirk crossed his face. I winced back in pain and covered my face as I watched Jace tackle him to the ground and hold him down by his neck.

Everything around me blurred as Jace's arm continued to swing never letting up on my father.

WAKE UP CALL
VICTORIA ASHLEY

Caleb attempted to stop Jace, but not even that would get Jace to stop.

"Stop," Caleb shouted. "You're killing him."

I shot up from the ground and that's when I noticed all of the blood that surrounded them. Looking at it made me feel dizzy. Then panic set in. I couldn't let Jace kill him. "Jace," I shouted.

As soon as the word came out, he froze. He dropped his arm to his side and looked up at Caleb. "You idiot. I should kick your ass for letting her get hurt."

Caleb stood there in shock as he watched Jace get back to his feet. Not another word was spoken between them as Jace brushed past Caleb and stood before me.

His handsome face looked pained as he reached for my hand and helped me to my feet. He slowly reached out his hand and delicately caressed my swollen face, as he looked me in the eye. His green eyes were strained and full of hurt.

"I promised to never let you get hurt," he whispered. "I failed you and I'm sorry."

My heart beat rapidly in my chest as his fingertips softly touched my face and trailed down to my lips. The touch of his skin made me feel safe and all that I wanted to do was curl up in his arms and get lost.

"It's my fault," I whispered. I threw my arms around his waist and buried myself in his firm chest. The smell of him was so familiar and calming. Being that close to him made me realize what I had been missing all along. Why had I been so stupid?

He squeezed me close to his chest and tenderly pressed his lips to the top of my head. "I will never let him hurt you again." Jace promised.

"Shit," Caleb mumbled, interrupting the moment.

We both looked over to see Caleb standing above my dad. He bent down and held his hand above his mouth. "He's barely breathing," Caleb panicked. "You better get out of here. Now, before I call the cops."

A small part of me wanted to run to my dad. To make sure that he was going to be fine, but the bigger part of me told me that I needed to get Jace out of there. He was only protecting me. He never meant to hurt him.

"Jace." My voice shook as I reached for his arm.

Jace took a deep breath and bit his bottom lip. "I didn't mean to hurt him that-"

"I know," I cut in. I knew that Jace meant well. He was taking care of me as he promised. Just as he did that day when Max touched me.

"Take that monster and get out of here," Caleb spat. "That's who you choose to be around? He's dangerous, Avery."

"He's not. He was-"

"It's fine, Avery. Let's get out of here." Jace said, pulling me into him.

I took one last look at my dad as he coughed and struggled, spitting up blood. My legs grew weak as I let Jace lead me outside and to his Mustang.

Jace opened the door for me and gently helped me inside before running over to his side and roughly shutting the door behind him.

He shoved the keys into the ignition and then reached over and cupped my face. He was silent as his eyes studied mine. My heart sped up. Both of us started to shake, as he looked me in the eye. "I'm going to take care of all of this. I promise."

I sat back in my seat and squeezed my eyes shut as Jace shifted the car into drive and took off. The tears rolled down my face leaving little wet spots on my shirt and jacket.

I could see Jace turning to look at me every few minutes, but I was in so much shock that I couldn't even get words to form.

I shook my head and slammed it into the seat. I didn't know what to think. If my father died then Jace would probably get thrown into jail, not to mention the fact that my mother could already be dead.

The car was silent as we pulled up in front of Jace's house. He took the keys out of the ignition and looked over at me. "I have something to tell you." He forced out. "I should've told you in the first place."

My whole body started shaking as I attempted to look over at him. The look on his face was one of worry and pain. I wanted to reach out and hold him, to comfort him. "Tell me," I said softly, wanting him to know that he could tell me anything.

Jace leaned his head back and squeezed his eyes closed. He nervously played with the steering wheel as he pursed his lips.

"That girl. The one that was in the picture that broke." He paused and looked away.

"Yes," I pushed.

"That was a close friend of mine. Zara was her name," he whispered. "Her boyfriend used to beat the crap out of her. She would come over at least once a week with bruises and cuts, crying and telling me all of the horrible things that he did to her. Finally, one day after I had enough and couldn't take anymore, I found him when he was alone. I found him and I beat the crap out of him." He stopped and looked over at me.

I nodded my head for him to continue.

He took a deep breath and ran his hands through his messy hair. "Zara came home just in time... she stopped me. He was barely breathing by that time. Fuck!" He slammed his head into the seat. "It was the same thing that happened tonight. I didn't mean to do so much damage, but something takes over me and when I care about someone I want to protect them."

I reached over with shaky hands and grabbed his face. I looked him in the eye, while rubbing his cheek. "What happened to her?" I questioned.

His eyes became glassy as he quickly turned his head away. "She felt bad for him so she stayed by his side. A week later he beat her...to...death." He choked it out. "I should've done more to save her. After that I promised to never let that happen to anyone that I cared about again."

My heart sank to my stomach as I sat there, mouth open in shock. I was speechless. Jace had probably spent all of that time blaming himself. That's probably why Max said that he hadn't changed. He meant his violence, but it wasn't fair. He was only protecting his friend. "It wasn't your fault," I blurted out, wanting to cry and hold him and tell him that it wasn't his fault.

He looked over at me with a look of shock. His eyes softened as he reached over and ran his finger over my lip.

"I missed you. I've been wanting to do this for so long now." He leaned in, pressing his lips against mine, causing me to become breathless.

My arms instantly went around his neck and squeezed as he pressed his lips closer to mine causing us both let out a moan of passion.

The kiss was broken up as loud knocking on the car window shocked us out of our own little world.

We both looked up in surprise to see a police officer with one hand on the window and the other gripping the top of his gun as if he was ready to pull it out at any minute.

His tall build leaned into the window as he nodded his head and waved his thick arm. "Jace Montgomery," he said stiffly. "Please step out of the car."

This can't be happening....

I watched in horror as Jace stiffly pressed his face into the steering wheel and huffed, before slamming his right fist into the roof of his Mercedes. "Dammit," he mumbled.

I felt sick to my stomach. *Caleb called the police! My father died? Jace is going to jail?*

I couldn't control my thoughts or emotions as I reached for the door handle, hands shaking as I pushed the door open. I placed one shaky leg after the other down to the dirty gravel as I attempted to get out of the car. My right leg gave out, but I quickly caught myself before I could fall down to the ground. "No!" I shouted. "Jace didn't do anything-"

"It's fine, Avery." Jace shook his head and looked toward the ground. "I will take full responsibility for what I did," He said while stepping out of the car and leaning against it, eyes glued to mine. "I'm sorry, Avery.

"No," I whined. "I won't let you go to jail." I looked up with pleading eyes as I stood in front of the police officer. "It's not his fault. You can't-"

"Look here." The police officer cut in. "I don't have all night to listen to you two whine about a ticket." He looked between the both of us and raised an eyebrow. "You both act as if you've never received a speeding ticket before," he grunted, while pulling out his pad of tickets.

My eyes wandered over to Jace as he relaxed and leaned into his car door. "A ticket?" He questioned.

The police officer stood tall, brown eyes concerned, with an annoyed look on his face. "Yes, a ticket. Did you expect that since you got away from me back there that you wouldn't be getting a ticket," he growled and rolled his eyes.

"I ran your plates and name. I knew you'd be coming back here sometime." He held out a pad of paper and pulled off the top sheet. "I followed you for almost five miles, with you going 20 over the limit. You better slow down and save a life, boy."

He did save a life. Mine.

My heart started beating at its normal rate as the police officer took Jace's information and made him sign for his ticket. A few minutes later the police officer was gone and on his way to ruin someone else's night.

Jace quickly walked around and wrapped his strong arms around me, pulling me close. He pressed his face against mine and softly kissed under my ear. "It feels so good to have you in my arms," he breathed. "I didn't want to have to give that up again."

I closed my eyes and pressed my lips against his scruffy cheek. I was just so happy that he didn't get arrested and all that I wanted to do was be close to him.

"Thank you," I whispered into his chest. "You have done so much for me. I don't know. I just don't. What would I do with without you?"

Jace cupped my face in his hands and looked me in the eye, eyes gleaming, as he rubbed his thumb over my lips. "You'll never have to find out."

With that, he firmly pressed his lips to mine, while snaking his arms around me and lifting me off the ground. My whole body relaxed into his as he carried me through the yard and into the house, his lips still pressed against mine.

Once inside he gently laid me down on the cool leather couch and pressed his body between my parted legs.

Moaning, his lips pressed further into mine as I gently snaked my arms around his neck, tangling my fingers in his messy hair. He smiled into my lips as he ran his fingertips up my sides and then rested them on my face.

"Jace," I breathed.

Jace kissed my lips once more and then gently ran his mouth over my neck. "Yes," he said softly, his breath tickling my neck.

I leaned my head back in delight as his lip ring brushed just under my ear, causing my whole body to jerk in satisfaction. "I - um," I moaned. "What if something happened to my father? Caleb might send the police here. Then what?"

The kissing stopped and Jace slowly pulled away looking me in the eye. He softly ran his thumb over my bruised eye and then turned away in disgust.

"I did what I had to to protect you. I would do it all over again too." He paused to take a deep breath. "I owe Dex everything for letting me know what was going on with you. I couldn't sleep because I was so worried about you. I sat up all night just thinking about you and ways to get you to come back home. Then to my surprise, Dex called me and told me his concern. I got there as fast as I could and it was a good thing that I did. If something happens to your father then I will take what I get." He smiled and reached for my hand. "All that matters is that you're safe."

I squeezed his hand, pulse racing and my head spinning. He made my heart melt. "I've never told you this, but... I only feel safe when I'm with you." I looked up into his beautiful emerald eyes and felt relieved that I had him in my life.

"You have no idea how happy you just made me." Jace grinned before he leaned in and placed a short, sweet kiss on my lips. "I wish that I could've done the same for a few others that I care about." He paused and swallowed, a look of regret in his eyes. "When I first saw you, there was something in your eyes that told me you needed me. I needed you too."

"I do need-"

We both pulled away as a red car pulled into the driveway, the headlights shining through the open door. I knew right away that it was Caleb.

Jace jumped up from the couch and raced over to the door. I could tell by the look on his face that he was willing to do whatever it took to get Caleb out of my life for good. He reached for the door and pulled it open with hate.

I followed close behind as Jace stepped out of the house and onto the lawn. My heart raced with every move that both men made.

Caleb cautiously stepped out of the car, but didn't come any closer. He glanced in my direction and then quickly locked his eyes on Jace. "I dropped her father off at the hospital." He paused and ran his hand over his forehead. "If I would've known how he was then I wouldn't have invited him in my home."

Jace clenched his jaw as he leaned into the porch. You could tell that he somewhat believed him, but didn't want to.

"It doesn't matter. You are still a piece of shit for not protecting her. She was in your home and you stood by like an idiot." He shook his head and slammed his fist into the side of the house. "I should kick your ass for not protecting her. Are you fucking stupid?"

Caleb shook his head back and forth as he slapped his forehead. "I was in shock. I was stupid. I don't know," he muttered. "I didn't know what to do. He was drunk and drugged up and-"

"So were you," Jace cut in. "You were drugged up and didn't want to deal with the cops. You knew that if you protected her that the cops could've possibly of gotten called. You were too busy protecting yourself."

Caleb turned his head and slammed his hand into the car door. Then he looked up at me with desperation in his eyes. "Avery."

"No, Caleb." I turned away, staring at the split wood on the porch railing. "I don't want to hear anything that you have to say. Just leave."

"I know where your mother's at."

Caleb's words made my heart stop. In all of the commotion, I had managed to forget about my mother and the fact that she could be dying. Both of my parents hurt and on the verge of death. "What," I questioned.

Jace looked back at me with a confused look on his face. "Avery," he whispered.

I forced my eyes to meet Jace's as I nervously ran my hands through my messy hair. "My mother is in the hospital." I pulled my eyes away from Jace and looked back over to Caleb. "Tell me," I demanded.

Caleb gave Jace a hard look before he bent into his car and then stood back up with a small folded up paper in his hand. He looked down at the paper and then back up at me. "I'll give it to you. Not him." he said nodding his head toward Jace.

Jace gave Caleb a dirty look before he pressed his head into his outstretched arm and gave me a nod.

I let out a nervous breath and took a step forward. All though Caleb hadn't physically hurt me I was still cautious around him. "Give it to me and go please."

I stepped up to Caleb with Jace keeping a watchful eye on us the whole time. Caleb gave me a weak smile and placed the paper in my open hand. "For what it's worth; I do care about you," he whispered, barely audible.

I closed my hand around the folded paper and took a step back. I didn't want to hear that Caleb cared for me. It suddenly made me feel bad for all that I had put him through. I would never show it though. He got his payback, even if he didn't mean to. "Bye, Caleb," I mumbled, taking a step back.

Caleb clenched his teeth as he backed away from me and shook his head. "Bye." He gave Jace one last look before he hopped into his BMW and drove away.

Jace was instantly at my side. He wrapped me in his arms and pulled my head down to his chest for comfort. His breathing slowed down as soon as Caleb was completely out of sight. "Would you like to tell me about your mother?" Jace asked as he softly rubbed my head.

I pulled my face away from his chest and looked up at him. "She's in the hospital." I felt the tears start to fall as soon as the words escaped my lips. "I think my father beat her. She needs me, Jace."

Jace leaned his head back in a struggle to control his anger. I could see how much it hurt him to see women being abused. It was something that he had dealt with in his past and I knew that he would put an end to it all if he could. "I'll take you there as soon as we wake up. I would feel better if you got a little rest first."

I nodded my head in agreement, just now realizing just how exhausted I felt. If it wasn't for Jace holding me, I would've probably of been on the ground. "Thank you."

Jace smiled and placed a kiss on my nose. Then he smoothly grabbed the paper from out of my hand and opened it. He read it to himself and then looked over at me. "She's only about 45 minutes from here. I'll get you there. Let's go inside and rest first. Just long enough for you to gain your energy. You're going to need it to be there for her."

WAKE UP CALL
VICTORIA ASHLEY

I gave him a thankful smile as he held my hand and led me inside.

Being back in Jace's home gave me that same safe, at home feeling that it always did. I had to admit that it felt great to be back. Jace and I may have still had a lot to catch up on, but at the moment the only thing that I could think about was my mother's safety. "Thank you," I said. "I owe you so much."

Jace pulled me into my old room and gently helped me into the bed. It was soft and cozy just liked I remembered and the faint smell of Jace's cologne still lingered on the blankets making me feel safe. He lay down next to me and stripped us both of our jackets before we got lost under the warmth of the blankets. "You being here is enough."

Chapter 14

I stepped into the shower and closed my eyes as the warm water splashed against my cool skin, causing my shoulders to relax. I slowly tilted my head back and ran my hands through my wet hair as my mind began to spin.

In less than two hours, I would hopefully be seeing my mother and I had no idea what to expect. *Was she still alive? Would she hate me? Has she missed me?* The thoughts were pure torture and honestly, I wasn't sure if I was ready to find the answers.

The sound of Jace entering the bathroom broke me of my thoughts as he turned on the sink water and grabbed for his toothbrush. The loud clatter was enough to grab my full attention. He always did have a thing with intruding on people's private shower time.

I poked my head out of the curtain being sure not to expose my naked flesh, as I smiled and shook my head at his carefree ways.

"Jace," I said, with a shake of my head.

He looked into the mirror and grinned back at me playfully as he ran a hand over his firm stomach. "Can I help you?" he teased. "You're interrupting my personal time."

I playfully hit the curtain and threw my head back. "Wait! I'm interrupting your personal time? "I questioned. "I'm naked behind this curtain if you care." I laughed and then attempted to look serious.

Jace slowly ran his tongue over his lip and then chewed on his lip ring, playfully. "I do care," he teased. "Trust me."

My face turned red as I pulled the curtain closer to me and laughed. "Stop teasing me and hurry up," I paused and stared him down. "You're making me nervous."

Jace gave me a serious look as I played with my hair. "Just remember that I'll be with you every step of the way," he paused. "Please don't worry too much." He stood there in just his low hanging briefs as he shoved his toothbrush into his mouth and shook his head at me. "You're not alone in this."

I took a deep breath, leaning against the back of the shower. Was it really that obvious? "I'm fine. I'm just tired and-"

"You're not fine," he cut in. "And I can't promise that everything will work out for you, but I can promise you that I will be there to pick up the pieces if they don't." He stepped up to the shower and ran his hand over the curtain, his eyes glued to mine. "I keep my promises."

My heart sped up, listening to his heavy breathing from outside of the thin curtain.

Suddenly, thoughts of Jace naked and sharing a shower with me clouded my mind and it was the only thing that mattered at the moment. I not only needed him, but I wanted him. I couldn't deny that fact anymore. The only thing that had been stopping me before was that I was scared. Scared of hurting Jace or possibly even myself.

"I care about..."

Jace's words trailed off as I slowly opened the curtain and gazed into his beautiful eyes.

He stood there looking shocked and confused as I reached out and grabbed his hand. I slowly trailed my fingertips over his hand, as I looked him in the eye. He was so beautiful. Inside and out.

Not a word was spoken as he stepped into the shower, still wearing his briefs and placed his hands on my face. His hands trembled as he slowly ran a finger down to my lip and bit his own. "You're so fucking beautiful," he breathed. "I want you to be happy. I want to make you happy."

WAKE UP CALL
VICTORIA ASHLEY

My heartbeat skyrocketed and my legs became weak as he leaned in and pressed his tender lips against mine. His touch was so sensual and the taste of his mouth was sweeter than sugar, causing me to run my tongue over his lips to get a better taste.

I watched, holding my breath, as the water dripped over his perfect body, soaking the briefs that he still wore. It turned me on.

The whole room suddenly spun around us as my hands trailed over his bare chest, rubbing his smooth flesh, before resting on the outside of his wet briefs. The feel of his hardness made me moan.

I felt my body start to shake uncontrollably as he gripped my wet hips and swung me toward the back wall, with passion in his eyes.

We both let out a low moan as he pressed me into the shower wall and roughly bit my bottom lip. "Are you sure that you're ready for this?" he questioned running his hands up my face.

I silently shook my head as I reached down and gripped his wet briefs in my small hand. Everything inside of me wanted to yank them off and toss them at the wall. To get a piece of him.

I stood there frozen in thought. Then suddenly my whole body shook with pleasure as Jace grabbed my hands, looked me in the eye and helped me strip him of his briefs. I was terrified of what was about to happen, but the sight of him naked was the most beautiful thing in the world. A moment that my eyes would never be able to forget.

Everything around me became silent and suddenly the only thing that I could focus on was the rapid beating of our hearts.

I stood there motionless and frozen in time before Jace grabbed my legs and wrapped them around his waist. He leaned into me, pressing his bare skin against mine. I got chills. "I don't want you to ever forget this moment," he breathed, running his lips over my neck. "I know I never will."

I knew that it would be a moment that I would never be able to forget. Every moment with Jace was something that I could never forget and something that I would never wanted to forget.

I shook my head, biting my lip as my eyes trailed over the smooth curves of everyone one of his perfect muscles, taking in the beauty of his body art. To me, jace was art and everything beautiful in the world.

WAKE UP CALL
VICTORIA ASHLEY

He moaned into my mouth as he took a piece of me. The one piece that I was able to give.

~•~

An hour later we were both dressed and on the road to finding my mother. Although, I was scared and nervous, the thought of being with Jace, managed to keep a grin on my face. Sure, I had experienced sex before, but nothing like that. I had never felt such happiness in my entire life and he made me feel things that I never thought to be possible. It was both a good and bad thing.

"Avery."

Jace's deep voice broke me from my thoughts as I turned away from the window and smiled. He looked so calm. "Yes." I smiled while twirling my finger in my hair.

The look on his handsome face was of pure happiness and I couldn't help, but to smile even bigger. "No matter what happens today with your mother I will always be there for you. I have been from the very beginning. Nothing will ever change that." He reached over and grabbed my hand, intertwining his fingers with mine, causing me to smile.

I glanced down at our hands and felt a wave of relief. His touch was so comforting.

Jace had been nothing, but truthful from the beginning and I couldn't see any reason to not trust him anymore.

I turned my head to look back out the window and rested my cheek against the hard, cold glass. It sent chills down my spine, but Jace's touch was enough to keep me warm. "Thank you," I paused to swallow. "For everything. For giving me a place to stay, for giving me a job-"

"I think you've already thanked me enough." He grinned. "That little thing that you do..." I laughed as Jace bit his bottom lip. "That was hot."

I flushed with embarrassment as I pictured it all in my head. I had to admit that I did have a few special moves, but nothing compared to the way that Jace made me feel. I'd gotten so weak in the knees that I'd almost fallen a few times. I had Jace to thank for being there to catch me.

WAKE UP CALL
VICTORIA ASHLEY

The car became quiet as the hospital came into view. *West View Hospital* was written on the front of the brick building. The sight was enough to make me feel sick from nerves.

My hand tightened around Jace's as he pulled into the parking lot and began to search for a parking space.

Jace noticed my rough squeeze and slowly ran his fingers over mine to help calm me down.

Suddenly, his touch wasn't quite enough to silence my racing heart. Somewhere in that building, my mother was close to death or possibly already dead. I hadn't the slightest clue how to act.

After what seemed like ages, Jace pulled the car into a spot in the middle of the parking lot and shifted the car into park. He turned off the engine and then turned around to face me. His eyes were full of concern. "This is it. Let's hope that Caleb wasn't lying to us," he paused. "I would hate to have to kick his ass. Well actually, no I wouldn't."

I pressed my hands to my head and shook my head. I'd never even thought about that.

I nervously ran my hands through my hair and leaned back into the seat. "Do you think that he would just make this all up? Give us a bogus address?" I started to panic at the thought.

Jace clenched his jaw and flared his nostrils. "The thought has come to mind, yes." He looked out the window and studied the brick building. "I didn't want to say anything because I wanted to have good faith for you. You deserve this."

I looked over at him and rubbed my forehead. "What's this?" I questioned.

A pained expression crossed his face as he reached for the door. "A happy ending," he said softly. "Let's go."

I carefully stepped out of the car and followed beside Jace, being sure to not fall as he grabbed for my hand and pulled me closer to him.

The cool wind hit us hard as we walked to the building and stepped inside. The numbing smell of Alcohol swabs and sickness hit me so hard that I felt nauseous and suddenly wanted to faint. I'd always hated hospital visits.

I was so nervous that I had to keep my eyes on the ground the whole way into the hospital and even up to the third floor, where my mother was. I was too afraid of falling over if I were to look anywhere else but there.

WAKE UP CALL
VICTORIA ASHLEY

When we stepped out of the elevator and onto the third floor, a dark haired woman in purple scrubs greeted us. She stood up from her desk and leaned into the counter. "How can I help you, folks, today?" she questioned with a friendly smile.

Jace lightly rubbed my back as he pushed me closer to the counter. "It's okay," he whispered.

I took a deep breath and leaned into Jace for support. "Yes. I am looking for my mother." I paused to look up at the friendly woman. "Joyce Hale."

The woman's expression turned frightened as she turned away and looked down at her desk. "I'm sorry ma'am, but she's not taking any visitors."

My heart sank. I was filled with mixed emotions. Happy that my mother was actually there, but sad that I wasn't even allowed to see her. I didn't understand. "Why not? Is she going to be okay?" I blurted out, not caring who was around to hear me.

The woman took a seat in her brown leather chair and nervously tapped her pencil on the desk. "I'm not allowed to give out that information," she said coldly. "Please don't ask any further questions.

I stepped closer to the desk. "But you don't-"

"Please leave." The woman cut in. She threw her arms up and then pretended to be busy. "I have work to do."

I stood there frozen in place as she typed away on her little computer. I wanted to scream.

Jace stepped forward and placed his hands on the front of the woman's desk. "Listen here ma'am," he said stiffly. "That woman that you are keeping from us is her mother. She has the right to see that she is going to live. Now why don't you just call for someone more important than yourself so that I can have a little chat with them."

The woman looked frightened as she reached for the stained phone and called for help. "I need some assistance please." She looked up at Jace and backed her chair further away. "Make it fast." She hung up the phone and stared and both Jace and I. "I'm only doing what I was told."

Jace let out a frustrated breath and smiled at the lady. "I understand that ma'am. What you don't understand is how important this is to her." He pointed back in my direction and grabbed my hand. "And myself. We must see her."

WAKE UP CALL
VICTORIA ASHLEY

The woman's expression softened as she picked up the phone again. She stared between Jace and me before pressing the phone to her ear. "Cancel that please." The woman hung up the phone and stood up from her desk. "Please follow me. I shouldn't be doing this."

Jace and I followed the woman down the brightly lit hall and stopped when she stood frozen outside one of the rooms. *328* was written in black lettering on the old oak door.

My heart sank as I looked to my right to see the door across the hall was fully open. A woman in about her mid-twenties sat in a chair with a cloth wrapped around her bruised and swollen face. She smiled weakly before I managed to turn my head away. I felt weak once again. Was that what my mother would look like?

The nurse placed her back against the door and huffed. "Look. I don't believe that you two had anything to do with this, but this woman was barely breathing when she arrived. We were lucky to get her steady. She has been here for three days and no one has come to visit or has called. I'm only trying to protect her, "she whispered. "We have no idea who did this to her."

A tear slowly rolled down my cheek when I realized the pain and suffering that my mother had to of gone through. I wanted that animal to suffer for hurting her. No one deserved what my mother had gone through. "I know who did it," I barely choked out.

The woman's eyes went wide as she reached for the handle and shook her head. "And you're willing to tell us?" she questioned. "There's a chance that if this person gets caught that they can go to prison for attempted murder.

Jace looked at me and ran his hand over my cheek for support. "You both deserve this. You have to protect her... before it's too late."

I reached up and gripped Jace's arm. "My father," I growled while gripping my hair in anger. "Henry Hale. He's a piece of shit," I sobbed. "I should have stayed. I could have helped-"

"No you shouldn't have," Jace cut in. "You did what you had to do. If you stayed, then this could've been you."

"No, Jace," I screamed. "I could have helped her. You don't understand. He did this to her to get me back. When I was around, he took most of his anger out on me. I left..." I cried out. "It's my entire fault."

The woman placed her hand over her mouth in surprise as Jace grabbed my face and pulled my forehead to his. "Don't you sit here and punish yourself," he growled. "Don't do this, Avery."

I pushed Jace away from me with all of my force. It didn't matter what he said. I knew that it was all my fault. His words wouldn't help this time.

I walked over to the door, placed both of my shaky hands on it, and stared at it. I felt helpless once again. "I was so selfish. She has to hate me now," I whispered mostly to myself. I ran my hand over the wooden door and choked back a sob.

I felt Jace's hand grip my shoulder before suddenly being jerked away from the door and pressed into Jace's chest. He wrapped both of his arms around me as he pressed his face to the top of my head. "I won't let you beat yourself up for this." He pulled my hair from out of my face and looked me in the eye. "What you did was brave. You did the best thing that you could do. You couldn't have protected neither one of you. He's a dangerous man."

The nurse stared at us both looking lost. Finally, she turned on her heels and started walking away with anger. "I'm reporting that man," she mumbled. "He's not getting away with this."

We both watched in silence as the woman hurried down the hall, almost tripping over her own two feet. I bet they'd be surprised to see that he got what was coming to him already. Most of it at least.

Jace reached down and pressed his lips to my forehead. They were warm and soft to the touch. It helped to calm the shivers that were running all through my body.

"Are you ready for this? He nodded at the door. "We have no idea what's behind that door."

I swallowed hard and then reached for the brass knob. "No," I mumbled. I gently turned the knob and pushed the door open. What I saw in front of me was frightening. Almost unrecognizable.

My mother lay in the oversized bed full of bandages and tubes hooked up to multiple machines. Bruises covered her once beautiful face and half of it was swollen beyond recognition. Her raven hair curled around her bandages and you could still see traces of blood that never got washed out. The sight made me sick.

"Mother," I cried out.

Her eyes shot open, but she didn't move.

My breathing became heavy as I stood there waiting for a sign from my mother. Her blue eyes, swollen and bruised, struggled to stay open as she lifted her head and groaned out in pain.

My mind spun as I stood there watching her in silence waiting for her next move. She didn't attempt to move though. Instead, she just closed her eyes and exhaled as she rested her head back down onto the pillow.

I held my breath and reached for Jace's hand for comfort as it lightly brushed against mine, sending chills up my arm. The feel of his soft skin made me remember to breathe again. If it wasn't for Jace's support then I would have fallen over in a weeping mess. There was no way that I could have done it without him.

"It's okay, Avery." Jace whispered. "You have to show her that you're here to support her no matter what." He gently kissed my forehead and gave me a slight push to get me going. "I'll be right beside you."

I slowly made my way over to the huge bed with Jace following close behind, but stopped before I got too close. I had no idea what I was going to say and I was honestly terrified.

I glanced beside me and smiled over at Jace as he stood there looking calm and relaxed, arms crossed over his chest as he smiled back. He seemed so put together and confident. How could he manage to be so perfect?

"Mother- I... I'm-"

"Avery," My mother cut me off, her voice weak. "Are you really here?" She whispered.

My heart raced as the sound of my name. It sent chills down my spine and reminded me of how much I had actually missed her in the last year. I didn't realize it until that moment, but I did. I missed the good times that we had. As few of times as there were, they made a difference in my life.

"I'm here," I whispered. A tear rolled down my cheek as my mother's hand reached out for mine. It was pale and badly bruised. It reminded me too much of my father and I had to fight the urge to not break down. It was enough to see my dad a bloody mess, but now my mother. It was all too much for me.

WAKE UP CALL
VICTORIA ASHLEY

My mother's hand was ice cold as she wrapped her fingers around mine and softly rubbed her thumb over my hand. "I'm so sorry," she cried. "Shit, Avery. I messed up. I really messed up." My mother struggled to open her eyes as she pulled me closer and wrapped her arm around my neck. "I'm the worst mother in the world. I should have been there for you," she breathed. "I never thought I'd see you again."

I fought back the tears that were threatening to form as I looked into her eyes and gripped her other hand. I hadn't expected an apology and my emotions were running wild. She had hurt me a lot in the past, but she'd had her good times as well. Maybe none of that was important anymore.

Since meeting Jace I had begun to realize that looking back was only going to keep me down. Starting fresh and working on being happy was the only thing left to do. "The past doesn't matter anymore," I whispered. "I'm here for you. I won't leave you again." I squeezed her hand and leaned in closer.

Suddenly my arms wrapped around her frail body and the both of us just let it all out. All of the hate, the hurt and the frustration that has kept us back for so long.

The tears rushed out and I felt a sense of relief. I felt safe there in her arms with Jace by our side. I could tell that by the way she held me that she felt safe for the first time in a long time as well. Maybe even, for the first time since she had met my father. It made my heart ache to think about it.

I didn't understand how she had gone through so much hurt and for so long. Maybe my father wasn't always a monster. Maybe he was good once and she was holding on to the hope and memories.

After a few minutes of silence, I felt Jace's hand on my back. His touch was supportive and gentle. It reminded me that he was there for me and he wasn't going anywhere. That thought alone was enough to make me smile. He was the light in the dark when I needed it the most and that moment was now.

I pulled away from my mother when she groaned out in pain again. I didn't even realize how much pressure I was putting on her. I was just happy to be close to her and I didn't want to let go. I had imagined the moment that my mother and I could let go of our fears and be close my entire life. I wasn't ready for the moment to end. "I'm sorry. I'm just happy that you're safe." I smiled, but felt bad for hurting her.

Jace rushed over and grabbed the back of my mother's head for support as she attempted to lie back down and get comfortable. "There you go." He smiled as he pulled the blanket up to cover her shoulders and then brushed the hair from out of her face. "Can I get you anything? Just relax, Joyce."

My mother looked a little confused at first, but managed to smile when she realized that Jace was with me. "Thank you. Um..." She paused searching for a name.

"The name is Jace ma'am," he said softly. "It's nice to meet you."

Seeing Jace being so polite and caring made my heart pound. I was amazed. *How does he do this to me?* He had everything that any woman could ever dream of in a man and yet there he was next to me.

Jace stood next to the bed and placed his hand on my shoulder. "Maybe I should give you two some alone time. I'll be out in the hall." He smiled down at my mother as she reached for his hand and squeezed it.

"Thank you," she whispered, looking him over. "I've never seen her look so... alive."

Jace nodded his head, a look of pain in his eyes, and then left the room.

It was silent as I sat there on the edge of the hospital bed. The temperature seemed to drop as soon as Jace left the room and it left me feeling cold and lost.

Should I tell her about my scumbag father? How would she react? Would she hate me? After watching her lay there in the bed with her eyes closed, curled up into a ball, I decided that it was probably better to wait. She had already been through enough and she deserved just a little moment of peace. I didn't want to be the one to ruin that for her.

I jumped out of thought at the sound of my mother's voice. I was so lost in thought that I hadn't even heard what she said.

"Avery?" She tried again. "Are you okay?"

"Huh?" I mumbled looking into her eyes.

My mother reached out and ran a hand over my face. "What happened to your eye?" she questioned. "Who hurt you?"

Shit! Please just drop it.

"I said what happened to your eye?" She sounded angry as she leaned back on her elbow and sat up. "Who did that?"

I turned my head away from her vision and pushed myself away from the bed. I didn't need her asking any questions. All of the answers would lead to her piece of shit husband and how Jace put him in the hospital. "It's not important." I smiled and squeezed her hand. "Get some rest and I'll be out in the hall with Jace..."

I got ready to walk away, but her arm reached out and gripped mine before I could manage to get away. "It was your father, wasn't it?" She squeezed my arm and a tear fell down her face. "Answer me," she screamed. "I need to know. Where is he?"

"It was-"

My words cut off as the door swung open and Jace rushed into the room with the nurse following close behind. Their presence seemed to shake us both up, causing our bodies to shake uncontrollably as we both looked up and studied the sight in front of us.

The nurse stood in the corner of the room as Jace nervously ran his hands through his hair. *I don't like this.*

Jace eyed my mother's hand with concern, as she squeezed it and took a step closer to us. "Is everything okay, Avery?" he asked cautiously.

"No," my mother muttered. "Where did this come from?" She pointed at my face and took a deep breath. "I know you guys saw him. Did he come for her?"

Jace bit his lip and turned to look at the nurse. "It's best that you step in now." He walked over to the wall and placed his head into his arm. He looked scared.

The nurse nervously played with her shirt collar as she eyed the gray linoleum flooring. "Ma'am your husband," she paused to swallow. "He died a few hours ago. I'm sorry," she breathed. "I'll be back to discuss the details a bit later. Get some rest." The nurse looked at me with a look of relief and then left the room. I knew that she felt he deserved death after what he had done to my mother, but what would my mother feel?

The look on my mother's face was of pure shock. All of the color drained out of her face and she looked as if she couldn't breathe. "What," she whispered. "This can't be happening." She looked around the room in silence before she set her eyes on me.

The fire in her eyes made my heart stop. I knew what was coming next. "What happened to him? You better answer me," she growled.

Jace stepped away from the wall and walked over to stand next to me. He protectively placed his arm in front of me and faced my mother. "It wasn't her fault." He looked down at me and cupped my face as I broke down in tears. "It wasn't your fault. Do you hear me?" He shook my face and then pressed me into his chest.

"I'm sorry," I cried. "I didn't mean for any of this to happen. I just wanted to stay away from him. He came after me. I didn't want him dead."

My mother sat up in the bed and squeezed the white sheet until the color drained from her knuckles. "What did you do, Avery?" she spat. "Please just tell me. I can't live without him." she sobbed into her hand. "Please."

I looked up at Jace not knowing what to do. I couldn't tell her the truth or she'd hate Jace and blame everything on him. Maybe even press charges and get him arrested. I couldn't let that happen. As much as it hurt, Jace was only protecting me.

I got ready to speak, but Jace silenced me by placing his finger to my mouth.

"It was me. I did it." He paused to look me in the eye. "I don't regret protecting you and I would do it all again if it means your safety. You deserve to be safe. I want to do that." He ran his thumb over my cheek and turned back to face my mother. He somehow managed to keep his calm. I wasn't for sure, but I was guessing it was for my sake.

"I didn't mean for it to go as far as it did, but when I walked in on them he was choking her. She couldn't breathe and I couldn't let him hurt her anymore. It was an accident."

My mother's mouth dropped open and she sat there looking surprised. She looked between the both of us and then pointed for the door, her hand shaking. "I need you to leave. The both of you." She threw her hands to her face and shook it back and forth. "Now!" She screamed.

My heart ached to reach out and hold her. I wanted to feel like I did a few minutes before. When she actually loved me and was happy to see me. Now it was gone. I was losing my mother again. "I'm sorry. Please-"

WAKE UP CALL
VICTORIA ASHLEY

"Just go," she screamed as she wiped at her face. "Please. I need to be alone."

Jace gripped my waist as my knees gave out on me. He pulled me close to him and walked me toward the door. "We need to give her some space. We'll be back." He grabbed my face and looked me in the eye. "Everything will be okay. I'm here for you."

I looked back at my mother right before we reached the door. Her face was pressed into the pillow that was now covered in her tears and drops of blood from the scabs that covered the side of her neck. She looked pathetic and weak once again.

My father always managed to do that to her. He still somehow managed to do that even in his death. To the both of us. He really was a monster.

Now what?

Chapter 15

An hour later, Jace and I were on the road once again and heading back to Jace's place. My mother refused to see us or even the nurse again and I knew that nothing would change her mind.

Thoughts of my father now poisoned my mother's every thoughts and that was a powerful enough thing to make her blind to the situation. It would be no use to try to gain her forgiveness. Not now. Only time would be able to heal the damage done. Even then, there was only a slight chance for forgiveness.

My swollen eyes wandered out the passenger side window as the nurse's words replayed repeatedly in my head. They were words that I never expected and that I would never be able to forget.

"Avery, your father has been battling cancer for over thirteen years now. His body has been shutting down slowly and all of the drinking has finally taken him down. He was admitted to the hospital earlier today after being attacked in an alleyway. It was then that they noticed the cancer had taken its toll. There was nothing that anyone could do to save him. He did this to himself. He was an addict."

"Avery." Jace's deep voice called out.

I slowly reached up, hands shaking as I wiped the tears from off my puffy cheeks. Then I turned to face him, keeping my eyes glued to my hands that were now moist from the tears that wouldn't seem to stop falling.

"Are you okay?" he questioned. His emerald eyes looked dark as they scanned mine and then set back on the road. "Would you like me to stop somewhere? We can take a rest and get something to eat."

My stomach growled at just the thought of food, but I knew that keeping any food down wouldn't be an option at the moment. "No," I whispered. "I'm not hungry. I just want some rest."

I leaned into the black leather seat and closed my eyes. I had no idea that my father had cancer and the thought made me sick. I had a feeling that not even my mother knew. All of those years he'd kept that huge secret to himself. One that had probably been eating at him and tearing him apart bit by bit as he died a little more each and every day.

Every day he had to live with the pain and face the fact that he was dying. Maybe he couldn't face the fact. Maybe that's why he was never sober. He turned to drugs and alcohol to numb the pain. That was why my mother stayed. She did know the good side at one point. She spent her life waiting for the good Henry to return. The one that at one time possibly adored her and maybe even myself. I was going to be sick.

"Stop the car!" I threw my hand to my mouth as the vomit threatened to spew through my parted lips. "Stop!"

Jace quickly pulled the car over and jumped out of the car right as I managed to swing my door open and fall out on my knees. The hard gravel dug into my bony knees as the world spun around me and the vomit escaped through my parted lips. The only thing that kept me sane was the feel of Jace's strong hand rubbing the back of my head. Nothing else in the world seemed to make sense at the moment. He was the only thing that seemed real to me. The only thing keeping me alive.

"I'm sorry... I'm sorry," I cried. "I should have stayed with you. I did this. Everything is my fault." I brought my knees to my chin and rocked back and forth, as he continued to rub my head. "I left to keep you safe and I still managed to mess things up. I'm nothing but a-"

"No," he whispered. "None of this was your fault. You had no control over your father or your mother for that matter. You have been through so much and it's time for you to move on. This is your chance." He pulled me into his arms and fell down on the ground next to me. "This is what it feels like to be loved," he swallowed. "Let me get you home."

I stared up at him in confusion as he jumped to his feet, helped me up and back into the car. All of the color drained from his usually tanned face as he wiped the ass of his jeans off and gently reached over to buckle me in. I wanted to question what he had just meant, but I couldn't seem to form any words. Not the ones that I wanted to at least. "Okay," I whispered. Thank you."

He looked down at me while chewing on his lip in frustration. He looked as if he had something to say, but decided against it at last minute. Then without another word, he jogged to his side of the car and jumped in.

We arrived back at Jace's house to find a little silver Honda now sitting in the driveway. Jace's eyes went wide as we pulled up behind the car and Jace nervously slammed the car into park. He looked lost as his eyes focused on the figure that now sat on his front porch. It was too dark to tell, but I was almost positive that it was a woman.

"It's my sister," he whispered. "She hasn't come to my house in over three years. There has to be something wrong." He ran his hands through his hair and exhaled. "Shit."

I sat there frozen in place as he jumped out of the car and hurried over to his sister. They both stood there in silence before Jackie threw her frail arms around Jace and he pulled her into his arms. I could see Jackie's body shaking as she fell to her knees and gripped his shirt. The sight in front of me brought me to tears. I could tell even from far away that they were both crying.

I never in my life had seen a man cry and it broke my heart to pieces. Jace was the strongest person that I knew and to see him cry crushed me. He really did have the biggest heart in the world. First, he was there to take care of me and now his sister. He had to have a heart of steel to be so strong.

I waited in the car until Jace looked my direction and nodded his head.

He smiled as I stepped out of the car, popped a piece of gum in my mouth and walked over to stand in front of him and

Jackie. "Go on inside and get some rest." He kissed his sister on the forehead and watched as she smiled at me and headed inside. She looked as if she had been crying for days. Her cheeks were swollen and red and she could barely even open her eyes. By looking at her, you would think that she hadn't slept in over a week. Jace really had his hands full with the both us.

I stood there feeling lost, but somewhat relieved as the door softly shut behind Jackie. Jace peered over his left shoulder to look at me. He nodded his head and then walked over to lean against the porch. His eyes scanned mine as he played with his leather jacket. "She left him, Avery." He let out a small grunt and then smiled. "She actually left that piece of shit." He looked down at the ground and a tear fell from his face. He didn't even try to hide it.

My heart raced as I ran over to him and threw my arms around him. For the first time in a long time, I was thinking about someone other than myself. "Don't cry," I breathed, wanting nothing more than to comfort him. "I don't like to see you look so..."

Jace looked up and cupped my face. "What?" he pushed.

I hid my face in his chest and gripped his jacket. I didn't want him to see my face. "Sad," I replied. "It makes me..."

"It makes you what," he whispered, "Tell me."

"It makes me sad and breaks my heart. Okay," I muttered. "It fucking hurts me to see you sad." I looked up into his eyes as his grip suddenly tightened around me. It gave me chills.

The look on his face was unreadable as he leaned forward and softly brushed his lips against mine. "That's how I feel about you every day." He pressed his soft lips to mine and then slowly pulled away. "My heart aches for you every day, but that won't keep me away. I wouldn't stop the suffering because I welcome the pain." He crushed his lips back to mine, causing me to lose my breath as I kissed him back with force.

A moan escaped my parted lips as I placed my hands to his stiff chest and squeezed. His heart pounded heavily against my open palm as he lifted me off the ground and set me down on the railing. He forcefully pressed his body between my legs and gripped the back of my hair with both hands.

I felt like I was falling, but I wasn't afraid. I had Jace there to save me. "You do something to me," I moaned against his lips.

He smiled and ran his finger over my bottom lip. "You do something to me too. Something that I'll never be able to explain..."

His words trailed off as he kissed me again while fighting to catch his breath. His breathing was heavy and forced as he placed his hand to my chest and reached for my hand with his free one. "This is the only way to explain what you do to me." He firmly pressed my hand against his chest to reveal the heavy beating of his heart.

I had felt it earlier, but it was beating much faster and harder at the moment, making me feel weak.

Seeing him, standing there so vulnerable and open made him sexy. Everything from the sultry look on his face mixed with pain to the way that his chest looked in his fitted black T-shirt screamed 'sexy'. In that moment, I wanted him.

"I want you," I moaned, rubbing my hand over his chest. "Every part of you."

Jace froze momentarily before his hands snaked under my ass as he picked me up and forced me to wrap my legs around his waist.

His body felt nice and firm underneath mine and I liked it. I never wanted to let go. I squeezed my thighs tighter around him for support as he carried me through the warm house and into my old bedroom. He gently placed me down on the bed and yanked his jacket and T-shirt off. He stood there shirtless with every defined muscle flexing as he fought to breathe. "Anything that you want is yours," he said huskily. "All you have to do is take it."

My heart pounded heavily as I reached out and gripped the waist of Jace's faded jeans. I unbuttoned his jeans with one hand while running the other one up his tight stomach. Suddenly touching him wasn't even enough. I had to get a taste to satisfy my burning hunger. "I need you, Jace."

Jace smoothly stepped out of his jeans before he crawled onto the bed and hovered above me, his bare chest heaving above my face. "I'm already yours," he moaned.

I snaked my arms around his waist as I slowly ran my tongue over his every muscle. He tasted salty, but sweet against my tongue.

WAKE UP CALL
VICTORIA ASHLEY

His stomach flexed as he watched my every move. Then suddenly he stripped me of my clothing and pulled me on top of him. I wanted him more now than ever. "You're beautiful," I moaned into his lips.

A smirk crossed his face before he took control of me, giving me the greatest pleasure I have ever known. The second time was somehow even better than the first. I had a feeling that it would only get better from there.

~•~

I awoke in the middle of the night to an empty bed. The room felt colder than it had before, but somehow I was covered in sweat. I felt down, shook up from the earlier events, and didn't want to be alone. Jackie was sleeping in his room and it made me wonder where he could've gone.

I crawled out of bed and threw on a pair of sweats and an old T-shirt. I sauntered down the dark hall and stopped when I heard voices in the kitchen. Jace and Jackie were sitting in the kitchen drinking tea. Feeling as if I might have interrupted, I spun on my heel ready to head back to the room. "I'm sorry," I choked out.

Jackie and Jace both stood up and smiled. Jackie waved me over and pulled out a chair next to her. "No. Please join us," she said in a soft voice. "Jace was just telling me about you."

Jace's face turned red as he bit his bottom lip and took a sip of his tea. "Sit down. Let me get you some tea." He shook his head at Jackie and then reached for a mug. "Sorry if we woke you."

I grabbed the mug from out of his hand and took the seat next to Jackie. Sipping the tea, I looked between the both of them. "It's fine. It wasn't you guys. I was just having trouble sleeping," I admitted.

Jace walked over to me and kissed me on the forehead. His soft lips lingered for a moment as he rubbed the back of my head. "I'm sorry. I wish that I could take back-"

"Jace." A smile spread across Jackie's pale face as she watched her brother's movements. "I wish that I had what you guys do."

Jace and I both looked over at her with confused looks.

"What!" She grinned. "I'm not blind. I can see that you guys love each other. Joe never truly loved me. I know this."

Jace swallowed hard as he reached out and poked his sister in the rib. "You should get some sleep." His jaw clenched. "You need to gain your strength back."

My heart skipped a beat as I glanced around the kitchen and then set my eyes back on Jace and his sister goofing off. *That's what love and family should be like.*

"Um... Maybe I'll go back to bed." I felt so confused. Why did my heart beat that way when she said that Jace and I love each other?

I stood up, but Jace placed his hand on my shoulder to make me sit back down.

"You should finish that tea first. You need something in your stomach." He glared over at his sister and rubbed his hand over his forehead. "Good night, Jackie." He laughed and nudged her in the side again.

Jackie looked back and forth between the both of us and laughed. Her face looked slightly better from earlier and she seemed to be doing okay. Jace managed to give us both hope. "Good night, kids." She stood up from the table and made her way back to Jace's room.

The room was silent once we were alone. It was a silence that made my heart race and palms sweat. I had never been so nervous.

Finally, breaking the silence, Jace set his mug in the sink and reached for my hand. "Let's get some sleep. I'll explain everything about my sister tomorrow."

I nodded my head in agreement and followed him back to bed. It felt good to have him back by my side. It made me...happy.

Chapter 16

I groggily made my way through the hallway and into the kitchen, which smelled of freshly cooked pancakes and syrup. A small smile spread across my face as I spotted Jace standing in front of the stove, spatula in hand, as he peered over his shoulder at me and smiled.

"Good morning, beautiful," he said softly. "Did you sleep well?"

My eyes wandered down to the kitchen table to see that it was set up for breakfast for three. In the middle of the table sat a plate of pancakes, corn beef hash and bacon. It looked and smelled absolutely delicious. It made my mouth water, even though I knew I wouldn't be able to stomach it.

"As well as I could manage," I replied softly. "I had a headache from hell that wouldn't seem to go away."

Jace gave me an apologetic look as he dropped the spatula on the stove and exhaled. "I'm sorry. I should have asked if you needed anything last night." He stepped over to me and wrapped his arms around my waist. "Is the headache gone? I can run to the store and grab-"

"No, I'm fine," I cut in trying to sound as believable as possible. "I'm all better now."

I smiled up in a daze at his sexy lips before pulling his face down so that it they brushing against mine. Our foreheads rested against each other's as my hands cupped his face causing us both to breathe heavier.

"Oh... I like this," Jace whispered against my lips. His hands tightened around my waist as he pulled me closer. "This makes me want you so bad," he growled, gripping my thigh.

My body couldn't fight the urge any longer. I had no control over my actions in the presence of Jace. He had me in a trance and I wasn't willing to fight back.

My lips eagerly crushed his causing us both to stumble into the stove behind Jace, almost knocking over the pan of sausage in the process.

Luckily, Jace reached out in just enough time to catch it before it could happen to fall. "Crap!"

"Whoa there!" Jackie called out. "Let's not burn the house down." She laughed, placing a hand to her temple. "This headache is kicking my ass."

We both looked over at Jackie as she brushed her black locks out of her face and pulled out a chair to sit in. The bruising had decreased significantly over night, making her face look much better than before.

"Morning, Jackie."

Jace watched Jackie as she continued to rub her head. "You're looking really good. I'm guessing that you slept well." He strolled over to the table and kissed Jackie on the forehead before pulling out a chair for me to sit in. "I hope that you're both hungry."

I nodded my head at Jackie and then took the seat between the two of them. Somehow, being in the middle of them made me nervous and at a loss for words.

The room stayed quiet while we enjoyed the well-cooked breakfast that Jace provided for us.

It took me a while to stomach the food, but I managed to put everything out of my mind and try to enjoy the first good meal that I'd had in days. I had to admit that it felt nice being there with Jace and his sister. It almost felt like a real family. One that I'd never had.

"So Avery," Jackie paused to smile. "I hear that you live here with my brother. That's great because I've been worried about him being lonely. I'm happy that you're here."

WAKE UP CALL
VICTORIA ASHLEY

Oh shit! I cursed myself realizing that I forgot to tell Jace about the apartment that I got. Not only that, but I also failed to mention the new job.

I looked nervously between Jackie and Jace as they stared at me waiting for a response. I swallowed hard and glanced back down at my half-empty plate feeling lost.

Jace's eyes went wide as he shifted in his seat and grabbed my hand. "Is everything alright?"

I took a deep breath and leaned back in my chair. "I have something to tell you." My heart pounded uncontrollably at the thought of being away from Jace.

Suddenly, I just couldn't do it. I couldn't tell him about the apartment. "I found a new job," I swallowed back the lump in my throat. "I'm supposed to start tomorrow morning."

The look on Jace's face was of pure hurt as he forked his pancakes and swallowed. "A new job," he mumbled. "Where at?" he asked looking back up.

I couldn't stand to look Jace in the eye at the moment. I felt sick to my stomach for making him feel the way that I knew he felt. I could see the hurt all over his face.

"It's at a little pizza restaurant called 'Jan's Place.' It would be Mondays, Tuesdays and Saturdays from ten o'clock a.m. until around six o'clock p.m. She wasn't quite sure of the hours," I said nervously.

Jace smiled and squeezed my hand, but the smile didn't reach his eyes. "I've been there plenty of times. Jan is a loyal customer of mine. A little hard to get along with, but you'll do fine."

He looked over at Jackie and nodded at her. "Maybe Jackie could fill in on those days for you at the diner and you could still work with us on Thursdays and Sundays."

Jackie looked taken aback as she looked up from her plate and looked between the two of us. "I... um... I don't know Jace," she mumbled, looking away.

Jace swiftly reached across the table and grabbed for his sister's hand. "This can be a new start for you. You can sleep here until we can get you a place and you can work in the diner. You never have to see Joe again." He squeezed Jackie's hand as a tear rolled down her cheek. "I promise you that things will get better. I love you." He turned his face away as if to hide it.

WAKE UP CALL
VICTORIA ASHLEY

The look on Jackie's face matched the screaming of my heart. Hearing those words come out of Jace's mouth had my heart aching. It sounded like the sweetest and most sincere thing that I'd ever heard in my entire life. It pained me to know that I'd never known those words.

Jackie's face scrunched up as the tears poured out uncontrollably. You could see that she was fighting as hard as she could to hide it, but it was no use. Jace had a way of making you feel everything. There was no hiding. "I feel so lost right now," she cried. "Why do I miss him so much?"

Jace jumped up from the table and ran over to his sister's side. He placed both of his hands on her face and squeezed it. "You don't. You just think that you do. Your body and mind is programmed to think that you miss him. What you miss is always knowing that you had someone to go home to." He shook her as she began to shake her head back and forth. "Trust me. You can still have that. You have Avery and me now. You don't need him."

Jace's words froze Jackie in her place. Her body loosened up as she took a deep breath and turned around to face me. "I trust you, Jace. I can see it in her eyes too. You've got a good woman here."

My mind was in complete shock as Jackie made her way past Jace and threw her arms around me. I sat there for a moment not knowing what to do. I felt like running, but a big part of me felt as if I could cry. I didn't do either. I just sat there stiff as a statue.

Finally, Jackie pulled away with a sad smile on her face. "I'm going to take a shower and find some clean clothes. Thank you for breakfast." With that she walked away leaving Jace and I alone in the kitchen.

Jace waited for Jackie to leave before he walked over and squatted down in front of me. "Thank you," he whispered, rubbing my cheek.

I gave him a confused look while trying to put myself back together. "For what?" I questioned.

He smiled and ran a finger over my bottom lip giving me the chills. "For letting my sister hug you. I know that you don't like to be touched."

I turned my head away and bit my bottom lip. I never actually came out and told Jace that. He was a lot smarter than most people that I knew.

He slowly broke my walls down bit by bit and knew all of the right times to touch me.

"You figured that out." I smiled impressed. "You're perfect." The words left my mouth before I could stop them. I threw my hand over my mouth and hid my face, embarrassed by my confession.

Jace cupped my face and forced me to look at him. "Don't be afraid of your feelings. I want to know how you feel." He leaned in and pressed his lips against mine. "Go and get ready." He smiled, his eyes sincere. "There are some people that want to see you."

I wasn't surprised when we pulled up in front of diner. My stomach still managed to do a flip at just the sight of The Indy Go. It hadn't been that long since I had been there, but it had felt like a lifetime. I was nervous.

Jace pulled the keys out of the ignition and looked over at me with concentration. The look on his face looked as if he was trying to figure me out. "Are you okay with coming here?" he finally questioned.

I thought about it for a moment before I responded. "Yes."

As soon as Jace pulled open the door to the diner, Stacy, along with her loose blond curls were bouncing around in my face. She didn't waste time before she threw her tiny arms around me and pulled me in for a hug. It was probably the tightest hug that I had ever managed to survive. She was quite strong for being so small.

"Holy shit, Avery!" she squealed. "I was so worried that I would never see you again. I'm so sorry that I didn't see you leave." She pulled away, but not before planting a soft kiss on my forehead. She really had a way with making a person feel at home. If I had to admit it, I would say that I have grown to be quite fond of her.

I nodded my head and patted her on the back. The softness of her sweater made me feel cozy and comfortable.

I was so lost in the moment that I almost didn't even pay attention to the fact that there were about three more bodies surrounding us. "It's okay," I managed to say.

Before I could take another step, I noticed Dex, Winston and Maple standing in a circle in front of the counter. Winston stepped away first and made his way to stand in front of me. "It's good to see you again." He offered his hand for a shake and I took it without a second thought. It felt good to see them all again.

I smiled and brushed my hair from out of my face. "It's good to see you too. All of you." I looked around nodding my head. "It really is."

Jace grinned as he cupped my face and looked me in the eye. "No one is happier than I am at this moment. It feels like home here and it isn't complete without you here." His eyes softened before he pressed his lips against mine and rubbed the back of my head. "Welcome back."

Everyone in the room looked shocked as Jace pulled me next to him and kissed the top of my head. Everyone acted as if they'd never seen Jace be affectionate with a woman before.

He just ignored all of the looks and walked me over to the counter. His hand held onto mine as he grabbed Dex's shoulder with his other hand. "I owe you my life, man." He pulled Dex's face close to him and squeezed his shoulder. "Let me know if you ever need anything."

Dex's eyes lit up as he grabbed Jace's shoulder and smiled. "You've already done enough in the past. I owed you, bro."

Dex's eyes turned to me and he smiled. "I'm glad that you're okay. You're in good hands."

I nodded and smiled. "Thank you."

I couldn't help but to feel warm and tingly inside from all of the love that seemed to be going around the diner. The feeling was so overwhelming that it brought tears to my eyes. I wasn't used to this feeling and it had me very confused.

"Are you alright, dear?" Maple questioned concerned.

I slowly looked up while trying to hide my moist cheeks. "I'm fine. More than okay."

The room was silent as everyone stood there watching me. I felt like a freak show.

"Well everyone," Jace said breaking the silence. "We're going to take off."

Everyone said their goodbyes and we headed back to Jace's house.

I knew that at some point I was going to have to tell him that I was moving into my apartment in just a few days, but it just wasn't quite the right time.

When we arrived back at the house, Jackie was sitting on the floor with the game Yahtzee sitting in front of her. She looked up with tired eyes.

It looked as if she had been crying again, when we were gone. She forced a smile and patted the two spots beside her. "Remember when we used to play this game?" She looked up at Jace with a childish grin.

Jace grinned back before he sat down next to her and grabbed for the dice. "I do. I remember we used to stay up all night playing. Mom never cared, but when dad got home... he would yell until we put it away and went to bed. We were so in love with this game." He smiled over at me. "Sit."

Jackie looked up at me as if she was still waiting for me to join them. "Do you like this game, Avery?" She waited for an answer as I found my way to the floor and took a seat next to her.

I thought for a second before I answered. I knew that they would both probably laugh at me. I would have. "I've never played it." I grabbed for a piece of game paper and looked it over. "How do you play?"

Jace and Jackie both smiled at each other before explaining the rules to me. It was a lot easier than I thought it would be and the game was actually fun.

We spent the next couple of hours just laughing and talking while playing Yahtzee. We never had games at my house back when I was living with my parents. I knew the main reason for that was that they didn't want to take the time to teach anything to me. The thought made me sad, but it was never too late to learn.

Hours later, Jackie went to bed leaving us alone in the living room. I was tired as well, but didn't want to leave Jace's side. It felt good being so close to him and the thought of being alone made me sad. I just wasn't ready yet.

"Tell me what happened with Jackie," I whispered while leaning into his chest.

Jace squeezed me closer to him until my head was resting on his shoulder. He lightly kissed my head and then played with the ends of my hair.

"Jackie was a... is a good woman. She got mixed up with Joe sometime after my father left and my mother passed away a few years later. She was uncontrollable at the time and he took advantage of her. He fed her lies, drugs and anything else that he said would make her happy again. She believed it all." He paused and shook his head. "I've been trying ever since to get her back. She's a tough one. Even now I can't be sure that she will stay."

I swallowed the emotions that were forming as I reached up and touched his chest. It felt warm and firm under my fragile touch. He had been through so much and... alone. "What happened to your mother?" I asked suddenly wondering if I had taken it too far.

Jace's body stiffened for a moment as we sat there in silence. His heavy breathing made me nervous.

"She kind of lost it after my father left. She got addicted to antidepressants until eventually she gave up on everything and got sick. I took care of her for as long as I could." A tear fell from his face as he squeezed his eyes shut. "She didn't make it."

My heart pounded heavily in my chest as I pulled him as close to me as I could. It broke my heart to think about what he had gone through. He deserved so much better.

"I'm so sorry," I whispered. I didn't know what else to say. I knew that nothing would be able to take the pain away. Mine was always there.

Jace reached out with trembling hands and cupped my face, his emerald eyes burning into mine as he as he shifted to his knees and pulled in closer to his face. "Be with me, Avery," he whispered.

My throat closed up. I tried pulling away from his firm grip, but it was useless. I was weak and powerless when it came to looking into his eyes. I felt as if I was drowning. I was sinking further and further under the water and it was getting harder and harder to breathe.

Jace sat there breathing heavily, chest heaving up and down as he stared into my eyes, his eyes burning with passion.

"Avery, I love you," he said breathless.

Chapter 17

Unable to think clearly, I clumsily scrambled to my feet, hands tangled through my hair as I fought to catch my breath. My whole body was trembling now and I had many mixed emotions. I wasn't quite sure, but it sounded as if Jace had just confessed his love for me. Maybe I was hearing things.

"Avery," Jace whispered moving closer to me.

I looked up in a daze, but didn't utter a single word. I was speechless.

"Did you hear me?" His eyes searched mine.

I shook my head back and forth while slowly backing up against the wall. I carefully leaned against it for support as I tried to calm my spinning mind.

"Huh," I breathed. "I...um." I dropped to my knees and reached for the tear that was rolling down my cheek.

"Avery." Jace dropped to his knees in front of me and reached for my face, but I turned away from his grip. I couldn't handle the feel of his touch at the moment. It wouldn't allow me to think straight.

"What is wrong with you," he questioned, his voice soft. "I love you. Is that so wrong of me?"

I forced my eyes up to meet Jace's and suddenly I got slammed with so many emotions that I lost it. I couldn't handle the fact that he could throw those words around so easily when he knew that I had been through so much.

He couldn't love me. I didn't even know what those words meant. How could he love someone that didn't even know the meaning?

"How could you even say that," I mused. "You're going to look me right in the eye and lie to me. Are you trying to hurt me?" I stood to my feet and pointed at my chest. "Look at me," I screamed. "If you could see right through me. Then you would see that this is empty. How could you love someone like that?" I was sobbing now. Sobbing like a baby.

Jace forcefully gripped my wrist and pulled me against his chest. "Why won't you just let me love you?" A look of pain flashed in his eyes as he ran a finger over my cheek. "I have never in my life told a woman that I love her. You have made me feel things that I have tried to keep locked away for so long. Just the thought of never being with you hurts. Do you get that? You have to believe me. I would never lie to you."

I closed my eyes and leaned my head to the right. His touch was making me weak and I didn't want to fall into his arms and drown in all of his lies. "I can't do this right now." I yanked my wrist from out of his reach and slowly backed away from him. "I can't listen to this."

Jace stood there in silence for a moment before he walked over to the wall and slammed his fist against it. The wall shook.

His jaw clenched as he ran his hand through his hair and stared at the wall. "Tell me something then, Avery. Tell me the truth." He paused to look up at me. "Do you have any feelings for me? Do you feel anything at all?" he asked breathless.

My body stiffened as my mind searched for answers. "Jace, I don't know how I feel," I whispered, searching for my own answers. "What I feel is very confused right now. I have never felt this way before about anything or anyone but when I'm around you, it's like... my heart hurts. I don't know how to describe the feeling."

I pressed my hand to my chest and squeezed it. My heart stopped at the sound of my own words, my stomach suddenly dropping.

Jace placed his hands to my face, hands shaking, as he gently backed me into the wall behind me. He took a deep breath and exhaled slowly. "Tell me this." He paused to swallow. "Do I even have a chance?" His eyes searched mine again.

My mind spun as I fought to figure out how I felt. The truth was that I thought about Jace every second of everyday and just the thought of never seeing him again hurt like hell. I had never felt anything like it before. It pained me too much to put it together now. The last thing I wanted to do was hurt Jace.

Jace's eyes hardened when I didn't respond.

"Nothing to say, Avery? I just poured my heart out to you and you can't even say one word, "he growled.

I closed my eyes and sighed. "Jace, I don't know-"

"Just stop there," he cut in. He pulled his hands away from my face and walked over to stand in front of the door. "I need to clear my head and cool off." He hesitated for a second before he reached for the knob and pulled the door open.

"Jace," I said under my breath. "I'm sorry-"

"No need to be," he cut in, his voice hard. "I just need to go." He gave me a quick look before stepping outside and into the light rain.

I ran to the door as I watched him walk through the chilly night and hop into his car. He didn't hesitate for long before he turned on the engine and disappeared from out of my sight.

I stood there for a while cold and speechless, heart pounding, as I attempted to think straight. I felt sick. Seeing him leave tore me apart.

Suddenly, it hit me. I couldn't lose him. The thought hurt too much. I still wasn't sure if it was love, but it was something worth fighting for. I had to let him know before it was too late.

I ran to my purse and struggled to pull my phone out. It got caught on the edge of the liner causing my whole purse to fall out of my hand as I finally got the phone out and searched for Jace's number. I kicked my purse to the side and ran over to the door. "Come on. Pick up." The phone kept ringing until finally it went to voicemail. *Dammit!* Now I was the one trying to reach him and getting no response in return. It hurt.

If I couldn't call Jace then I needed to get to him as soon as I could. Jackie was already sleeping and the last thing that I wanted to do was wake her up and explain to her that Jace and I had gotten into a fight and he left. She already had enough of her own problems to deal with.

WAKE UP CALL
VICTORIA ASHLEY

I decided on calling for a taxi. That way none of Jace's friends or family had to get involved. I messed up big time and I was feeling the pain. The pain that I had caused both Jace and myself. I had to make it right.

It was pouring rain by the time that the taxi arrived and it would probably be close to impossible to see the roads through the mess. It didn't matter to me though. I just needed to get to Jace as quickly as possible. Even if I had to walk.

I ran through the heavy rain and jumped into the back of the taxi, slamming the door behind me. "Just drive. I don't know where I'm heading just yet," I announced, shaking the rain off.

The heavyset man glanced back at me, looking me over, before stepping on the gas and taking off. "Your wish is my command," he muttered.

I just shook him off, running my hands through my wet hair while staring down at my phone. *Ring! Please. Just ring.*

I sat with my face smashed against the frigid window in search of Jace's car. It was close to impossible to see anything through the rain and it was really starting to frustrate me.

Taking a deep breath, I reached for my phone again and dialed Jace's number. Come on. Come on. My hands started shaking as the call went straight to voicemail this time.

I threw my phone down in anger and looked up just in time to notice some flashing lights just ahead of us. A surge of fear shot threw me at the thought of Jace being hurt. "Slow down," I yelled frantically.

I pressed my face back into the glass to get a better look. That's when I noticed three police cars, two ambulances and then a little black car that was smashed up on the side of the road. Jace's car!

"Stop! Stop the damn car," I screamed, my voice shaking. My whole body trembled as I reached for the handle and struggled with opening the door. "Shit! Shit!" I cried. Finally, I managed to push the door open to jump out of the taxi.

The cold rain hit roughly against my heated face as I ran over to the crowd of people and pushed my way through. It was hard to tell, but it looked as if two of the ambulance drivers were pushing a stretcher that was covered with a blanket. I couldn't make out if it had a body underneath or not.

Panic set in as I roughly pushed my way through the crowd to find someone that could help me.

"Move," I shouted while pushing bystanders out of the way. "I need to get through. Move!" I didn't stop until I was standing breathless and sobbing in front of a police officer.

The officer quickly looked up from his paper work and attempted to push me back behind the orange cones. I pushed his arm away.

"I'm sorry ma'am, but you can't be in this area," he said with a sound of regret. "Please step back."

I gripped onto the officer's jacket and started shaking his arm. "No! You don't understand. I need to know what's going on," I cried. "What happened to the man in the black car? Please!" I pleaded, my eyes wet.

The officer froze. His whole body stiffened and he turned away from my view. That couldn't mean anything good.

"There were no survivors." He turned away, hiding his eyes from my view. "I'm sorry, ma'am. The driver was going at least 60 mph when his car slid and crashed into that pole. There was nothing that anyone could do. He died instantly."

My body shut down instantly, causing me to crash down onto the filthy, wet ground. I dug my hands into the mud as the tears flooded my eyes. It can't be true. Jace can't be gone.

"No! No! No!" I cried, "There has to be something you can do. Save him," I screamed in rage. "He might still be breathing. You gave up too quickly."

The officer shook his head and attempted to cover the hurt in his eyes. "It was impossible. I'm sorry," he said softly. "We did all that we could do."

I sat there in shock. I didn't want to live without Jace. I couldn't live without him.

An intense pain shot through my chest as my head quickly spun. My breathing became very heavy and then suddenly my ears started ringing.

"Ma'am are you okay?" The officer questioned. He bent down and reached for my arm. "Someone better get a stretcher over here. This woman is going down." His voice echoed through my head.

My body hit the ground in what felt like slow motion. Then suddenly my breath got knocked out.

WAKE UP CALL
VICTORIA ASHLEY

~•~

I jumped back startled as the bathroom door swung open to Jace standing there in his boxers. A sight I had grown used to.

He looked me up and down, his body covered in sweat, as he fought to catch his breath. I didn't understand what he was doing.

It made my heart race. "Jace, what are you doing in here?" I took a step toward the door to escape but he grabbed a hold of my wrist stopping me in my place. My heart sped up and my breathing became heavy. "Jace."

He looked me dead in the eye and without saying a word; he picked me up and sat me on the edge of the sink. He gripped my face and roughly pressed his lips against mine, causing me to moan. His lips were soft and sweet, just as I had imagined. Although, I wouldn't admit it. Not even to myself.

The taste was too overwhelming; causing my whole body to shake as he gently ran his fingers through my hair and pressed his body in between my legs. I could feel his hands trembling as he placed them on the inside of my bare thighs while sucking my bottom lip.

Suddenly, he pulled away and we both sat there panting and fighting for breath. His eyes were unreadable as he looked me in the eye and shook his head. My body leaned forward involuntarily, and it almost felt as if I were falling off the sink. I braced myself, pulling myself upright again.

"Jace..." I breathed.

I slowly opened my eyes, throwing my hands to my head, as an intense pain shot through my skull. I noticed right away that I was in the local hospital as I blinked my eyes rapidly, fighting to stay open. I could smell the room even before I could manage to see it.

Tears instantly rolled down my puffy cheeks at the fresh memory of Jace and our first kiss. For a second I had almost forgotten that he was gone. *Jace is gone. He's never coming back.*

I forced my body to roll over as I gripped my pillow and slammed my face into it. "Jace," I cried. "I'm sorry. I'm so sorry."

WAKE UP CALL
VICTORIA ASHLEY

I heard the sound of footsteps as someone slowly approached the bed, but I refused to look up. I just wanted to be alone.

"She's awake," said an unfamiliar voice. The soft voice of a female nurse was my guess.

"It's been a few hours. Give her some more pain medicine," another voice replied. "It should help her be more comfortable when she fully awakens."

I felt something cold shoot through the IV in my arm, causing my body to flinch. It made the tears flow even faster. I felt dazed and sore. I wanted to scream at the top of my lungs for jace, but I knew it would be useless.

I wanted to reach out and touch him. Feel the warmth of his soft skin against mine. It hurt like hell knowing that it would never happen again.

I buried my face into my tear-stained pillow and listened as the nurses left the room, leaving me alone in my silence.

A few minutes later, I heard heavy footsteps. I was too weak to attempt to look up. So I didn't move. I didn't have the will too.

The footsteps stopped in front of my bed and suddenly I felt a hand touch my arm from through the blanket. It made my chest hurt and I wanted to scream. I didn't want to be touched.

"Don't touch me," I said, voice shaking.

It was silent for a moment as the person slowly removed their hand from my arm.

"Avery," a voice called.

I ignored it. I couldn't make out who it was. No one else mattered to me except Jace and now he was gone.

"Avery."

I felt someone grab my arm again, but this time they didn't let go. They pulled my body so that I was facing up again and then cupped their warm hands around my face.

I looked up with blurred vision before blinking away the tears. I knew that touch from anywhere. My whole body shook as I broke out in a sob. "Jace!" I cried, still trying to focus my eyes.

"I'm here for you," Jace said. "I told you that I always would be." He rubbed my cheek.

I was in so much shock that I couldn't even manage to speak. I knew what I wanted to say, but I couldn't. *How could he be here in front of me?*

"It's okay, Avery." He bent down and pressed his lips against mine, causing my heartbeat to quicken. "The nurse said that you just bumped your head pretty hard. You're going to be fine. You can leave later today."

I gripped his face as hard as I could before running my hands over every inch of his perfect face. I wanted to be sure that I wasn't just seeing things. "I thought that... you... you were dead. How did..." I squeezed my eyes shut before opening them again and pulling his face down to mine. "I thought that I had lost you."

A smile spread across Jace's face before he trailed a finger over my lip and then kissed me. "You'll never lose me," he said simply. "I was on my way home when I got stuck in traffic because of the accident. I got out seeing what was going on and that's when I noticed you on the stretcher. I ran over to you, but you wouldn't wake up." He pressed his lips to my forehead and then grabbed both of my hands. "You have no idea how happy I am that you're okay."

I was so relieved to see Jace alive that I suddenly burst into laughter. I was worried about him dying and yet he believed that I had no idea how happy he was to see that I was okay. I had only bumped my head. "I have never been so happy in my life," I laughed, feeling a bit dazed from the medicine kicking in. "I really-"

"I'm sorry to interrupt, but I just wanted to let you know that the medicine should wear off in a few hours and you will be all clear to go then." The older nurse turned, but then stopped to look back at us. "Oh and the medicine can make her a little..." She stepped closer to Jace. "Loopy," she whispered and then smiled. "That will go away soon."

Jace nodded his head in understanding and smiled at the nurse as she grinned at him. "Thank you for your help."

The nurse nodded back at him and then walked out of the room, softly closing the door behind her.

As soon as we were alone, I got the sudden urge to laugh. I had no idea why, but I just burst into a fit of laughter. "You're okay," I laughed. "You're... I'm in the hospital."

Jace leaned in closer to me and rubbed my head. "It's okay. It's just the medicine," he laughed. "How's your head feeling?"

I grabbed for Jace's hair and ran my fingers through it. "Jace, you are so beautiful. I have something that I really need to say."

Jace went silent. His body stiff as he reached for my face, looked me in the eye and waited for me to speak.

"I love you, Jace," I whispered. "I really love you."

A look of happiness crossed his face, but then was quickly replaced with pain. He looked as if his dog had just been hit by a car. "I know that the nurse said you will be a little loopy from the medicine, so I'm going to guess that it's the drugs that are talking. Maybe you should just get some rest." He smiled and then gently kissed my hand. "I'm sorry for leaving."

My heart broke as soon as I realized that he was serious. He didn't even believe that I loved him. How could he after all that I had put him through? I didn't even believe him when he told me how he had felt. "I do-"

"It's okay, Avery." He smiled and rubbed my face. "Get some rest and then we can go home."

I grabbed his hand and kissed it. Making him believe me now would just be useless. He was right. I really did need some rest.

"Okay," I whispered, my voice pained.

Jace crawled into the bed next to me and threw his arms around me. He snuggled his body against mine and pressed his lips to my ear. "I'll wake you in a few hours."

I nodded my head and reached for his arms for comfort. It was the best feeling in the world. He was the best feeling in the world.

Chapter 18

I sat at the kitchen table lost in thought as Jace gave me a loving smile and carefully slid a mug of tea in front of me. I stared down at the little blue mug and stifled back a grin. Things weren't what I'd expected.

The events of last night replayed repeatedly in my mind and I couldn't believe that Jace was still there, in front of me, and breathing. When I thought that I had lost him, I would have given anything to get him back. I would never be able to forget that feeling.

"Jace," I whispered, looking up at him as he ate his food.

Jace looked up from his plate and reached for my hand. He softly ran his fingers over mine and smiled. "Are you feeling okay?" he questioned.

I nodded my head and looked him in the eye. I wanted to scream out that I loved him, but I didn't know if I had the courage to.

I swallowed hard and said the first thing that popped in my head. I hadn't even told him yet and I felt so ashamed. "I have a new apartment," I blurted, my heart racing.

Jace's eyes widened as a look of hurt crossed his once relaxed face. He turned his head away, taking a deep breath before biting down on his bottom lip. My heart dropped as I watched him. He looked hurt.

The room stayed silent. I didn't know what to say. We both sat there looking down at our plates, until Jackie entered the kitchen wearing a fitted black suit. She looked back and forth between the both of us and then leaned against the counter. "Well, everyone seems a little out of it today," she mumbled. "What's going on?"

Jace gave me a weak smile before looking up at his sister and motioning for her to join us at the table. "Everything's fine." He squeezed my hand and pulled my chair closer to his. "You look nice today, Jackie. Do you have some special plans that we don't know about," he questioned, trying to sound excited.

He was right. She looked great. Her black suit fit her perfectly and she had her hair pulled back into a tight bun, with a loose strand of hair that hung perfectly around her face. She looked very professional. She was quite beautiful.

She flashed us a huge smile and dug into her food. "I'm going job hunting today." She shoved a forkful of eggs into her mouth and then slammed back her whole mug of tea. "I'm really nervous, but excited at the same time." She sat back in her seat. "I've been doing a lot of thinking and I'm ready to change my life. Joe has kept me back for so long and I haven't even experienced life yet." She looked over at Jace and reached for his shoulder. "I can't do this without you, little brother. I really need your help." Her eyes watered as her bottom lip began to quiver.

She really did need his help. She needed his help much more than I did now. Maybe me getting the apartment was perfect timing. Jace's place was only big enough for two people and now, Jackie was the one that needed him the most.

Jace wrapped his arms around his sister and pulled her in close for a hug. The sight made my eyes water. Jace was the greatest and most loving person that I'd ever met. Jackie and I were both lucky to have him in our lives.

"Jackie," I said with a slight smile.

Jackie peered over Jace's shoulder and smiled back. "Yeah."

"I'm moving out today. My old room will be empty if you'd like it." I glanced over at Jace and he nodded his head in approval.

"I have enough money saved up so that I can buy a new bed and a few other things to get me started. You should take my old room and be close to Jace." I paused. "You guys need each other."

Jackie's eyes fell down to Jace's shoulders before she pulled away and looked Jace in the eye. "I don't know. I don't want you guys to think that Avery has to move just to make room for me." Her face scrunched up as a tear fell down her cheek. "I can't-"

"It's not like that. I would have let you stay no matter what." He said firmly. "I would have been perfectly fine on the couch or in Avery's room." He looked over at me and smiled. "Avery just needs to be on her own for a bit. She's been working really hard to get on her feet and now is her chance to do that. It's not a problem, Jackie."

Looking at Jackie, I suddenly got the urge to reach out and give her a hug. She felt like a big part of me now. Maybe that was because she was the biggest part of Jace. I wanted Jace and everything that came with him.

I stood up from my chair, pushing it under the table, before walking over to Jackie. I looked down at her and then slowly bent down and wrapped my arms around her. Her hands felt stiff for a moment before she squeezed me close to her and rubbed my back. "I'm so happy that you are here with Jace."

Jackie grabbed both of my arms and looked me in the eye. "You have no idea how happy I am to be back. Jace was the only place that I had ever really felt safe. He took care of the whole family for so long. He was the glue that held us together." She turned her head away and squeezed my arms. "I lost that for a long time. Don't let that happen to you."

We both looked over at Jace to see him staring in shock at the both of us. To be honest, I was in shock myself. I never really felt the need to hug anyone in my life before. Jace had changed me. Love had changed me. The feeling scared the living crap out of me. I never wanted to feel that I needed someone to be happy. Or that I needed someone to be close to. Now, even the thought of being out of Jace's arms broke my heart into a million little pieces

Jace cleared his throat and then stood up from the table. "Well ladies. I'll do these dishes." He kissed Jackie on the forehead. "Good luck." Then he walked over, grabbed my face and pressed his lips to my cheek. "Go and get ready so I can buy you a few things for this apartment of yours." He smiled and then looked down at the ground, his eyes looking sad.

I just stood there staring as Jackie walked out of the kitchen and Jace stood in front of the sink with his back toward me.

The whole kitchen spun around me as I tried to put my life together. In just a few hours, I would be on my own, in my own apartment, and with two decent jobs. No more crappy apartment or job as a stripper. I felt... normal for once and alive. More alive than I have ever felt.

"Avery."

The sound of Jace's voice broke me from my reverie. I shook my head and looked up. "Huh?"

He chuckled at my expression and turned off the sink. "Are you alright?" He walked over and lightly rubbed my shoulders. "Are you going to get dressed or do you need another day of rest?"

I placed my hands on his bare chest and took a deep breath. His skin felt so soft and warm against my bare hands. It made me want to lose myself in him. "No." I shook my head. "No, I'm fine. I told the landlord that I would show up today with the deposit and first month's rent."

Jace ran his hands up my arms, lightly tickling me, as he smiled. "It's okay, Avery. You don't have to be upset or worried," he breathed. "At first I was sad that you were leaving, but now that I've had time for it all to sink in; I realize that it's a good thing for you. We can still be together anytime that we want. It's all just a part of a new beginning for you. One that you've needed for so long."

I swallowed hard and stifled back tears. He always had a way of making me feel as ease. "I know, but-"

"No buts," he cut in. "Everything is going to be... perfect." He pressed his lips to my forehead and then kissed all the way down to my lips. "I promise. Now go get dressed."

~•~

An hour later, we both stood inside of *Bergstroms* a small furniture store, about twenty minutes away from Jace's place.

Jace held my hand as he took me around the store and showed me the various couches and beds that they had on display.

The prices seemed to be fairly decent for the quality that they offered, but I was overwhelmed. I didn't even know where to start.

"This is nice. It almost looks like ours... I mean mine." His words stopped my heart as we both stood there looking at each other. *Ours?*

Jace coughed and pulled my arm, bringing me over to stand in front of a black leather sectional. He was right; it was almost identical to his. It was beautiful.

"This is very nice." My eyes wandered over the leather couch before settling on the price tag. "Thirteen hundred dollars! Oh no." I shook my head back and forth and stepped away. "That is way too expensive."

Jace ran his hand over the arm of the couch and smiled. Then he waved one of the workers over. "I think this one is actually better than mine."

A man in about his mid-thirties walked over with a welcoming smile on his pudgy face. His red polo shirt clung tightly to his round belly, but was entirely too long for his short body. Even his khakis seemed to be excessively long for his legs.

He held out a short, hairy arm and reached for Jace's hand. "Good morning, sir." He nodded his head at me. "Ma'am." He looked at us both, anxious to make a sale. "I see that you are interested in this couch. My name is Tom. Can I answer any questions that you may have?"

Jace ran his tongue over his bottom lip and then grinned. "Yes. How soon can you have this couch delivered, if we purchase this today?"

I lightly elbowed Jace in the side. "I can't afford this," I said soft enough for only the two of us to hear.

Tom ignored me and set his full attention on Jace. "Depending on the location we can have it delivered and set up in an hour. Where would the drop off be?"

Jace scrunched up his face and looked lost in thought. Then he turned to me and rubbed my cheek. "What's the address?"

"But-"

"What's the address?" He cut in.

WAKE UP CALL
VICTORIA ASHLEY

I huffed and reached into my purse to pull out the envelope with the address on it. I glanced down at it and read it aloud. "5324 Victory Lane."

A huge smile spread across Jace's face as he nodded his head at Tom and repeated what I said. "5324 Victory Lane. What's the verdict, Tom?"

Tom smiled and shook Jace's hand again. "An hour at the latest."

Jace wrapped his arm around me and then leaned in to kiss my neck. "We have a little more shopping to do first. We'll find you when we find our next purchase. Thank you, Tom."

I watched in horror as Tom walked away with the sales tag in his hand. "I really can't afford that. I only have $600 to spare."

Jace gave me a sincere smile and pulled me close to him. He softly ran his hand under my hairline and gripped the small of my back with his free hand. "Just because you're on your own, doesn't mean I can't take care of my woman. The couch is on me."

My breath caught in my throat and I started choking.

"Are you okay?" Jace softly rubbed my back and held my arm above my head. "Breathe." He chuckled.

I got my breathing under control once again and managed to look Jace in the eye. I was in complete shock that he had just called me his woman. I was speechless. "I don't... you don't have... thank you," I just finally whispered.

Jace laced his fingers through mine and pulled me beside him. "I have more than enough money to help out. I've been saving for years now. It's not a problem for me and it shouldn't be for you either." He kissed my hand. "Let's go find you a bed."

~•~

We arrived at my empty apartment, thirty minutes later, with a 42-inch TV, a black coffee table, a glass entertainment center and little black dresser. The couch and the queen-sized bed would arrive within the next forty minutes. The excitement was starting to settle in and I couldn't help but to smile.

Jace and I both looked around the small apartment, checking out all of the rooms. The living room was complete with caramel shag carpet, burgundy shades and black windowsill and trim. It was the perfect size to fit all of my new furniture in it. It actually felt like a home.

Jace ran his hand along the freshly painted wall and smiled. "This place is perfect. I really like it." He pulled up the shade and looked out the window. "I might even spend most of my time here. It's...cozy."

I laughed and reached for Jace's hand. It felt good to see that Jace approved of my new place. "I really like it here. It seems peaceful. It's like having my own place for the very first time. The last apartment never felt like home." I ran my hand over Jace's chest and grinned. "I'm just not so sure that I should allow boys into my first place."

Jace chuckled as he gripped my hips and hoisted me off the ground. "I'm not just any boy." He smirked. "At least, I'd like to not think so."

I reached out and cupped Jace's face, the same way that he always cupped mine. "Trust me. You're not just any boy." I roughly pressed my lips against his, desperate to get a taste of his sweet mouth. Everything about Jace was sweet.

He squeezed me tightly, while walking us into the kitchen. He stopped in front of the stove before setting me down on top of it. Our lips didn't separate as he wrapped my legs around his waist, pressing his crotch into my inner thigh. It sent chills all through my heated body and made me want to rip his clothing off. He had a way of turning me on, that I couldn't even explain.

Jace roughly bit my lip, while pulling my jacket off and tossing it down onto the white linoleum flooring. Things were getting heated and I wanted nothing more than to be with him. "I want-"

We both stopped and looked up in shock as Jackie came strolling into the kitchen holding a huge box. She just eyed us both, with raised eyebrows and laughed. "Well... a little help."

Jace snapped out of the stare and playfully ran his hand through his hair. "Of course. Sorry," he said. He gave me an apologetic look before pulling away from me and grabbing the box from Jackie's arms. "How did you know where Avery's apartment was? Did you have any luck on the job search?" he questioned. "And what's all of this stuff?"

Jackie walked over and grabbed my arm, helping me down from the stove. "Dex stopped over looking for you two. I told him

that you were helping Avery move into her new apartment." She
grinned and walked over to the box. "No luck yet, though on the
job. I hope to hear back soon," she answered with a smile. "I
went through some of mom's old dishes that she never really
used, along with some other kitchenware."

She reached into the box and pulled out a toaster. "I found, a
toaster, a can opener, some plates, silverware and her old
microwave is in the car." She reached back into the box. "Oh and
I even went and picked up a four pack of these purple cups." She
smiled holding up the cups. "Purple is my favorite color."

Jace walked over toward the door and shook his head in
disbelief. "Where did you find all of this stuff?"

Jackie laughed and gave him a dumbfound look. "In your
basement. You don't remember storing mom's things down
there?"

"I forgot." Jace gave Jackie a grateful look and walked outside
to fetch the microwave.

I just watched Jackie as she continued to pull things from out
of the box. I couldn't believe that she was treating me so much
like family. It made me feel... good. "Thank you, Jackie." I
grinned and started helping her. "You really didn't have to."

Jackie brushed a strand of hair behind her ear and smiled.
"Anything for family." She looked me in the eye, making me feel
like crying, before she opened the fridge and frowned. "You don't
have anything in here. We're going to have to get you some
groceries later. We'll just order pizza for lunch."

I shook my head, not knowing what to say. Then a smile crept
over my face as Jace entered the kitchen, holding the microwave.
"Thank you, both," I beamed.

Jace set the microwave on the black countertop and then
watched as Jackie grabbed my arm and pulled me with her.
"Show me around your new place."

I walked her through the living room and then into the decent
sized bedroom. The bedroom was pretty much painted the same
as the living room, except the carpet was a bright shade of white.
It also had a walk in closet that was big enough to fit a single bed
in and still have room. It was even bigger than the room that I
had at Jace's. I loved it.

Jackie nodded her head and crossed her arms. "I like this
place. Maybe one day, I will come and take this place from you."

WAKE UP CALL
VICTORIA ASHLEY

She paused and gave me a sad smile. "After I'm stronger, of course. I couldn't manage to live alone right now. Joe has a very strong influence."

I reached out and gently grabbed her arm. "It will happen one day. You just have to be strong." I surprised, even myself with my words of encouragement.

Less than two months ago, I was the one in dire need of help. Now I was the one trying to give someone else the hope that I never had.

Jackie let out a small laugh and then reached out to hug me. "I know. I realized that, after seeing my brother and you at the bowling alley that day. I saw how happy you guys made each other and I missed being that happy. It made me miss my little brother." She smiled and then headed for the door. "Let's see this bathroom of yours. Is it just as nice as the rest?"

She didn't even wait for me to answer before she took off, strolling to the bathroom. I followed close behind her as she stepped into the bathroom and ran her hand over the glass door that surrounded the shower. She nodded her head in approval and then stepped over to the oval sink. She reached above her and screwed in the fourth light bulb that didn't seem to shine as bright as the rest. When the light flickered and then brightened up, she grinned and waved her hand in front of it. "All fixed."
"The couch and bed are here."

Jackie and I both laughed and then walked into the living room together. It took the movers a total of twenty-five minutes before they had both the bed and the couch set up and ready for use. It was slowly coming together before my eyes and I felt so happy.

Jace walked the movers outside and thanked them both for their help before handing them each a ten-dollar bill. He really knew how to handle everything and make everyone happy. I was very thankful.

Jackie and I both went into the living room and sat on the couch as Jace started putting the entertainment center together. I had to admit, he looked masculine and sexy, down on the floor putting my table together. I could have sat there and watched him all day.

Finally, Jace glanced up from the table and looked over at Jackie. "Why don't you take Avery to the store and get her some stuff to put into the fridge. I'll order a couple of pizzas and everything should be ready before you two return."

Jackie stood up from the couch and grabbed my hand. "Perfect. We'll be back in thirty."

Jace stood up from the floor and dropped his tools. Then he walked over and grabbed me by the waist. "You girls take care of each other." He pressed his lips against mine and then playfully slapped my butt. "Have fun."

~•~

We arrived back at the apartment with soda, bread, butter, milk, cheese and a few frozen boxes of chicken. It wasn't much, but it was all that I really needed to get me through the next day. After work tomorrow, I would have to go and get a few more things for the house. It was exciting.

Jackie walked in front of me the whole time, pushing the door open for me and holding it open. I stepped inside to see Dex, Stacy and Jace all standing in the kitchen. The counter was covered with plates, cups, napkins and pizza boxes. It made me smile to see everyone.

I tossed the bags onto the empty space on the counter and laughed. I was completely surprised. "Hi everyone!"

Stacy grinned and bounced over to me. "I love your new place. Now we'll have to start hanging out more." She leaned in and gave me a hug. "It won't be as awkward as me trying to invite myself to the boss' house." She giggled and looked over at Jace.

Jace just shook his head and laughed at her innocent ways. "I didn't realize that the boss was so big and scary."

Dex patted Jace on the back and laughed. "Trust me... you're not, bro." Then he walked over to stand in front of me. "This is apartment is great. I'm glad that you decided on this one."

I looked around the place and at everyone that stood around chatting and smiled. "Me too," I said. "I really owe a lot of thanks to you. You helped me in more ways than you know." I turned around to look at everyone. "All of you have helped me more than you even know. Thank you."

Jace walked over and grabbed me by the waist. Then he gently rubbed away the tear that I hadn't even noticed had fallen.

"You are so special. You're special to all of us." He ran a finger over my lip, while biting his own. "I-"

"I love you," I cut him off. "I really, truly love you." My heart raced, as I looked him in the eye, in shock that I had found the courage to say those words again. He almost looked as if he could fall over at any moment. It was true though. I loved him. I knew that now. A big part of me had even known for a while. I had just been too afraid to admit it.

Jace cupped my face with trembling hands as he pulled my face close to his. "I love you too," he whispered. "More than you will ever know."

I tangled my hands through his hair and pulled his lips to mine, crushing him with my desire for him. He wanted me, just as badly as I wanted him.

Suddenly, I heard whistling, clapping and shouting from behind us, followed by laughter.

"About damn time." Stacy laughed. "Holy shit! I never thought I'd witness Jace in love."

Dex patted Jace on the back and then looked over at me. "I knew it, bro. I knew it." He smiled and then grabbed a slice of pizza. "I could tell from the very first day that I met Avery."

Jace just shook his head and laughed at our friends. Everyone had something to say except for Jackie. That was when I noticed that she wasn't even in the room. I tilted my head at Jace and got ready to question where she had been. "Where-"

My words were cut short when I heard barking coming from right outside the kitchen door. I gave Jace a questionable look and then reached for the door handle.

Jace just smiled and looked up toward the ceiling as if everything was normal.

The door swung open to Jackie standing there with a beautiful Siberian husky in her arms. She looked up at me and then handed me the puppy. "Look what I found in the back of Jace's car," she laughed. "Weird, huh?"

I took the puppy in my arms and looked behind me at Jace. "Holy... what is this?" I asked amazed. I had never had a dog or any other kind of pet before and I really didn't know how to react.

Jace smirked and walked over to stand next to me. He reached out and rubbed the puppy's head before kissing my cheek. "I couldn't let my lady be alone, when I'm not around. I want you to always feel wanted and needed. Just like you are."

I set my lip into a pout and rubbed the dog's soft fur. It looked up at me with beautiful baby blues and whined. "I don't know what to say." I set the puppy down in the kitchen and it took off running around in excitement while taking turns being sure to jump up on everyone. The sight made me giggle. It was so playful and free. "Thank you, Jace."

Jace grabbed for a slice of pizza and handed it to me. "You're welcome." He grinned and then grabbed a slice for himself. "Go look in that closet." He pointed over to the closet, next to the pantry and then took a bite of his pizza.

I looked around at everyone as they all stared at me. It actually made me somewhat nervous to have all eyes on me.

"Okay," I said nervously. I walked over to the closet and pulled the door open. The bottom shelf was full of puppy food, puppy treats and puppy toys. Then right above that, were the puppy dishes and leashes. They were all blue.

"A boy," I said with a laugh. "Thank you. Thank you for all of this. You didn't have to."

Jace walked over and reached up on the top shelf. "That's not all." He smiled as he pulled down a huge puppy bed and handed it to me. "He needs somewhere to sleep as well."

I looked down at the soft bed, smiled, and then set it down next to the fridge. "What is his name?"

Jace looked down at the puppy that was now jumping all over Stacy as she giggled in delight. Then he looked back over at me, leaning against the fridge. "What do you want it to be?"

I pointed to myself and shook my head. "I can't name him. You-"

Jace grabbed my hand and placed it on his chest. Then he ran his hand over my face and sucked his bottom lip in. "He's yours. You name him."

I looked down at my new puppy and laughed as he came running over to me, slipping across the floor in the process. "Look at you. You're so darn cute." I crouched down and picked him up as he licked the side of my face. "Lucky. That will be your name because I'm lucky to have all of this." I waved my arms out in front of me and ended up falling back as Lucky jumped on me.

Jace bent down next to us and patted Lucky's head. "Lucky," he paused. "I like that name."

"Lucky," Jackie called.

Lucky glanced behind him, but didn't make a move.

Jace stood up and watched as Lucky plopped down in front of his feet. He shrugged his shoulders and smiled at Jackie. "Well... it will take him a little time to get used to his name."

Jackie waved a dismissive hand at Jace and then reached for her cell. "I'll be right back," she said nonchalantly.

I just stood back and watched as everyone enjoyed each other's company, laughing and telling stories. It was an amazing feeling and things were starting to feel complete.

I felt complete...

Chapter 19

I rolled over as I felt something moist touch my cheek. I had slept so well in my new apartment that I had almost forgotten about having Lucky.

I ran my arm over my face and yawned as Lucky pawed me in the face and whined. "I'm awake." I laughed.

Lucky jumped up on my chest, knocking me back into the mattress, as I attempted to sit up and stretch. The cute little cuddle bug had spent most of the night curled up on my feet, even though I had tried numerous times to get him to settle down in his new bed. I had to admit, I really liked having him around. It made me feel warm and... cozy inside.

I froze and took a deep breath.

A smile slowly crept to my lips as Jace leaned against the door shirtless, arms resting at his sides, as he smiled at me. He looked so beautiful. He always did. "Good morning." He grinned.

I softly bit my bottom lip and ran a hand through Lucky's soft fur. "Good morning, Jace," I whispered.

I patted Lucky's back and watched him as he jumped off the bed and ran through the hall. I looked up at Jace and shook my head. "What was that all about?"

Jace pushed away from the door, smiled, and stepped out of his snug boxer briefs. My eyes hungrily scanned his naked body as he stepped up next to the bed and grabbed me by my sides. "I knew he had to be just as hungry as I am," he breathed. "He'll be occupied for a while.

I let out a soft moan as Jace's hands tightened around my body, pulling me close to his warm chest. I gently placed my right hand over his heaving chest and smiled. "If you're hungry, then maybe you should cook us some breakfast." I laughed.

Jace's eyes wandered down to my legs as he chewed on his lip ring. "Nothing can satisfy my hunger, quite like the taste of you." He ran his hand down the front of my camisole, before yanking on my hips, pulling me back down to the bed. "I'm not letting you leave."

I threw my head back and giggled as Jace pressed his soft lips to my neck. It tickled, but at the same time, felt so damn good. "Never?" I questioned.

Jace pressed harder into my neck while gripping onto my right thigh. "Never." He paused to look at me. "Okay, well maybe not never. That could be a little creepy." He laughed and then pressed his mouth against mine.

My fingers lightly tangled through Jace's messy hair as he hovered his body above mine, barely brushing mine, and gripped the back of my neck. His touch was so caring, yet strong at the same time. He made my whole body want to melt into his and get lost.

"Jace," I whispered. "I meant what I said."

Jace's body stiffened as he pushed me down into the soft pillow. His beautiful eyes studied mine, before he pressed his body into mine and cupped my face. "I know." He smiled, his finger grazing over my lip, as he squeezed my hip with his free hand. "I believed you the first time."

I playfully pounded my fist into his chest as he grinned at me. "You jerk," I shouted. "You were messing with me?"

Jace's hand gripped my flying fist as he pulled it around his shoulder and kissed my arm. He ran a finger down my belly and then yanked my top off. He stared down at my bare body and then into my eyes. "I felt that it was real, but I was too afraid that I was wrong. I didn't want to get my hopes up and then lose you." He bent down, pressing his lips to mine. "I wanted to wait until you said it again. I wanted to hear it, when it came from here." He pointed at my heart. "That was when I was sure that the first time was real."

WAKE UP CALL
VICTORIA ASHLEY

A tear rolled down my cheek at the thought of that night. I was so afraid that I had lost Jace, that he was probably right. I would have said anything at that point. Not to mention that the medicine didn't help me think more clearly either.

"I was so scared." I looked up, but set my gaze on his lips. "The thought of never seeing you again made me... it made me..." I got the courage and looked him in the eyes. "It made me feel as if I was dying. I suddenly couldn't picture a life without you in it and I wanted to die with you. You were the only thing that was keeping me breathing. I had nothing before I found you. I was nothing-"

"Don't say that, Avery," he cut in, his voice soft. "You were always something special. You were just too blind to see it. You were brought up to believe that you were nothing. Like no one could ever care for you." He grabbed my hand and kissed it. "That was all wrong. Do you hear me? You are... everything to me."

My heart fell to my feet. I shifted on the bed and looked down at the floor. "Jace-"

"No, Avery," he blurted out.

He stood up from the bed and walked over to the window. "You have been everything to me since our first kiss. I felt something that I had never felt with anyone else. Suddenly, the only thing that mattered to me was your happiness. I wanted you to be happy and I wanted to be a part of that happiness." He turned away from the window and brought his eyes up to meet the ceiling. "You're all that I think about. When you left... you..." He bit his lip in frustration. "You broke my fucking heart. I looked everywhere for you. Everyone told me that it was fine. That you would return when you were ready. What nobody knew... was that I was afraid that you would never be ready. It scared the shit out of me."

His words broke my heart. The pain in his voice was almost enough to bring me to my knees it hurt like nothing else before.

I scrambled from the bed and jumped to my feet. I needed to show him how much I loved him. I threw my arms around him and roughly pulled him to the bed. I stared him in the eye while pushing him onto the soft mattress. "I love you. I fucking love you so much that it hurts." I placed my finger to his mouth and leaned down so that my face was inches from his, his heavy breathing tickling my lips. "I want you more than anything else in life and I will do anything to prove that to you. Please don't ever give up on me. Please," I pleaded, looking in his eyes.

Jace grabbed my head, closing the distance between us, as we made love. What I just experienced with Jace was love. True, undeniably, passionate love.

~•~

An hour later, I found myself standing outside of *Jan's Place*. Jace had dropped me off and offered to come inside with me, but I felt as if it was something that I had to do alone. Knowing that I was about to start a new job, made me so nervous that I didn't know whether to laugh or run away.

I took a long, deep breath and reached for the handle.

I stepped inside to a quiet, dark restaurant. At first I thought that maybe I had arrived early, but after checking the clock, I saw, that I was only ten minutes early. I took a few steps inside and looked around. I didn't see Jan anywhere in sight. "Hello," I called out. "Is anyone here?"

It was silent for a few moments until finally I heard tiny footsteps behind me. I turned around to see Jan standing there with a frown on her face. She reached out and placed her hand on my arm. "Come on, girl. Let's get started."

I smiled and nodded my head as Jan explained everything that I needed to know to get started.

I was surprised to find out that she had practically spent over twenty years running the Pizza restaurant by herself, after her husband Frank had passed away and her only child had took off and left her all alone. I could tell that she was lonely and really needed the company. I almost felt sad for her.

A few hours into my first shift, I was already getting anxious to get off and see Jace. I kept my cell in my pocket, occasionally texting both Jace and Stacy, wondering how things were going at the diner. I was very happy and grateful for Jan giving me a job, but I couldn't help but to feel an empty feeling in the pit of my stomach. Every time that my phone vibrated in my pocket, I couldn't help but to think of how I could have been there with them.

"Hey, girl."

WAKE UP CALL
VICTORIA ASHLEY

I dropped the towel onto the empty table and peered over my shoulder to see Jan standing behind me. "Is everything okay?" Her forehead wrinkled in concern as she waited for my response. "There is a handsome young man here to see you. Maybe that might cheer you up," she groaned.

A smile crossed my face as I studied the look on Jan's face. Jace hadn't even mentioned that he was coming to see me. "That's got to be-"

"Hi, Avery." The voice sent chills up my spine.

"Caleb." I froze unsure of what to say next.

Jan looked back and forth between Caleb and me before disappearing into the kitchen, leaving the two of us alone.

Panic set in causing my head to spin. I wanted to scream at the top of my lungs until he left. I took a few calming breaths and continued to clean off the table. "What are you doing here?" I questioned.

Caleb took a step forward, but then stopped before he got too close. He looked nervous.

The smell of his Joop cologne filled the air as he threw his hands up in defeat and grunted. "Avery, look. I know that I messed up. I messed up big time and I'm sorry." He paused and reached for my shoulder, but I shook it off. "I didn't know that Henry was a piece of shit. Pam started coming to me months ago. She was a good client... so when she mentioned that she was your aunt and that your father had been searching for you, I thought that I was doing you a favor."

I threw the towel back down on the table, pressing my hands to my forehead. I was beyond frustrated and I just wanted to move on with my life and leave the past behind me.

"Caleb, I understand that you didn't know what you were doing. I guess that I can't really blame you for bringing my father back into my life." I glanced up at Caleb and then threw myself into an empty chair. "I really can't."

"You're right. You can't." He agreed. "I didn't know anything about your past and that was because you refused to tell me. I wanted to know. Trust me. I did."

I shook my head, knowing that he was right. A lot of the pain that I had gone through was my own doing. I could had let him in from the beginning and told him everything. I didn't. I kept it from him. Then I hated Caleb for even trying. I was horrible to him. "I wasn't ready. It hurt way too much," I whispered.

Caleb crouched down, placing his right hand on the ground, and his left one on the side of the chair. Suddenly, I didn't feel as much hate as I did in the past.

"You didn't have to go through it alone. Yes, I had feelings for you, but I would have settled for an actual friendship. I wasn't just in it for the sex. I still saw the good in you, Avery."

I turned my head away as a tear rolled down my cheek. I felt a huge sense of relief and I was actually kind of glad that Caleb had come to see me. Maybe making things better with Caleb was a part of my healing process. It was as if a weight had been lifted off my shoulders, but there was still one thing bothering me. "Why didn't you tell the cops about Jace? You had a chance to get him arrested, but you didn't. Why?"

A small smile crept to Caleb's lips as he stood back up and fixed his wild hair. "Henry deserved what he got." He paused to look down at the floor. "That ass was right."

I looked up at him in confusion. "What do you mean?"

Caleb brought his eyes back up to meet mine. "Jace. He was right. I was too chicken shit to fight back." He laughed. "I'm a drug dealer, Avery. I couldn't afford to get busted. That made me realize that I wasn't the right one for you. If I cared as much as I thought I did, well... then I would have done what Jace did. I didn't, so I did the next best thing."

I allowed myself to smile as I pushed my way out of the chair and grabbed Caleb's arm. "Thank you. You did the right thing."

Caleb glanced down at his arm and smiled. "So... your mother?" he questioned.

My heart ached at just the thought of her. As much as I wanted to make her understand, I knew that it would take time. Just like it took me time to figure things out. Her day too would come. "She's alive," I huffed. "She hates me, but she'll live."

Caleb nodded his head, looking relieved before turning on his heel. "Take care, Avery." He flashed me his dimpled smile and then headed for the door.

"You too," I said softly, still a little overwhelmed by the whole situation.

I waited until Caleb was completely gone before I went back to cleaning the tables. My heart still raced in my chest at the thought of Caleb showing up. I had expected the worst, but ended up getting the best. It was shocking. I guess that good things really could happen if you just allowed them to.

"Who was that young man?"

I looked up to see Jan enter the dining room. She blankly stared at me while waiting for an answer. It was hard to tell whether she was upset with me for already getting a visitor. The last thing that I wanted to do was get Jan upset and stress her out on my first day. "I'm sorry-"

"For what?" she cut in. "You're allowed to have friends come in. I'm not some grumpy old bat." She grinned. "Do I look like a grumpy old bat?"

I smiled back while shaking my head. "No. Not at all," I lied.

"Good. Now get back to work," she said.

I laughed to myself and then prepared to take care of a group of smiling customers as they filed in and took a seat at one of the back tables.

~•~

When I arrived back at the apartment, Jackie was lounging on the couch. She looked up from her bowl of popcorn and smiled. "How was your first day?"

I looked over at Jace and he just shrugged his shoulders. "I don't know. She loves it here," he whispered. Then he pressed his lips to my neck and laughed. "So... how was your first day?"

I plopped down next to Jackie on the couch and reached inside the bowl of popcorn. "It was fine. Jan had her moments. It will take some time getting used to, but I will manage."

Jace smiled and then jumped on top of Jackie's lap reaching his hand into the bowl of popcorn. "Don't you have places to be, or jobs to apply to?" He teased.

Jackie pushed Jace out of her lap and playfully slapped his arm. "Nope! I can sit here all day. I haven't had any call backs yet."

I sat back and watched as Jace and Jackie teased each other. I couldn't help but to laugh when Jackie slapped him in the back of the head. The look on Jace's face was priceless.

"Ouch. Is that how you treat your little brother?" He jumped to his feet and rubbed the back of his head. "Did-"

"I have something to tell you," I cut in.

The room grew silent.

"Should I sit down for this?" Jace teased.

I reached over and slapped him on the arm. "No." I laughed.

"Ouch. The abuse of you ladies." He chuckled, while grabbing both his arm and his head. "Maybe I will just sit down. Over here." He pointed to the end of the couch.

Jackie narrowed her eyes at Jace and then set the bowl of popcorn down. "What is it?" she questioned.

I wasn't really sure how Jackie and Jace would react to me seeing Caleb today and it made me really nervous. I ran my sweaty palms over the side of my favorite shirt and exhaled. "Caleb came to see me today."

Jace's body stiffened as he sat up and gave me his full attention. His jaw tightly clenched as he ran a hand through his hair and frowned. "What happened, Avery?" Jace jumped up from the couch and grabbed my arms. "Are you okay?"

I smiled as Jace gripped the back of my neck and looked me in the eye. He was always so quick to comfort me and it gave me a feeling of security. I loved him for it. "I'm fine."

Jace loosened his grip on me and let his breath out. "What did he want?" he questioned.

"He just came in to apologize. It was really weird," I breathed. "But things are good now. I guess in some way I kind of needed the closure. You know?"

Jace nodded his head, but didn't speak. I could tell by the look in his eyes that he felt a sense of relief as well. "Yeah. I know." He leaned in and softly kissed my nose. "I understand."

"I'll be right back guys."

Jace and I both looked over at Jackie as she jumped up from the couch and ran toward the door.

"Jackie. What's going on?" Jace yelled after her.

"Nothing! It's fine. I just have a call." Jackie's voice shook as she answered back. "I'll be right back."

I pushed my way out of Jace's arms and followed Jackie to the door. I knew what she was doing. "Jackie! Don't do this," I pleaded. "He is no good."

Jackie gave me a blank look and then stared down at her phone. "I dont know what you're talking about," she mumbled. "It's just a- it's a friend."

WAKE UP CALL
VICTORIA ASHLEY

I gripped Jackie's shoulder just as she reached for the door handle. I knew that she was lying and I wasn't about to let her go back to Joe and hurt Jace. "Jackie, I know how hard it is to leave your past behind. Trust me. I beat myself up every day for letting myself drown in my misery. You have to keep him out of your life. If anything... do it for Jace."

Jackie's whole body shook as she looked back down at her phone as it vibrated in her hand. "He won't stop! He won't ever stop," she cried.

I slowly reached down and grabbed the phone from out of Jackie's firm grip. "I'm here for you. You will be fine." I threw my arms around her as she rested her head against my shoulder. "I promise. Jace promises. You have us both now."

Jackie's grip tightened around me as her body began to shake. "I can't do this. I just can't do this," she whined. "It hurts so damn much."

"Yes you can." I shoved the phone in my pocket and looked her in the eye. "We both can do it. Together."

Her eyes wandered down to my pocket before looking up to land on Jace.

Jace stood there in the kitchen with his eyes glued on the both of us. Then he walked over and placed a hand on Jackie's shoulder. "I love you, Jackie. You know that. I always have and always will."

A smile crept over Jackie's face before she broke into a laughter that was soon followed by tears. She stared up at Jace before jumping up and throwing her arms around Jace, body shaking, as she fell into him. "I love you too... punk." She smiled weakly. "I love you so much. You're all that I have left."

Jace softly rubbed the back of her head and peered over Jackie's shoulder to look at me. He smiled and gave me a loving look. "We'll change that soon. I promise."

Jackie looked over at me and gave me a look of confidence. "I'm trusting you to take care of me." She grinned, hopeful. "Don't be surprised if you see me here every day." She stepped toward me and reached her hand out. "Let me see that phone."

I hesitated for a moment before reaching in my pocket and gripping the phone in my hand. "Jackie-"

"It's fine, Avery." She paused to look at Jace. "I'm fine."

Jace gave me a nod as I softly placed the phone inside of Jackie's open palm. "Let's go grab some dinner." He said calmly, trying to change the subject. "Jackie's buying."

Jackie reached over, slapping Jace in the head, as Lucky jumped in the middle of them yelping.

I leaned against the counter and closed my eyes.

Looking over at Jace, Jackie and Lucky, told me everything that I needed to know. Everything that I had been hoping for my entire life.

I am okay now.

Chapter 20

Six years later....

The warm wind playfully blew through my freshly curled hair as I happily stared into the clear afternoon sky.

The sun lightly kissed my already pink nose, causing me to laugh at the thought of how severely my nose had gotten sunburned last summer. It was so bad that, the skin had shed for three weeks, even though everyone had warned me ahead of time to wear sunscreen. I was just too stubborn to listen, and so for that, I paid the price and everyone made fun of me for weeks. I looked absolutely horrible.

"Mommy."

I laughed to myself and shook my head. *Silly me...*

"Mommy."

"Huh?" I questioned, unaware that anyone had been talking to me.

Zari leaned back in the swing, chestnut hair flying around her smiling face as she struggled to look up at me. Her big green eyes flashed with joy, reminding me of Jace.

She playfully giggled, while reaching for the chain on the swing. "What are you doing, mommy? I've been talking to you." She pouted, her lip sticking out.

WAKE UP CALL
VICTORIA ASHLEY

I slowly stopped the swing, walking in front of my daughter, to cup her little round face in my hands. She was my pride and joy. It was her fourth birthday and I wanted her to enjoy each and every moment. "I'm sorry, baby girl." I gently tickled her. "What were you saying? Mommy is listening now."

Zari pushed my hands away from her face and jumped from the swing. "I said that grandmas here. Hurry mommy," she said excitedly. "Grandma always has the best gifts."

I stood back for a moment and watched as Zari took off running through the soft grass. Jace playfully jumped in front of her and reached for her arm, but Zari dodged his reach and ran straight to my mother's arms.

She had always been close with my mother and nothing could ever come between them. It made me happy. So happy, that sometimes I found myself crying at my mother finally turning her life around and being in our lives. It took her about a year after Henry's death for her to start coming around, but when she did, Jace slowly broke her down. Just as he did with everyone.

"Avery," My mother called. "Come join the party." She flashed me her loving smile and reached her arm out. "I have something to show you." She patted Zari on the butt and pushed her toward Jace. "Go with your father and I and mommy will be there in a few minutes."

Zari nodded her head and reached for Jace's outstretched hand. "You lovely ladies take your time." Jace winked at me and smiled at my mother. "We'll try not to eat the cake without you."

I threw my hands to my hip and laughed. "Very funny. I'm telling you right now that if you eat that cake without us that you will be wearing that cake," I teased.

Jace playfully bit his bottom lip and raised an eyebrow.

"Not in that way," I laughed. "We'll be right there."

Zari tugged on Jace's arm. "Daddy." Jace bent down and placed a finger to her chin. "You better listen to mommy. She might just beat you up again," she teased, laughing in her father's face.

My mother and I broke into a fit of laughter as Jace attempted to hide his blushing face. "She didn't...," he started. "Oh never mind. You girls always win." He hoisted Zari off the ground and threw her on his shoulders. "Let's race."

WAKE UP CALL
VICTORIA ASHLEY

Zari playfully tugged on Jace's hair and giggled as he took off running. "We can't race with me on your shoulders." She laughed. "Daddy..."

My mother reached out, placing her hand on my shoulder, for attention. I quickly turned away from my two angels and smiled. "What is it, mother?" I asked.

My mother's eyes glazed over as she reached into her handbag. "Avery." She paused and smiled. "I have something that I have been meaning to give you your whole life. I know that I haven't been-"

"It's okay, mother. That is the past, "I whispered." We don't need to discuss it anymore. I'm happy, you're happy, the family is happy. Let's stay that way."

My mother shook her head and pulled her arm from out of her bag. "This means the world to me." She grabbed my hand and placed something in it. It felt a lot like some kind of chain. She closed her hand around mine and shook her head back and forth. "This locket..." She turned her head away and wiped at her cheek. "Is very important to me. I slept with this locket every night. This was the one thing that Henry couldn't take from me, no matter how screwed up I was. He would have had to pry it from my cold dead fingers."

I slowly opened my hand, nervous to see what the locket held.

I gripped the silver locket with shaky hands and lifted the cover to the case. My fingers lightly traced the circle as my eyes watered. Inside was a picture of my mother looking young and beautiful with a baby in her arms. I knew right away that the baby was me. I threw my hand to my mouth and forced back a sob. "Mother. How... why-"

"You were my world," She stated, shaking her head.. "I was just lost in another world for a while. I knew I would eventually find my way back. If it wasn't for you and your husband," She paused. "I would still be in that world, mourning someone that ruined both of our lives. A monster. He broke us."

I threw my arms around my mother and squeezed her tightly. She had been the best mother and grandmother for the four years and I never wanted anything to ever come between us again. She supported jace and me so much and it meant the world to me. I think she even cried more than I did when Jace proposed. It probably reminded her of the good days that she had with Henry.

One day, she promised to sit down and tell me about their past and how they met. I told her to only share with me the things that she felt comfortable with. Maybe someday soon, I would understand why my mother fell in love with Henry. The guy that changed my life and caused me to find my world.

"Avery," Jackie called. "Zari said to say this exactly." She threw her hands to her hip and huffed. "Mommy, I already stuck my finger in the cake. It was really good and I want more. If you don't hurry then I'm going to let daddy push you in the pool. He said that he was going to." She removed her hands from her hips and rubbed her round belly. "That message came directly from the princess. I think she means business."

"Mommy, why did you run off?" Little Jaxon poked his head around the sliding door and whined. "Hurry."

Jackie shook her head and laughed. "Go find your daddy, booger. Mommy will be right back."

I reached out and placed my hand on Jackie's belly. She was twenty-nine weeks pregnant with her second child. A little girl that was to be named after Jace and Jackie's mother, Olivia Anne.

"She's restless. Olivia kicks me every time that I touch your belly."

Jackie laughed and grabbed my hand. "She's just happy to meet her aunty." She looked down at her belly and rubbed it. "Right, baby girl?" She made little baby noises as we made our way inside to join the party.

Jace looked up from the table and reached for my hand. "I thought you girls got lost. I was going to send a search party." He winked and kissed my cheek. "Jaxon attempted to shove his face in the cake at least four times. I had to stand and guard it."

I laughed at the thought of our silly family. I had almost forgotten just how much they all loved cake. "I'm here now. I'm here." I laughed.

Dex laughed as he teasingly nudged Jace. "This guy is fooling you all. It was Jace that tried shoving his face in the cake." He reached out and placed his hand on Jackie's belly, before kissing her cheek. "Are you going to let your uncle pick on your brother, Olivia? Huh?" he teased.

"Guys," Zari whined. "It's my birthday." She threw her hands up and squeezed her tiny fist. "You guys always make me wait too long. It's not fair."

Jaxon jumped up on the chair next to Zari's and grabbed her hand. "Can I blow out the candles?" He leaned in and reached for a burning candle.

Jackie threw her hands out in front of her as Stacy quickly reached out and slapped his hand. "I don't think so, handsome." She placed Jaxon's hands to his sides and patted his head. "Keep her hands right there."

Jackie nodded at Stacy and exhaled. "Thank you." She placed her hand to her heart and took a deep breath. "That boy is going to give me a heart attack someday."

Jace placed his hand on his sister's back and smiled. "He's a boy, sis. He's tough. Now let's get this cake eating started."

Lucky looked up from his bed and tilted his head.

"Not you, Lucky." I laughed.

Lucky got up and walked outside. That dog was spoiled as it was. Thanks to Zari, of course.

~•~

After cake, ice cream and gifts we all made our way back out to the backyard. A few of Zari's friends showed up and the kids were taking a swim in the pool that Jace had put in last summer.

I sat up from the lounge chair when I heard a whistle. Jace was standing in front of me in his favorite green swim trunks.

He grinned and reached for my hand. "Hey, beautiful." He ran his hands over my back and pressed his lips to my neck. "Will you go out with me?" he questioned.

I pulled away from Jace's grip and smiled. "Excuse me?" I laughed.

Jace pulled my body against his and cupped my face. "You're beautiful and I want to take you on a date." He smiled as he ran a finger over my lip. "What do you say? Is it a date?"

I felt my heartbeat quicken as I looked into his calming eyes. Everything about him was so perfect. Even though I had been with Jace for over six years, he still managed to make every day feel new. I knew that no other man could've ever made me feel the way that he did. I was on top of the world when I was with him. He made me the woman that I was today. The sweet, caring, loving mother and wife that I have become.

When he asked me to marry him five years ago, I almost fainted. I knew that my life would be complete with him in it. What I didn't know then, was that Zari would storm into my life and make it even better than I could had ever imagined. She was a lot like her father and I was glad for that. She was strong, sensitive and loving. They were both beautiful.

I smiled and reached for Jace's face. "I would love to go on a date with you." I pressed my lips to his and laughed.

"Gross," Zari screamed. "Why do you two always smell each other?" She crossed her arms over her chest and tugged on her purple swimsuit. "That's weird."

Jace and I both looked at each other and then back at Zari. "We don't smell each other. We're showing each other how much we care." I smiled. "Now go play, baby girl."

Zari made a disgusted face and pulled out her wedgie. "So you have to smell someone when you care about them?" She walked over to Jaxon and grabbed his hand. "Come here so I can smell you."

Jaxon pulled away from Zari and stuck out his tongue. "Gross. Leave me alone." He took off running with Zari following close behind. "You can't smell me."

Stacy plopped down in my empty chair and laughed. "Come here, Avery. I want to smell you." She teased.

Jace laughed and slapped my butt. "Go play with your friend. I'll smell you later."

I crossed my arms and pursed my lips. "Real funny. Now our daughter is going to go around smelling people."

Jace waved his arm and took off toward Dex and Ace. "Nah. I'll explain it to her later. We'll let her enjoy the party for now."

Stacy and I both smiled as Ace looked over and waved at Stacy. Stacy had met Ace a few months ago and they had been inseparable since. She dated Will for a couple of years, but eventually found out that he was cheating on her. She hadn't really tried with another relationship until she met Ace.

Ace had showed up at the diner one day and Stacy was his waitress. He returned every day for a week straight until he had gotten the courage to ask her out. It was the cutest thing I had ever seen. It made me happy that she was happy.

"Isn't he adorable," she questioned. "I just want to eat him up. I'm going to have his beautiful babies someday."

I looked over at Ace and she was right. He was adorable and they would make beautiful babies. His curly blond hair and piercing blue eyes were adorable. He was definitely the perfect man for Stacy. "Does he know?" I questioned.

Stacy pulled down her sunglasses and looked me over. "Know what?" she asked confused.

I nodded over at Ace as he smiled. "That you're having his babies." I replied.

Stacy sat up and blew Ace a kiss. Then she leaned back and threw her glasses back on. "Not yet." She grinned.

"Avery."

I looked behind me to see my mother throwing her purse over her shoulder. "I have to go. There's an issue at the restaurant. Jan needs me to take care of it right away." She smiled. "That's part of running a restaurant, I guess." She threw her arms around me and then kissed the top of my head. "I love you."

I gave her a quick hug and shook my head. "Okay, mom. I love you too. I'll stop by the apartment with Zari later."

My mother nodded as she waved to Stacy. "Bye, dear."

"Bye, Joyce." Stacy grinned.

I looked around me as the kids laughed and played, the boys hung out in their little circle, and Jackie sat in the shade rubbing her belly. It was beautiful and it all happened in our house. It was perfect.

I moved into Jace's room, when my mom took over the apartment. By that time, Jackie was already seeing Dex and was mostly staying at his house anyways. It was the perfect time to get married and start a family. To start my new life.

The feel of Jace's arms around my waist made me jump. "Crap! You scared me."

Jace pulled my hair away from my neck and pressed his soft lips under my ear. "I just had to come over and tell my beautiful wife how much I love her and appreciate her. And that she means the world to me," he whispered. "Her and our beautiful daughter."

I threw my head back and laughed. "Oh yeah," I teased, "I'll be sure to tell her when I see her."

Jace gripped my waist and turned me around to face him. "You be sure to do that." He kissed my nose and then my lips. "Also, be sure to tell her that I accidently broke her favorite Vase."

"What!" I playfully slapped him as he laughed. "How-"

"I didn't," he said calmly. "I love you, Avery." He pressed his forehead to mine and looked me in the eye. "I truly do."

I reached out and touched his soft face. It felt so good under my palm. It still felt like a dream world to me. "I love you too, Jace. More than you can ever know."

"Mommy! Daddy!" Zari yelled. "Come swim with us." She brushed her wet locks from out of her face and laughed at her friend Ellie. "Come on. Please," she begged.

Jace looked at Zari and then over to me. "Anything for my princess."

Jace hoisted me over his shoulder and walked toward the pool.

Lucky followed behind us barking the whole way. He was very protective of us girls.

"Oh no! No you don't." I slammed my fist against his muscular back and screamed. "No, Jace. Don't throw me in. Don't think that I won't-"

Jace walked over the edge of the pool, with me on his shoulders, and soon we were both sinking into the deep end. The warm chlorine water surrounded us as he cupped my face and pressed his soft lips to mine. Even under the water, his kiss was perfect.

My family was perfect.

Made in the USA
Lexington, KY
04 March 2015